IN DARKNESS,
DELIGHT
MASTERS OF MIDNIGHT

IN DARKNESS, DELIGHT
MASTERS OF MIDNIGHT

EDITED BY:

ANDREW LENNON
& EVANS LIGHT

CHARLOTTE, NC

In Darkness, Delight: Masters of Midnight

"Letters" © 2018 by Michael Bray
"Mirrors" © 2018 by Billy Chizmar
"The Pipe" © 2018 by Israel Finn
"Every Lucky Penny is Another Drop of Blood" © 2018 by Joanna Koch
"In the Ground" © 2018 by Patrick Lacey
"Run Rabbit Run" ©2018 by Andrew Lennon
"Kruze Nite" © 2018 by Lisa Lepovetsky
"One Million Hits" © 2018 by Evans Light
"Violet" © 2018 by Jason Parent
"Pulsate" © 2018 by Espi Kvlt
"Dogshit Gauntlet" © 2018 by John McNee
"Tattooed All in Black" © 2018 by Mark Matthews
"One Thousand Words on a Tombstone: Dolores Ray" © 2018 by Josh Malerman
"Refuge" © 2018 by William Meikle
"Angel Wings" © 2018 by Paul Michaels
"Who Are You?" © 2018 by Ryan C. Thomas
"Rules of Leap Year" © 2018 by Monique Youzwa

Cover by Mikio Murakami.

Interior formatting by Lori Michelle of
The Author's Alley.

For more information, please visit:
www.corpuspress.com

TABLE OF CONTENTS

MASTERS OF MIDNIGHT

WHO ARE YOU?

Ryan C. Thomas

MASTERS OF MIDNIGHT

As I GET OLDER I find my memory is as reliable as a pothead friend who says he'll help you move a couch. My lapses are doubly worse when the spring heat waves arrive, such as they had been lately. So it shouldn't have registered with me that the woman behind me in line at the grocery, with her gray-streaked oily hair and schoolmarm olive green dress, had been the same woman behind me in line at the bank one day earlier.

Strangely enough, two days later, as I was coming home from the gardening store, where I had purchased some sprinkler parts for my home irrigation system, I saw her again. She was walking by the small duck pond near the on-ramp to the Interstate. She wore the same green dress. She carried no purse. Her hair shined like a wet towel, impervious to any wind or humidity. A few oily strands hung sadly down her back, like running paint on a wet canvas. I noticed the way her arms barely moved as she walked, as if they'd been stapled to her ribs. There was something almost waxen about her. If it got any hotter out I thought she might just melt into a puddle right there in the street.

She glanced over and caught me staring, and perhaps out of embarrassment broadcast a half-heated smile at me that revealed a parade of oversized horse teeth.

I drove by, watching her in my rearview mirror, noting the way she kept her eyes on me as I put distance between us. "Stop following me," I muttered. "And here Mom said I'd never grow up to be popular." I laughed at my own lame joke because I am a sad, lonely soul—my brother's words, not mine.

At home I turned on the news and chewed my own tongue watching a report about politicians trying to solve crime rates in

1

inner cities around the country. They splashed the usual statistics onto the screen, as if they meant anything. Crime was up, always up, never stopping. I thanked my stars I lived in a good neighborhood. Beyond a solitary incident in which a teenager stole my neighbor's car a few years back—joy riding, he told the police—we had not had any criminal activity in a long time.

A couple days later, when the marine layer had rolled in and dropped the temperature to something tolerable, I went out into the backyard and fixed the sprinkler system with that PVC I'd acquired. I dug down around the lines and saw that the gophers had come back. They always flourished when the heat rose. I talked down their tunnels: "Stop coming into my yard, assholes."

I swear one of them responded: "It was our land first, you dick."

I thrust the hose down there and tried to drown the bastard out but after several minutes of wasting water I gave up and went back inside the house.

Over lunch that same day I saw a man walk in front of my house. He wore a dark brown suit and a fedora, which I found peculiar since his young age seemed inappropriate for such anachronistic dress. Perhaps in his twenties, though he sported the kyphotic frame of an elderly woman. Bent forward, stiff arms by his sides, walking with a forced smile. I figured him for a religious missionary of some sort, and watched him move down the road until he was lost in the heat wave. He did not leave any pamphlets in mailboxes or knock on doors.

I should have forgotten about him, especially in the blistering heat that lasted all through the next week, but I saw him again at the donut shop on Sunday morning. I proffered a cordial, "Hey," as I got in line behind him. He tipped his hat to me and smiled.

A wide, crooked smile that seemed to wrap around his head like a crack expanding in a sheet of glass. And inside that smile, a row of pearly white, massive horse teeth.

Christ, I thought, those teeth . . . .it's like some disease that's going around.

I saw him again several times over the next couple of days. At the grocery, at the Home Depot, at the high school football game on Friday night. He sat one row in front of the woman in the green dress. They remained statuesque throughout the game, neither cheering nor booing nor checking their phones like the other people in the stands.

My house was just three blocks up past the high school parking lot, and so Friday night games helped pass the time these days. I'd tried online dating, but aside from two dates to get coffee, nobody seemed to want me. My brother, who called me once a week, told me, "It'll happen when it happens. Don't rush it, Tim. Remember how I met Jillian?"

"At the doctor's office." I'd heard the story so many damn times I wanted to reach through the phone and punch him.

"At the doctors. She has gout. I have gout. So I said, 'Would you like to *gout* with me sometime?" He chuckled like a moron.

"That's really . . . a dumb joke." I hung up on him.

It was almost nine o'clock when the game ended and I was wiping sweat off my forehead, wondering how high my electric bill was going to be with all the fans I had on at home, when both the man and woman stood and walked down the bleachers, onto the grass, and disappeared into the night. Neither of them moved their arms when they walked. It was weird. Why didn't anyone else seem to notice it?

Surely it had to seem weird to others?

As the concession trucks rolled away, and the players ventured into the stands to see their friends, I decided to head home. That's when I noticed the little girl sitting by her father. She

3

was maybe nine or ten, wearing a pink and yellow dress, a white bow in her hair, and she studied the high school crowd like she was observing salamanders in a terrarium. There was little to no emotion in her face, which was neither here nor there. Except, it felt off. She wasn't bored, or tired, or anxious to leave, or confused, or content. She was blank. Her father looked back and caught me staring, and I quickly looked away, but not before I saw he was wearing a T-shirt that read Vista Police Athletic League Softball.

He was a cop.

I waited a full minute before looking again, at which point the girl's father asked if she was ready to leave.

She nodded. Smiled. She had the giant teeth. I swear I was seeing those teeth everywhere.

"Who are you people?" I whispered to the night.

I saw her a few days later, at a bookstore where I'd ordered the latest mystery by some author my brother had gotten me hooked on. She was standing in the Young Adult section, looking at the spines of the books. Not reading the spines, mind you, just staring through them, expressionless as a porcelain doll.

I looked around for her father but did not see him. It was just as well, since I'd be hard pressed to explain to him why I, a fifty-six year old man, was eyeballing a kid.

Did I mention she wore the same pink and yellow dress? She did. She walked down the aisles without moving her arms. Did kids do that? I didn't know. Eventually a worker asked me if I needed help finding a title and I had a momentary vision of bashing his brains in with a hammer. Way to ruin my stakeout, pal!

As I'd feared, the girl turned toward me, waiting to see what I'd say.

4

"No, just browsing," I replied.

Her dead eyes gave me the heebie jeebies, so I left.

The very next day I was back at the bank to discuss a fraud charge on my debit card. My brother kept telling me I needed to take better precautions with my money. But screw him, it's not like he was paying my mortgage, right?

"Just give me access to your account," he'd say. "It's hard doing it all by yourself. Believe me, I know. Jillian has to help me with a lot of our finances because I keep forgetting to set up our auto pay."

"Get lost," I always told him. As if I needed another greedy hand on my money.

The bank manager took me to one of the desks and we went over the charges that week. "That one," I said, indicating a purchase in India. "Obviously I wasn't in India four days ago."

"So you didn't spend $286 in Delhi?" She spoke to me like I was an idiot.

"Do I look like the type of guy who goes to Delhi?"

"Okay, we will flag that one and you should see the money reimbursed in a day or two. In the meantime I'll need to get you a new temporary bank card. Just wait here."

She left me alone at the desk. In walked the man in the brown suit and fedora. He stood in line for a few seconds, then looked around, saw me, and gave me his overzealous grin just like that day in the donut shop. I smiled back, watching him, waiting for him to speak. He waited his turn and then reached the teller. He handed her a withdrawal slip. The teller read it, said, "Do you want that in twenties?"

The man nodded. When the teller asked how his day was going, he merely shrugged.

"Here is your card, Mr. Garmin. You should receive your permanent one in the mail in about a week. Is there anything else I can help you with?"

5

"Yeah, "I said, before I could help myself. "That man in the hat who just left. I think he lives in my neighborhood. I wanted to say hi but I don't know his name. Do you?"

"I'm sorry, but I can't give out anyone's personal information. Perhaps if you just say hello when you see him next. Maybe you can catch him now if you hurry?"

I took her up on her advice and raced outside into the heat, but he was gone. The trees and flowers in the back parking lot were dead or dying from lack of water. I swear it looked like the clouds were melting. Would the sun ever turn off?

I was driving home from the bank when I saw all three of them sitting on a bench at the local bus stop. The girl, in her pink and yellow dress, the man in his brown suit and fedora, and the stringy-haired woman in her green dress. They were looking at me as I drove by. The hairs on my neck stood up, though I couldn't tell you why.

"What're you all looking at?" I whispered, pulling my truck into the next side street. I did a three-point-turn in the closest driveway (okay it was more like a thirty-point-turn) and backtracked to the bus stop. The bus was pulling into traffic and the three people who had been on the bench were gone. I surmised they had gotten on the bus, and so I followed it for several blocks while it made stops, hoping one of them would get off. After an hour I realized it was getting late and I was going crazy—following a bus with people who had done nothing wrong other than to look a little odd. It wasn't a crime.

I shook my head like a wet dog. "Tim, you're brain is melting like a scoop of ice cream shoved up a gorilla's asshole. Go home and read your book in front of the fan. Get some sleep."

And so I did.

I had one date the next month. I met her on a dating app my nephew urged me to try. The app was mostly full of young women looking for a casual hook up, which was fine by me, but of course none of those women wanted me. Couldn't blame them either. I was overweight, balding, and still had a home phone. I was a geezer. But Miranda answered my chats asking if she'd like to go to a poetry reading downtown. I had noticed she had poetry as one of her interests, and so I quickly Googled around to see what was going on locally. There was a "Night of Spoken Word Wonder" going on at the local library, and it said there would be cookies and coffee, so I figured, if nothing else, I would not go home on an empty stomach.

She responded and said she was planning on going to the event anyway, but that we could meet there and talk. Truth be told I would rather have my dick gnawed on by rats than go to a poetry reading, but I was tired of only talking to my house plants.

I got there early, and met Miranda near the door. She was my age, dressed well, and had fiery red hair, all of which seemed a plus to me. We made small talk for a few minutes, and I got her to laugh once or twice. She had a mouth like a pirate but I didn't mind. Straightforward women turn me on.

The first reader droned on about wishing she was a lizard or some such nonsense, and both Miranda and I chuckled a bit behind our raised hands. The second reader told of growing up gay in the south. I felt bad for him, but his prose was shit so unfortunately I didn't care about his work. It was during the third reader, an older gentleman with a bad comb-over, that I noticed the woman in the green dress walk into the library. She made her way to the coffee and poured some into a Styrofoam cup. I watched her intently, ignoring the reading, even ignoring a couple of sotto voce comments Miranda made toward me. Why was she here, this woman? Was she following me? Why did she keep appearing in my life?

The woman in green never took a sip of the coffee. She looked at the ground for a moment, then lifted her head and stared at me. I felt a chill run down my spine.

I couldn't sit still, not with her blank face locked on mine, so I excused myself from Miranda's presence and made my way to the coffee. As I drew up next to the woman in green I could smell something earthen and cold in the air. I leaned closer to her. She smelled like mud. With a slow turn, she met my eyes. I felt my scrotum shrivel in fear, though I still couldn't explain why. "I'm Tim," I said. "Who are you?"

The woman in green said nothing, just smiled for a half second, revealing those giant teeth again.

"Are you . . . are you following me?" I asked her.

She slowly shook her head no, without breaking eye contact, put her cup of coffee back on the table and exited the building.

"Wait!" I yelled, racing after her. My voice apparently caused some stir with the reading, but I was out the front door before I heard what was said about me. The woman in green was already out on the street at yet another bus stop.

"Who are you? Why are you following me!"

She got on the bus and it drove off.

I felt a presence behind me, and when I turned around Miranda was there with her red hair swaying in the hot, spring night. "You okay?"

"I . . . that woman. She . . . " I had no idea what to say.

"You interrupted that guy's reading. Kinda douchy. Just saying."

"I'm sorry. I didn't mean to. It's just . . . I keep seeing that woman. I've been trying to follow her but—"

"Follow her? If you're so into her, why did you come on a date with me?"

"No, it's not like that."

"That's what they all say." She went back inside the library.

8

I apologized again after the reading was over, and she was pleasant enough, but I could tell I'd blown it. It didn't matter, though, because the next day I saw on the news that Miranda had been killed in a car accident. Her head was crushed upon impact with the truck that hit her. The windshield was smeared with red and bits of white, and the news apologized for the grisly images, but I knew they were banking on it getting them viewers. The shot lingered long enough to see tufts of hair in the congealed bits of brain on the glass.

The driver of the truck, also a female, was also dead. She was being called an "unidentified citizen" due to the fact they had not yet recovered any ID. But when they showed the truck driver's picture, half her face caved in, all my breath seemed to leave my body. It was the woman in the green dress.

The Friday after I watched the news of Miranda, I decided to go to the football game at the High School, get my mind off things. The Beavers had made it into the playoffs, though they'd need a miracle to beat the Grizzlies, who were ranked number one in the county.

The night was hot, as it had been for months now. I bought a bag of chips and some sweet tea at the concession stand, and then sat at the top of the bleachers so I could see the whole field.

The Beavers were up by three at the end of the first quarter, which was when I saw the little girl in the pink and yellow dress. She was sitting with her dad down near the field. I watched her scanning the people sitting near her, watched the way she studied them, like they were alien to her. I noticed again her tiny frame, how thin she was and thought on how it was pretty trusting of her father to let her go and take the city bus alone like she did.

9

I gave a determined scan of the bleachers until I saw the man in the fedora. He was only three rows ahead of me, and he was doing his usual "stare into nothing" type glare. Occasionally he moved his head as if he was following the plays on the field, but I could tell he was not really watching the game.

At one point, he and the little girl exchanged eye contact, lingering on each other more than I would have liked. There were no expressions of recognition, but they didn't turn away from each other either.

"The hell is going on?" I whispered. I wanted badly to find out why these freaks were in my neighborhood.

I moved down next to him, cleared my throat. "This seat taken?" I asked.

He turned his head but didn't speak. He smiled a little, looked at the seat, and faced forward again.

When I was seated, I took a moment to collect my thoughts, and then said, "I saw you on my street not long ago. You live around here. My name's Xavier. Xavier Garmin. And you are . . . ?"

He said nothing, left my hand shake hanging in mid air. Just then the whistle sounded and the game ended. People stood up like it was suddenly raining money from the sky. The man in the fedora gave me one more smile, then stood up and began walking down the bleachers. I had just a second to notice the little girl in the pink and yellow dress was also looking at him before I realized I was going to lose him in the crowd.

I stepped down the bleachers, pushing my way through the throng, until I hit the grass of the field. I caught sight of the man far out near the parking lot. Either he had sprinted when I lost sight of him, or he'd slipped through a time warp somehow.

I raced after him, losing him as cars cut me off. I weaved around a couple of SUVs and a Mustang, thought I saw him at the edge of the lot near the street, but as I raced closer I saw it was just a high school kid in a surfer hat.

"Fuck."

I headed back across the lot toward my house.

I was a block from home when I saw him again. He was down the side street about three houses, standing on the front porch. I turned and headed toward him, intent on finally getting his name and confirming he lived in the area. If he did, I was going to feel foolish, but that didn't mean I was crazy, did it?

He opened the front door and stepped inside. I raced to catch him before he shut the door and locked it. But he never shut the door, just left it wide open. I jogged up the front walk and onto the porch, stuck my head in the front door.

"Hello?" I asked.

There was a thud from somewhere inside, followed by a series of grunts.

"Everyone okay?" I wouldn't normally enter another person's house, but it sounded like someone was hurt. I made sure to keep announcing myself so I wouldn't startle him.

"Hello? It's Tim. We met at the game. Are you okay?"

I heard more grunts and groans and a feeble yelp. When I got to the kitchen, I found an elderly man on the floor. His head had been bashed in with what I could only assume was the frying pan laying next to him. The wide gash over his right eye exposed gleaming white skull and flaps of pink skin. Dark blood pooled beneath him. Next to this, the man in the Fedora was bent over a woman. She too was covered in blood. Her nightgown had been slashed and a gouge ran down between her elderly breasts. Blood ran out of the gouge like someone had left the sink on. The man in the fedora was holding a butcher knife.

I stood stock still, my mouth quivering. "Oh my God," I said.

I backpedaled a step and watched the man in the fedora stand up slowly. He took the butcher knife, which was covered in the woman's blood, and jammed it into his own neck.

"Holy Christ!" I spat.

The man gurgled, spasmed, and fell to the floor where his feet twitched for a good minute. Then he stopped, and the only thing I could hear was the tick tock of the antique grandfather clock in the hallway.

I realized then that I was standing at a murder scene, and everyone was dead except me. And I had no way at all to explain how and why I was in the house.

Shaking, confused, and terrified beyond words, I made my way back to the front entrance, stepped out into the cool night air, and did my absolute best to walk home without looking suspicious.

I stayed inside my house for the entire next week. I eventually saw the news of the murders on TV. The cops were ruling it a breaking-and-entering gone bad. The finger prints on the murder weapons matched the man in the fedora, who, again, was being identified as an "unknown assailant" owing to the fact he was not carrying any ID. The news was asking anyone who recognized the man to call the police.

So I did.

I told them I'd seen the man at the bank. I hung up quick. I did not want them to look into my own story further, having been in the house during the murder and all.

After many days, I couldn't shake the thought of the little girl.

She was stuck on my mind like dirty adhesive tape. And why shouldn't she be, for she was also one of them. This much I knew for sure. At least I thought I did. There was no other explanation for her behavior.

I debated telling the police, but had no idea how to relay my theory. I had no evidence of a threat. I also couldn't go to the police because her father *was* a police officer. (Maybe he was one of them too—though he did not walk the walk nor were his teeth of any significant size.) One can't just accuse a small child of being a murderer, especially when no murder has yet taken place. They'd lock me up and throw away the key. And yet I knew, without a doubt, that she was going to cause someone harm, or even death.

I knew I was going to have to take care of her myself before she killed whoever she'd chosen as a victim.

So I did what any good citizen would do. I tracked her down.

It wasn't hard. I happened to see her father leaving the local Wendy's one afternoon. I followed him to a house only six streets over from my own. He disappeared inside for several hours, then came out again to drive his police cruiser back to the station. To make sure it was his house, that he wasn't just sleeping with the home's owner, I waited outside on two different nights until I saw him arrive home in his Jeep Cherokee. The little girl in the pink and yellow dress and white hair bow also got out. Together they went inside and I watched through their front window as they ate a dinner of spaghetti. Well, he ate. She did not touch her food.

"She wants blood," I muttered.

I slept in my car overnight, and when the father left for work in the morning, I followed the girl. She gave it an hour and then left the house, walked to the bus stop, and took the bus to the strip mall two miles away. She waited on the walkway and watched the people coming and going from the mom and pop stores.

13

"She's choosing one," I said. "She's finding a victim."

And so it was with careful planning that I returned to her house that night with the intent of stopping her. I failed to see what other options I had. I didn't own a gun, but I owned a hammer, and I figured that could be easily discarded in one of the local strip mall dumpsters.

I waited until her father left for work, and then kicked in the front door. She was sitting on the couch staring at the TV. A teen drama was on. I didn't recognize it. She looked up and saw me. She screamed, which was very much out of character for her, but I knew it was just a ruse.

I chased her into her father's bedroom and held her on the floor.

I don't remember much after that, but I remember her acting skills, the way she was able to generate real fear in her eyes, the shriek in her voice as she yelled trough her horse teeth, "Who are you? Who are you?"

To which I responded, "No, who are you?"

And then there was blood.

The blood was mine. I think. Maybe it was hers. It's hard to tell. I remember swinging the hammer, but I also remember getting slammed into the wall. I remember the girl's father standing over me with his gun drawn, screaming at me. And then an ambulance came and at one point I was being laid on a stretcher, wondering if I'd killed that alien kid, wondering if I'd saved humanity, listening to some neighbors talking.

"He lives a few streets over. Xavier something. He, you know, lives alone, keeps to himself."

"It's always the ones that keep to themselves."

Then I was in a hospital and there was a lot of talk about a bullet in my back.

All the doctors walked with their arms down. I think. They all looked at me like they were studying me, like I wasn't even human. They were one of them, I'm pretty sure, one of those demon people out to kill humans.

"Did I kill her? Did I succeed?," I asked the nurses later. They just ignored me.

"You have to stop her!" I wailed. "I was just trying to stop her! To save people!"

It was years later, after much time in various mental health facilities, that I was allowed to return home. My brother, my tether to reality, had purchased my house and used it as a rental property for my time away. The equity had increased three-fold, and he made a nice profit from the renters over the years, and so he kept the deed in his name but let me move back in for a generous rental fee. What a dick.

I received visits from county workers who gave me tests and asked me about my days. They asked me where I went during the day, if anyone came to the door, if I spoke to my brother—which I did, every day.

I did not go to the football games, nor did I venture out to the coffee shops much. Needless to say, between my new life as a monitored hermit and the passing of years since my "incident," I saw no evidence that the horse-teethed people still existed.

That is, until six months later. I was lying on the living room couch, trying to read, the low watt bulb of my tableside lamp doing it's best to light my pages, when the front door opened.

I jumped up, my hairs on end, my tongue dry. Shaking, I dropped my book as I watched the man in the fedora enter my house. His massive smile turned toward me, and he nodded. He took steps into the living room, and I lost my breath. I couldn't

15

scream, couldn't run, so affixed to the rug I was, frozen in abject terror.

Behind him, the woman in the green dress appeared. She too, entered the room, came to stand before me, her horse teeth yellowed by the dim reading bulb.

"No," I finally uttered, falling back into the couch. "Please no . . . " I shut my eyes, waiting for these strange beings to finally do me in.

Lastly, behind her, the little girl in the pink and yellow dress entered. Her giant teeth glowed sallow under the light of my reading lamp.

I heard their footsteps creaking my hardwood floors, all of them coming closer. But they did not stop before me, rather continued past me, into the hallway. They walked their stiff-arm walk, smiled their big-teeth smile, ignoring me.

I moved down the hall, looking for a weapon. Still terrified, I shook my head at them, saw them standing still now, looking at me.

"What do you want?" I finally shouted. "Who are you?" My mind was reeling. I knew this was real. Despite everything the doctors had told me about my own brain playing tricks on me, I knew this event was happening.

It took all my courage to step toward them, ready to fight. They moved toward the doors in the hallway, he toward my bedroom, she toward the guest room, the girl toward the bathroom. Simultaneously, they opened the doors and stepped into the rooms. Then each door slammed shut, shaking the house with such force the lights flickered.

"Get out!" I screamed, racing down the hall. I flung open my bedroom door and flipped on the light. I nearly fell from the weakness in my knees when I saw the room was empty. I checked in the closet. I looked under the bed. The man in the fedora was gone. Only he wasn't completely gone his fedora was on the dresser. I snatched it up and crumpled it in my hands.

"No no no no no no," I stammered, and ran to the guest room. Here too I flung open the door and turned on the light. It was also empty, and my search under the bed and in the closet yielded absolutely nothing. But here too, a scrap of green dress hung on the doorknob.

In the bathroom I found nothing but the bow from the little girl's hair.

They were all gone, but I had pieces of them in my hands.

I returned to the living room, holding my keepsakes from my unwanted visitors.

I stayed there for three days, the lights on, my eyes wide open, waiting for them to come back.

On the fourth day my county worker arrived and asked me how I was feeling. I showed her the fedora, bow and scrap of green dress.

"What do you see?" I asked.

"A hat and some cloth," she replied, eyeing me with concern.

"Exactly! They're real," I said. "They came into my house. They're here right now. Watching me. Waiting."

"Who?"

"The ones with the teeth."

She cocked her head, somewhat frightened of me. But she kept her voice steady and unwavering. "I don't see anyone."

"They're here," I said. "They're in the walls. In the walls of the house."

"Mr. Garmin, are you taking your medication?"

I saw where this was going, knew I'd be back in a home with bars on the windows if I kept this up in front of her. So I laughed, pointed at her as if to say, *gotcha!* "Joking," I said. "Just testing you. Of course I'm taking the meds. And you have nothing to worry about, I'm fine."

But I wasn't fine. And when she left twenty minutes later, obviously concerned about me, I sat in the middle of the living room, the fedora, bow and swatch of green in my lap, gripping a steak knife in my hand, waiting for my visitors to come back out of the walls.

For that is where they are. In the walls. In the walls, watching me.

They're in the walls. And they're real. But who are they?

And can they withstand a house fire?

We'll see, soon enough.

IN THE GROUND

Patrick Lacey

MASTERS OF MIDNIGHT

TWO DAYS AFTER his father's funeral, Noah Tucker started digging a hole.

He woke early. The sleep he'd managed the night before was filled with nightmares, slithering and crawling things he wished he could forget, though they were still fresh in his memory.

He dressed and made his way downstairs, tip-toeing across the hall so he wouldn't wake his mother. Her door was halfway open, and he could hear her snores. He'd seen a bottle of something called Valium on the kitchen counter and deduced that it helped her sleep better without his dad next to her. Noah had considered taking a pill himself, but he didn't like the idea of being unable to wake from one of his nightmares, trapped while things with appendages chased him down a never-ending hallway.

Downstairs he made a bowl of Cheerios and sprinkled sugar until it tasted like a bowl of candy. He looked outside toward the yard. His father had been planning on making a small pond in the corner for Noah. All you needed were a couple of trash bags and a shovel. Dig a hole, lay the bag on the soil, and hide the edges with more dirt before pouring the water.

"Can we do it tonight?" Noah had asked on the ride home from school last Monday.

"It'll have to wait for the weekend. I've got a meeting in the city, remember?"

Noah had nodded and thought Saturday couldn't come fast enough. The next day his father had been blown to bits in the explosion.

Staring at the yard, as the sun began to light up the grass and the lilac tree and the line of bushes at the far end, Noah thought, *why not dig a hole now?*

21

The ground seemed to call him. He headed for the shed where his father kept his gardening tools. Grabbing the nearest shovel, he walked to the corner of the yard, the place where they'd planned on installing the pond.

He imagined his father's resting place: ruined skyscrapers and broken windows. No body to bury beneath the stone his mother spent a fortune on. He thought of all the other dead people in the world, those that were so old they didn't *have* stones to mark their resting places. Right here under his feet, there could have been bones and rotting skin, some unidentifiable corpse.

He lined the shovel up and brought his foot down. The soil was darker underneath the surface, fresher, and it was as if the ground had a voice. Loud and clear in his ears.

Keep digging.

Noah rubbed at bumpy skin despite the early morning heat, telling himself he was tired and hearing things.

Yet he obeyed the voice and brought the shovel down once more.

"Whatchya doing, kiddo?" his aunt Sarah asked an hour later. She'd been stopping by every day to check on his mother since the planes hit the towers.

"Digging a hole." He wiped at sweat, leaving behind dirty streaks on his forehead and cheeks.

"Is your mom up?" Aunt Sarah asked, as if reading his thoughts.

"I'm not sure. She wasn't when I came out here."

"I'll go check on her. How are you feeling?" She kneeled and rubbed his back. She was younger than his mother, and he'd always thought she was quite pretty and nice and from time to time he'd imagine what it would be like to have *her* as his mother.

"I'm okay." He tossed another load of dirt onto the pile.

"You're not just saying that? You'd tell me if you were really, really sad, right? Because that would be okay. Heck, that would be *normal*. And you wouldn't even need to feel embarrassed. You'd tell your aunt, right?"

"Right."

"One more question. What's with the hole?"

"I don't know," he said and it was the truth.

His aunt hesitated and then seemed to accept his answer. She kissed the top of his head and went inside.

He admired his work in progress.

Not bad but he had a long way to go.

A long way to go? What did that mean?

He wasn't sure but the soil seemed so inviting.

By the end of that first day, the hole was much wider and deeper. Noah's skin blistered from being outside the better part of six hours. He made a note to wear sunscreen when he came out tomorrow.

And he *would* be out here tomorrow. It was what the soil wanted of him. He couldn't explain the analogy, but he knew it was true nonetheless.

If he was going to build a pond, now would be the time to stop digging and start constructing but some part of him rejected the thought. This was no longer *about* the pond.

"Noah," his mother called from the back porch.

He tossed the shovel down and followed her into the house.

On the kitchen table were two bowls of tomato soup and two grilled cheese sandwiches. He ate the sandwich in three or four bites, and within minutes he was slurping at the last of the broth. The day's work had left him ravenous.

"Here," his mother said, pushing her bowl toward him.

"You're not hungry?"

"Not in the least." She forced a smile, and he supposed Valium took away your appetite. Or maybe death did.

He finished her soup and let out a belch she would've scolded him for under other circumstances.

"What've you been up to out there? You look burnt to a crisp."

"I was digging a hole."

"A hole? Any particular reason?"

"Nope. Just digging."

"Noah, I hope you know everything's going to be okay. Your mom's a little crazy right now, but we'll get through this. It's what your dad would want." At the mention of his father, her voice cracked and soon there were two matching tears sliding down her cheeks.

"I know," he said. He wanted to tell her he'd like to cry as well, that he'd give anything to break down, to feel *something* since he'd gotten the news, but instead he held his stare and tried to offer a smile of reassurance.

"Come here." His mom held out her arms and he held her tightly. "I'm going to get some sleep. You come get me if you need anything. And I mean *anything*."

"Sure." He watched her open the bottle of Valium and pop one into her mouth like a Flintstones vitamin. Then she headed upstairs, and after a few minutes of quiet crying, she fell into a snore-filled sleep.

He looked outside to catch another glimpse of the hole but it was too dark to see.

24

More nightmares. Different this time. There were still slithering and crawling things, odd-looking creatures his dream-self couldn't make sense of, but among them stood his father. Surrounded by rubble and smoke and blood. He placed a hand on Noah's shoulder. "How's that hole coming, kiddo?"

"It's fine." He tried to make sense of his surroundings. "I thought you were . . . this is where it happened."

His father nodded. For the first time Noah noticed his face. The skin was mostly missing, revealing charred bone beneath. His eye sockets were both empty. "You see that right there?" His father pointed to a section of the building that had landed on the other side of the street, leaning against a half-toppled parking garage. "That wall was outside our boardroom, just above where the plane hit. It cut off the stairwell. We were having a safety meeting. Can you believe that?"

Noah wasn't sure what to say. He wanted to tell his father to come home with him, out of the dream and into real life because then they could go see a matinee and drink sodas and eat popcorn, but the realization that Dad wasn't ever coming home was the cruelest thing he'd even encountered.

"You keep digging, kid. You keep digging." His father squeezed Noah's shoulder one last time and headed toward the epicenter of the rubble, where the slithering and crawling things seemed to culminate.

"It's just a phase," his Aunt Sarah said from the deck, unaware that Noah could hear. "To get his mind off things."

"You mean a coping mechanism," his mother said.

"Exactly. Better than playing video games all day or lashing out. It's harmless."

"But he needs to face it soon or else he'll keep it bottled up.

Sometimes you *need* to break down. It might be a phase but it's already overstayed its welcome."

Noah stopped listening, too intent on his work. Sweat poured down his face and into the hole, which was bigger now—so much bigger. He figured he could stand inside and just barely touch the surface. Soon he'd have to retrieve a ladder from the garage.

Someone grabbed his arm. He spun, ready to be back among the rubble, ready to see whatever hideous thing lay before him, but it was just his aunt. She held a glass of lemonade. From her pocket she presented a tube of sunscreen. "You look like you could use both of these."

He nodded his thanks, grabbed the glass, drank it in three big gulps.

She made a circular motion with her finger, telling him to turn around. He bit his lip as she applied sunscreen.

"How's it coming along?" she asked.

"It needs to be deeper. A lot deeper."

"Why's that, honey? What's down there, and why is it so important?"

He studied the hole again. A centipede lay half buried, pushing itself out of the dirt. "I don't know, but it wants me to let it out."

She froze, hand still on his shoulder. A look of concern replaced the usual cool-aunt smirk. For the first time ever, he thought that maybe she wasn't all that different from his mom.

"Noah, maybe you ought to knock off for the day, huh? You should spend some time with your mother."

"All she does anymore is sleep."

"Her husband just died. They were together for fifteen years."

"I don't care. Just let me finish." He pushed away and grabbed the shovel.

From behind, he could sense her presence for another few minutes, watching in awe as he worked faster, digging and smiling.

26

He didn't go inside until late evening.

No food on the table this time. His mother was passed out on the couch.

"Keep at it," she said in between snores and in a voice that was not her own. "You're almost there."

Noah went upstairs and watched the hole through his window. The moon cast bright light onto the backyard and he tried not to blink, hoping he wouldn't miss anything.

Noah might have slept longer had it not been for the crunching sound.

He stretched, yawned, and froze when he made the connection.

Running to his window, he pounded his fists against the panes.

His mother stood in the yard, wiping away sweat in the morning heat as she threw dirt into the hole.

He didn't bother slipping on his sneakers as he ran downstairs and headed outside. "Stop. You're ruining everything!"

She continued to fill it in, his beautiful creation. She had no right. Tomorrow he'd return to school and fidget in his seat all day, trying not to notice the stares and hushed whispers, and all he would think of was the hole and the voice and whatever dwelled down there. She was taking away the one constant in his life.

He grabbed the shovel. "Don't. I mean it."

"You *mean* it?" His mother yanked the shovel from his hands.

"Watch your mouth. I'm still your mother, you know. You're making a mess of the yard. It was fine for a while but this isn't exactly the healthiest way to cope."

"I'm not *coping*. It just wants to be let out."

She froze. "What did you say?"

"Nothing. I didn't say anything. I just like digging. That's all."

"No, you said something wanted to be let out. What does that mean? Are you okay?"

She felt his head as if he was simply feverish, as if all his problems could be solved with aspirin and chicken soup. "Noah, what wants to be let out?"

He didn't answer.

"I know this has been hard for you and I haven't been much help, but I think you ought to talk to someone. You've got to *deal* with this. You're better off being a mess like your mother than keeping it inside. Would you like that? Would you like to sit down with someone and talk about your feelings?"

"No. I wouldn't like that at all. I just want you to stop filling in the hole." He cried and cursed himself for being a baby. Whatever rested beneath seemed impossibly distant now.

She took him into her arms. "I'm so sorry," she whispered again and again, rubbing his sore back, telling him everything was okay as she cried tears of her own.

He stared at the soil, waiting for a voice that did not speak.

It was near midnight when his mother finally came upstairs and retired.

When he was certain she was asleep, he made his way back outside and started from scratch, digging with speed and determination, digging with a reserve of energy he hadn't known existed.

When he finally stopped, it must have been late. The sky was the blackest he'd ever seen it. He noticed the absolute stillness of the night, noticed the way the moon cast a dark blue hue over everything.

From beneath his feet, the voice spoke again.

Don't stop.

He tossed scoops of soil onto the ground like they were weightless. Managed to surpass the depth from the past two days. He dug and dug and without warning, the shovel broke through the dirt and hit nothingness, as if there were a cave down there, an empty space that was not dirt or soil.

He tried to make sense of it, but his thoughts went elsewhere when the shovel was pulled from his grip and *into* the ground.

Thank you.

Then came the hand. It reached through the opening. Black fingers, horribly deformed, leathery.

"What did I tell you about this?"

Noah stifled a scream at the sound of his mother's voice. She pulled him away. "I worked for *two hours* to fix your damn mess and look what you've done. Is this what you want? To drive your mother insane now out of all times? Because you're doing an awfully good job."

She grabbed his wrist, and he struggled. Somehow, she didn't see the hand, reaching farther upward, revealing an elbow and the start of the skeletal shoulder. It wouldn't be long now.

"Let go," he said as he pushed her away.

"I'm not going to let you give up on me. We're all we've got now."

The thought resonated with him. His father was gone and tomorrow, when he came home, there would only be his mother. The house would seem just as quiet. Just as *foreign*.

His mother started to say something else as the hand grabbed

29

her ankle. Another set of fingers covered her mouth, dampened her screams.

It dragged her head first into the ground, into the place where *it* lay dormant for so long. Her feet kicked before they vanished altogether.

Noah pushed aside loosened soil, searching for that entrance to the other place. For the creature or his mother or *someone* because he did not want to be alone for even another moment.

The soil gave way to more soil and he grew faint. Screamed. Neighbors watched through windows, stared from porches. Sirens sounded in the distance.

Noah reached into the soil, pushed with all his strength, and his hand finally broke through.

He recoiled when something dry and rotting clenched his fingers, struggled for only a moment before he remembered the house and the night and the empty world above ground.

He stopped fighting after that.

THE PIPE

Israel Finn

MASTERS OF MIDNIGHT

As Derik Ames guided his car north along Ninth Street, he wondered for the hundredth time if this meeting was a good idea. It would be awkward. But Joe Johnson had swayed him with that last cryptic statement, *"Don't do this for me, do it for Sara,"* before hanging up on him. It was enough to get Derik out of his apartment and into his car, his hands sweaty on the steering wheel despite the air conditioning and his head full of wild speculation as he navigated across town to Irwin's seedy south side.

He pulled up in front of a decrepit shotgun house nestled incongruously between a laundry mat with soaped-over windows on one side and a boarded-up brick warehouse on the other, parked his Honda behind a rust-eaten Ford pickup truck, and got out of the car. Immediately the humidity wrapped itself around him like a heavy wet blanket. He glanced around. He saw no other vehicles, and the only other houses on the street were obviously deserted, their windows smashed, their weathered frames covered with graffiti, and weeds growing knee high in their mean little yards. No wonder Sara never wanted to bring him here. Across the street was a derelict junk yard surrounded by a high chain-link fence with a rusty sign that said NO TRESPASSING, and back the way he had come he could see the Ohio River between some gray and brown buildings. He could smell it too, even from here, a muddy, metallic odor. Everything seemed to have fallen still under the oppressive Indiana summer heat. The scene reminded Derik of one of those spooky Edward Hopper paintings.

From the pocket of his athletic shorts, Derik removed his silver Zippo (a birthday gift from Sara) and a crumpled pack of cigarettes. He shook out the last one, making a mental note to buy another pack on his way home, and lit it. Engraved on the lighter's face was the Libra glyph which looked to Derik like the setting sun. Or maybe it was the rising sun? Sara was the astrology nut. Either way, he loved it because it was from her.

Dropping the lighter back into his pocket, he remembered the day she presented him with it, saying only half-jokingly, "If you're going to kill yourself, you might as well do it in style, babe." He balled up the empty pack and tossed it absently into the gutter with the other accumulated debris.

Derik took a deep drag and exhaled smoke into the blue-white sky. Butterflies—hell, *bats*—careened about inside his stomach. After a couple more pulls on the cigarette to steady his nerves, he dropped the butt onto the sidewalk at his feet and crushed it under the toe of his Nike. He headed toward the house on shaky legs, watching the windows (one of which had a whirring fan set in it) and getting an absurd but undeniable impression that they were watching him right back.

When he'd reached the half-way point between the car and the house, the front screen door swung open with a protesting screech and slammed shut again as a white man traipsed out onto the porch. He wore a Lynyrd Skynyrd T-shirt, blue jeans, and a greasy white ball cap with a black bill that covered his longish gray hair. Johnson descended the steps and advanced on Derik with an outstretched hand and a grin that flashed like a knife blade. "Derik?" he drawled.

"Uh . . . yes," Derik said.

"I'm Joe Johnson."

"Nice to meet you, Mr. Johnson." Derik reached out, and when Johnson seized his hand, he squeezed it like a vise and held on long enough for Derik to feel uncomfortable before finally letting go. Derik noted the tattoo of the coiled snake above the caption: "Don't tread on me" on his inner forearm.

Johnson waved his hand dismissively. "Call me Joe."

Derik nodded. "Joe, then."

Johnson stood there grinning at Derik, saying nothing, and the moment stretched out like warm taffy. Despite the late morning sun beating directly down on them, Derik noticed the man's face darken like an eclipsed moon. The humidity had already plastered Derik's T-shirt to his back, and he felt sweat trace its maddening way down his sides to his waist.

"Where's Sara?" Derik asked, trying to sound casual.

Johnson's face appeared to go even darker, though the grin remained. "She's around."

"I'd sure like to see her."

"I'll bet."

Derik didn't like the sound of that.

"I'm a little confused," he said. "What's this about?"

The grin slipped, and Johnson's expression looked injured. "I think a man has a right to meet the person his daughter intends to marry," he said. "Don't you?"

"Mr. Johnson . . . "

"Joe," the man corrected.

Derik sighed. "Joe. Not meeting you was Sara's idea."

"I know that."

"Well, then—"

"But a man should have enough respect for another man to ask for his daughter's hand. A *man* would have the balls."

Okay, tread lightly here, Derik cautioned himself. The thought reminded him of Johnson's tattoo. "And if I had asked you," he said, "would you have respected *me* for it?"

"Respected?" Johnson appeared to give this some thought. Finally he nodded. "Oh, yeah."

"But you still wouldn't have given us your blessing, isn't that right?"

The grin appeared again. "Right as rain."

35

"And why is that?" Derik asked. But of course he knew.

Johnson gave him a sly look. "Come on now," he said. "You're a smart boy."

It was Derik's turn to smile, but there was no humor in it. He shook his head in rebuke, saying, "Then what would be the point in asking your permission in the first place?"

Joe Johnson's eyes widened in surprise, then narrowed in disdain. "The *point*" —He stabbed a nicotine-stained finger into Derik's chest—"is doing the proper thing."

Derik pushed the hand away. "Don't do that," he said.

"The *point*" —Johnson took a step toward him—"is paying respect to your betters."

And here we go, Derik thought with resentment. *Another day, another douchebag.*

"My betters," he said.

"That's right."

"And what makes you my better?"

"Like I said, you're a smart boy. I don't need to spell it out for you."

Derik's jaw tightened as he ground his teeth together. This redneck son-of-a-bitch wasn't just pushing his buttons, he was hammering them. *Well, Sara warned you about him, didn't she? So why are you surprised?*

"Are you sure you *could* spell it out?" Derik asked, his voice trembling with barely contained fury. *So much for treading lightly.*

"What the hell is that supposed to mean?"

Derik said, "You're a smart boy. You figure it out."

Johnson frowned. "You're gonna make me mad, and this will be over too quick," Johnson growled.

"What?"

"Never mind." Big wet patches had blossomed at Johnson's armpits and chest. He smelled like sour whiskey and unwashed flesh.

Derik mopped sweat off his brow with his forearm. "It's too hot for games, man."

Johnson's watchful eyes fixed on Derik's. "You're wrong. It's a perfect day for games."

Derik knew he'd made a big mistake in coming here. He should have called the cops. But what would he have told them? *Hello, police? My white girlfriend's father just called and asked to meet with me. Can you send a car out?*

"Where's Sara?" Derik demanded. "I want to see her. Now."

Johnson seized him by the bicep. "Who the hell you think you're talkin' to, boy?"

Derik tore his arm from Johnson's grip and headed back toward his car. There would be no reasoning with this asshole. And punching him, albeit tempting, was a bad idea. Johnson was a white man, after all, and this was Indiana, and Derik was wise enough to know how that scenario would likely play out. He was out of here.

He had taken maybe three steps when Johnson gave a shrill whistle and Derik heard the screen door spring open and slam shut again, followed by the sound of something frightfully large scrabbling across the yard toward him. He flashed on a line that had stuck in his head from a poem he'd read a few years ago: *Beware the Jabberwock, my son! The jaws that bite, the claws that catch!* In a panic, Derik put on more speed. He was ten feet from the car when the biggest goddamn German shepherd he'd ever seen cut him off, stopping him in his tracks and snapping at the hand that was already reaching for the door handle.

"King!"

The dog drew back at his master's command, then held its ground between Derik and his car. It growled low in its throat and fixed him with sharp, hate-filled eyes that challenged: *Try to get past me, I dare you.*

Derik froze, but his heart was going gangbusters in his chest.

37

He tried to slow his breathing, terrified his heaving chest would provoke the animal to attack.

Johnson sauntered up beside Derik and placed a companionable hand on his shoulder.

"Darky like yourself come knocking on my door six summers ago—campaigning for that Muslim in the White House, he was—and ole King set on him like there was no tomorrow. Tore him up pretty good before I finally stepped in. I tossed him in the back of Henrietta there"—He nodded toward the old pickup—"and drove him over to the emergency room. He was back on his feet in no time, minus a couple fingers. But do you think he'll ever set his black feet on my property again?"

Johnson gave a satisfied chuckle as he squeezed Derik's shoulder.

Ever so slowly, so as not to bait the dog, Derik turned his head to face this man. "You're insane," he said.

Joe Johnson grinned at him. "Nope. I'm just done fucking around." Then he gripped Derik by the upper arm again and jerked him toward the walkway between the empty laundry mat and the house. "Let's go."

"What?" Derik protested. "Where?"

"Not far."

The dog at their heels, Johnson led Derik through the overgrown backyard between an abandoned washing machine and a collection of discarded car parts and out past a low metal gate to an alley. In the middle of the alleyway was a rusted rectangular grate. Johnson let go of Derik and bent down, hooking a thumb and forefinger through two of the grate's square holes, the muscles of his forearm popping up and making the tattooed snake writhe. He squinted up at Derik and said, "Give me a hand with this."

Derik snorted. "You've got to be fucking kidding me."

"I'm serious as a heart attack, champ."

Derik scanned Garfield Avenue past the south end of the alley, the sunlight bouncing off the river several blocks away and stabbing at his eyes. No help that way. Across the alley from the backyard a tall chain-link fence topped with barbed wire guarded a dilapidated brick building on a weed-choked lot. Derik turned and glanced behind him toward the other end of the alley. Not a soul in sight.

Johnson read his mind. "Shout if you want to. Whole damn neighborhood cleared out back in oh-eight. Might be some junkies squatting in one or two of the houses around here but they don't give a shit about nothing but their next fix. Cops don't even cruise here anymore."

Derik looked doubtfully at him, then Johnson startled him by suddenly yelling for help at the top of his lungs. He went on like that for ten seconds or so and when he stopped, the silence seemed even heavier than before, the air hotter and denser.

"Now get down here and help me, like I told you."

Derik still hesitated.

Johnson heaved a sigh, then said sharply, "King!"

The German shepherd lunged at Derik's ankle, its teeth flashing in a white blur. Derik felt an immediate and searing pain rush up his entire leg to his balls and he cried out in fear and anger. *"Call him off! Call him off! Call him off!"*

"King!"

The dog retreated, licking blood off his snout. Derik groaned and stared down at his ankle which now bled shockingly red rivulets onto his bright white Nike. "Goddamn it," he hissed.

"I'm not gonna tell you again," Johnson warned.

With grunts of effort (during which Joe Johnson let loose a loud fart and snickered like a kid) they lifted the grate from its casing and held it upright. Derik stood looking down into a crumbling concrete space about seven feet deep and four feet per side. About halfway up its south wall the round mouth of a concrete pipe yawned. Opposite this a metal ladder attached to the wall descended to a foot above the floor.

Standing there in the unbearable heat, Derik felt an icy tingle run up his spine.

"Get on down there," Johnson said. "And don't test me, or I'll let King there chew on you some more, only this time I'll let him finish the job."

While Johnson balanced the grate on the lip of the casing, Derik climbed to the bottom of the hole, his ankle on fire and his mind numb. How could this be happening? Where was Sara while it was going on? Why wasn't she calling the police, or coming out to demand that her crazy father put a stop to this madness? *Because she's not in the house. It was just a lie to get me here.* He even grasped at the possibility that this might all be a dream. But of course he knew better.

"Now, you got two choices," Johnson said. "You can stay down there in that hole, in which case you'll be dead from the heat in no more than two days, 'specially without water. Or you can get in that drain pipe and start crawling for the river. It's around three quarters of a mile, so your chances of making it are slim to none, but you never know. If you *do* make it, the pipe empties out about three feet above the waterline. All you have to do is wade over to the boat ramp and you're home free."

Derik stared at the opening to the pipe, his head spinning. "This thing can't be more than thirty inches wide," he said.

"Twenty-four," Joe Johnson said. "But you're a skinny buck."

Still contemplating the mouth of the pipe (and that's just what it was—a mouth, ready to swallow him whole) Derik said, "I'll never make it."

"Well, not with that attitude," said Johnson.

Derik shot him a look. "What's stopping me from going to the police if I make it through?"

"Not a thing," Johnson answered. "But I'm willing to bet you *won't* make it through."

"You're willing to bet your freedom?" Derik said. "Your *life*?"

Joe Johnson threw his head back and brayed laughter at the sky. "My life, he says." When the laughter died down, he rubbed tears from his eyes with his free hand. "What life is that?" he said to Derik. "You took my daughter away from me. My Sara."

Derik made one last desperate plea. "Don't do this, Joe. Let me up out of here. You can still do the right thing."

"You took her away."

"I love her, Joe."

"You took her away."

"Joe, please."

Johnson lowered the grate. And in that moment before it came down Derik observed over the man's shoulder a commercial airliner inching its way across the sky ten thousand feet up, its contrails drawing out behind it. He thought about the people on board, being served their refreshments, plugging their ear buds in to listen to music or cracking open a fat new novel, settling in for the long flight, and he wished harder than he had ever wished for anything in his life that he was on that plane.

After the grate was down and Johnson walked away, the dog appeared above, hiked its hind leg and proceeded to urinate down on Derik's head. He threw himself against the wall in revulsion, covering his head with his arms, but the grate slots caused the stream to spray every which way. "Ugh. Fucking mutt!"

Then he was alone in the half-light, sweat and dog piss dripping down his skin and burning the wound on his ankle. He cried out in fury and frustration.

He leaned against the wall and stared up through the slots. After a little while he had an idea. If he waited until dark, he might be able to climb the ladder and create enough leverage to

41

force the grate open with his shoulder, slip away and escape. The sonofabitch had to sleep sometime. There was the dog to consider, but still . . .

Derik heard the rattle of an engine approaching. A moment later the vehicle rolled onto the grate, where it stopped, its tire parked several inches above his head. A door opened with a squeal and slammed shut again. Derik caught the jingle of keys and receding footsteps. Then he heard Joe Johnson remark, "Just in case."

Derik screamed.

Ten minutes later, after cursing Joe Johnson to hell, cursing himself for getting his ass into such a fucked-up mess, and screaming himself hoarse (a mistake which left him terribly thirsty) Derik started his reluctant journey through the drain pipe.

After the first few feet, he fully understood what an ordeal he was in. The pipe was so constricting he could not take a full breath, and this triggered a low-grade anxiety he strove not to focus on lest it spiral out of control into full-blown panic. His arms stretched out in front of him, Derik crawled forward by dragging himself along with clawing fingers and flexing toes. In no time at all his lower back began to protest, then fiercely ache, and he tried to bend his spine to relieve the pressure, but the limited space would not allow it.

Soon even the diffused light was gone, leaving Derik in solid darkness which only increased the suffocating claustrophobia taking hold of him. The pipe descended at a slight angle and he assumed the temperature would drop the deeper he forged. He was wrong. The pipe's confines became explosively hot and that, together with the fact that he could only take half breaths, quickly turned his plight insufferable. *My Zippo*, he remembered suddenly. *Shit*. He could have used the damn thing as a torch to light his way, but getting it out of his pocket now would be impossible.

He crawled on. Before long he had scraped his knees and elbows raw, every few feet leaving more of his flesh behind him on the concrete. At one point he experienced a wave of panic so cold and paralyzing that he lay there in the dark, still as a corpse, for an interminable length of time. When he realized he was once again moving forward he couldn't even remember resuming. Derik wondered how long before he lost his mind in here.

Sweat dripped down his back and between his legs, causing a maddening itch made ten times worse because he couldn't scratch it. It made him think of Tantalus, the Greek god he learned about in high school Lit class. *Why does your brain come up with useless shit like that in moments like this?* he wondered.

The air was thick and heavy, the humidity clinging, and sweat continuously ran down his face and burned his eyes. For a while he rubbed at his eyes to clear them, but it was hopeless as well as pointless and he soon gave up. He thought he would sell his soul for a drink of cold water.

Farther on he came to a stench so strong it was like a physical blow. He halted, wincing as he tried not to imagine what caused that ungodly smell up ahead, and imagining it anyway. He peered into the darkness and willed himself to see the horror waiting for him, calling him onward with its sweet rotted breath. It was no use. He was blind as a mole.

With a sigh that was nearly a sob, Derik started forward again. The smell was appalling. It surrounded him, seeped into his pores and made its way up his nostrils and down his throat, becoming obscenely intimate, a malevolent companion embracing him there in the dark. Inevitably he arrived at the source, his hands coming down in a gooey mess at the base of the pipe. At first he jerked back, crying out in revulsion. Finally, though, there was nothing he could do but continue on through the slippery muck. As he crawled over it, the slime sucked at his hands and arms with wet slurping sounds, releasing him only grudgingly. He slid across the rot on his knees and elbows, feeling its foulness mix with his own blood. Pieces of skin and coarse hair stuck to his sweat-soaked face and limbs. Somewhere in the midst of the mess he vomited, then crawled through that too.

Then suddenly there were things on him, crawling all over him. On his arms, legs, and face. In his hair. Under his clothes. Biting him. He knew right away what they were. Carrion beetles. One tried to scuttle up his right nostril. Another one wriggled at his ear hole. Derik howled and rolled frantically back and forth and slapped at his head like he was on fire, the relentless stinging bites over much of his body feeling like dozens of hot match heads being held to his skin. They were everywhere, trundling over his body by the hundreds, the *thousands*, and in their agitation making a collective clicking sound he thought would drive him mad. In a frenzy he scraped them off by the handfuls, crushing their carapaces in his fists and flinging them away. But they kept right on coming.

In a mindless effort to escape them he scrambled forward as fast as the narrow space would allow, for as far as he had the strength to go before he needed to stop and rest. The beetles continued to crawl on him, to bite him. But he thought there were fewer of them now. And once he resumed his passage through the pipe, he felt them on him less and less the further he went.

Derik summoned Sara's face, pictured it suspended in the darkness before him, and crawled toward it. The illusion didn't last long though.

Something large scurried toward him from out of the dark. Before it reached him it halted a few feet away. Derik sensed it watching him in the dark, measuring him.

"Go away," he hissed at it.

Instead it came closer, then something bristled across Derik's outstretched fingers. He snatched his hand back in horror, screaming an incoherent warning at the thing. It scrambled away a short distance, then stopped. He felt it regarding him again.

Derik needed his Zippo.

He began gradually drawing his left arm back toward his body. It only took him a few short inches to realize he couldn't move it straight down along his side—there just was not enough room to maneuver. So he rolled his shoulder under him and dragged his arm backward beneath his torso. The pain in his shoulder was immediate and excruciating. The position of his arm under his chest forced his back up against the ceiling of the pipe, and now he couldn't breathe at all. Even worse, his chest now pinned his arm beneath him. He wrenched it forward, then back, then side to side, succeeding only in painfully scraping his flesh with no real movement of the limb.

He didn't panic. What he did was brace the rubber toes of his shoes against the concrete floor and push. Once, twice, three times. He well knew his forward motion brought him closer to the thing in front of him unless his noisy progress along the pipe's floor had frightened it away. He doubted it. Either way, he had to get a hold of the lighter. His arm rolled agonizingly beneath him, and for a few seconds he was sure it would pop out of its socket, but at last his hand fell against his hip. As he dug inside his pocket, something heavy crawled onto his right hand. Derik screamed and flung it away. He seized the lighter and yanked it out. But as he brought his arm forward it got stuck against his chest again, and this time he had no leverage to force it out in front of him. He couldn't draw a breath.

You're stuck like a cork in a bottle, babe, Sara spoke up in his head. *What're you gonna do?*

Good question. What *was* he going to do? He could already see little red motes floating in the dark space before his eyes from the lack of air to his lungs. He would soon suffocate.

Then he remembered one time when he was about twenty-one, he had stopped breathing in his sleep one night for some odd reason. He'd sprung awake in a blind panic, leaping out of bed and reeling through his apartment, gasping for air. But it was no use. His lungs were locked shut. He recalled as he bent over with his hands on his knees, fighting for breath, his mind screaming, *I'm going to die alone here and now. And I haven't done a damn thing with my life.*

What saved him was when he stopped trying to breathe in at all and instead exhaled forcefully what little air remained in his lungs. This had a triggering effect, and all at once his chest heaved as his lungs let in the biggest and sweetest breath he had ever taken.

He did that now, pushing as much air out of his lungs as he could manage. Even as he slipped into unconsciousness and experienced thoughts that might have been the beginnings of death dreams, he dragged his arm instinctively forward, the lighter clutched in his fist. He came back to himself with half a breath of sweltering air, his hand thrust out in front of him.

Derik flipped open the Zippo and struck the flint wheel with his thumb. In the sudden glare of orange-red light, the first thing he noticed was his knuckles scraped to the gleaming white bone. The next thing was a huge fat rat five feet away, its baleful black eyes fixed on Derik in the flickering light. The fire apparently didn't frighten it in the least. It stood up on its hind legs and sniffed at the air, its snout nearly touching the pipe's ceiling, then dropped back on all fours. Lowering its head level with the floor it stretched its neck out toward Derik, opened its mouth and made a high-pitched chattering sound. Derik felt ghostly fingers play along his spine.

The rat advanced.

Derik screamed, whipping the flame back and forth across the width of the pipe as tendrils of oily black smoke unspooled in the close space around him. He kept on screaming, hoping his voice as well as the fire would hold the damn thing back. It did . . . for a moment. Then the rat hissed at him and charged despite the flame. It streaked between his arms and snapped at his face and Derik felt a stabbing hot flash of pain in his bottom lip and tasted the coppery tang of fresh blood on his tongue.

He cried out in horror and disgust, striking at the rat with both fists, but the thing had already retreated. Drops of Derik's blood stained its teeth and clung to its whiskers. Derik tried to scream a warning at it again, but couldn't draw enough breath into his lungs now. He started hyperventilating, then lowered his cheek to the concrete, exhausted. The rat took advantage of this, scurrying onto Derik's shoulders and compressing its sleek body impossibly flat to steal across his back and buttocks to the floor behind him. It immediately began to gnaw at his right calf. Derik kicked his legs like a swimmer and scrambled forward a couple feet before quickly spending his strength once more. Sweat poured off him in buckets. The rat went at his leg again and all Derik could do was drag himself onward, inch by torturous inch, as it fed on him.

After a while the lighter's flame sputtered out, returning him to the awful darkness again.

He heard a voice up ahead. It echoed faintly along the pipe. *"Deriiiiiik."*

He stopped, straining to hear, and it came once more. *"Come to meeeeee."*

It was Sara's voice, calling to him from out of the dark, and he did as it told him.

At one point the rat slipped up the left leg hole of his athletic shorts to his crotch and began to sample what was there. At first Derik bucked and thrashed at the horror—the *violation*—of it. But at last he could only crawl forward and weep as he felt parts of himself being pitilessly consumed.

"Deriiiiiik."

47

"I'm coming," he croaked, his throat on fire. But eventually he grew numb to everything around him and time became meaningless and he lost all sense of himself.

Awake again.

There was a faint light ahead. He made for it, feeling stronger now. Unconsciousness must have given him his second wind. He realized he had lost the Zippo somewhere and didn't give a flying fuck. The rat also appeared to have departed and for this he was grateful.

The light got brighter and before long Derik was climbing out the other end of the goddamn pipe. He tumbled headfirst into the warm brown water of the Ohio and then stood with it sluicing down his body, rinsing his abrasions and lapping red around his waist. He inhaled great lungsful of fresh air and gave his back a long luxurious stretch. The pain was already subsiding.

He thought he must have been in the pipe for a long time because much of the light had bled out of the day. The sky overhead was the color of ashes. He looked west along the river and saw a dull and dying sun.

He waded toward the boat ramp. When he got there, he stopped dead.

High up on the wooden cross arm of a telephone pole sat Sara staring down at him, the long white gown she wore wafting around her dangling feet, though there was no breeze. On either side of her were a row of black crows, their bright dark eyes observing him with interest. As Derik watched, Sara slipped off the cross arm and drifted gently all the way to the ground.

As she glided down the boat dock toward him, he heard the crows cackling and whispering in human voices. Derik held out his hand to her and when Sara took it in her ice-cold grasp, he understood.

In his head, he was there. The dim interior of a shabby living room. A TV in the corner showing *The Price Is Right*. The greasy smell of fried pork chops coming from the dingy kitchen.

"I forbid you to see him again," Joe Johnson saying.

"Forbid me? I'm a grown woman, Dad. I'll see anyone I want." Sara heading out the door with a suitcase in her hand.

"I said no!" Johnson grabbing her by the arm.

Sara saying, "You can't stop me. I love him and that's all there is to it."

"I said NO, GODDAMN IT!" Johnson wrenching her backward and jarring the suitcase from her hand, it dropping onto the threadbare carpet. Sara stumbling over it, toppling, her head slamming down on the corner of the end table next to the couch. All of it over so fast, her life ending in an instant.

Derik understood other things too. Things that would flabbergast and horrify the creatures wandering oblivious through this world, consumed by their trifling differences and irrelevant concerns.

But there would be time enough to think on these things later.

For now, he and Sara were together again, and that was all that mattered.

It was time to go home.

Joe sure would be surprised to see them.

ANGEL WINGS

Paul Michaels

MASTERS OF MIDNIGHT

"AND IF YOU'LL LOOK HERE—*please* don't crowd the case, children, and *don't* touch the glass—you'll see what has been verified as a genuine piece of the very Ark Noah himself built on instruction from God."

Verified? How?

To Bobby Granger, there didn't seem to be too much crowding going on around the exhibit but being at the back his view wasn't the best. However, if the rest of the class felt the same as he, their boredom thresholds had long since been breached. Not that he'd had much enthusiasm to begin with. When their teacher had announced the trip to a local museum of unusual and religious artifacts it had been met with a desultory chorus of groans, boos, and sighs from the class, which Miss Appleby had shushed in irritation.

None of that had really registered with Bobby. He took the news with the same numb detachment he greeted most everything with these days.

His interest *had* been mildly piqued when their school bus had pulled up alongside the ramshackle wooden building on the outskirts of town, even though Bobby had been expecting grand classical architecture the likes of which he'd only ever seen on TV. But even that slight blip of interest had melted as soon as the group swapped the oppressive heat outside for an even more sweltering interior.

Bobby's spirit had wilted like a paper doll before a flamethrower as they were led around by the museum's curator, a thin, prissy-looking man in a bow tie, winding their way through a bewildering array of items which ranged from alleged holy relics to bizarre carnival sideshow attractions.

They'd stopped to look at a two-headed snake which Carl Taylor said looked like a badly-stuffed puppet, and since his father was a taxidermist, he should know. Then they'd examined a yellowed letter which supposedly was the actual order for Jesus Christ's arrest, despite the writing being faded to the point of illegibility. There'd even been a ball of elastic bands bigger than Bobby's head, an item whose significance or relevance he couldn't begin to fathom.

Now they were being given a glowing introduction to a piece of broken wood that by all appearances could have come from any construction yard, yet were supposed to accept that Noah and all the animals had once sailed upon a ship built with it?

Bobby wasn't much for religious fervor. Even though he'd been raised in a predominantly Christian house and community, he'd always found church tedious, even from a young age.

At the grand old age of eleven, he was of the opinion that God most probably did not exist. Even if he did, he was not the sort of God Bobby would want much to do with. Recent events had both reinforced this view and somewhat muddled its certainty in Bobby's mind, and he found himself oscillating between complete and despairing unbelief and childish wishful thinking.

Just as he felt this tour was going to crush the last sliver of life from him, his boredom and despondency scattered like dust blown from an old book when he saw the next exhibit.

Bobby's eyes widened and his heart stuttered. In front of him, within a large glass case, was a pair of wings, bigger than any he'd ever seen on any bird, either in real life or on film. The hubbub of the other students around him faded to a background murmur as his full attention was consumed by the glorious wings in the case before him. As the droning voice of the curator petered out of Bobby's awareness, he managed to catch the words, " . . . *wings of an angel, found on an archaeological dig . . .* "

Angel's wings.

He'd never imagined angel wings would look anything like this. For a start they were black, though not the midnight black of crow feathers but dusky, with a touch of gray. When he turned his head slowly, Bobby detected flashes of luminescence, a rainbow of transitory colors which disappeared the moment he saw them.

He stood transfixed, his vision narrowing until all he saw were those wings in that case, their depth of color sharpening and intensifying as he took them in, heightening their solidity. They seemed more real than their surroundings; or perhaps it was more that everything around them was drab and dull in comparison. They were majestic, proud, the wings of some forgotten angel warrior long turned to dust.

So taken with them and what they might represent, Bobby didn't notice the rough stitches and loose threads running up the insides of the wings, nor the very mundane and modern harness which bound the wings together. Even the gaps where feathers had come loose were lost on him. Such minor details were irrelevant to him. Or perhaps he simply ignored these flaws, lost as he was in the grandeur of something so magical to him.

He wondered if it could possibly be true. Could these objects have *really* once adorned the back of a celestial being? All at once his soft atheism—spoken of to no one but himself—seemed a meager nothingness in the presence of such ethereal majesty.

His small frame shuddered as he found himself on the verge of tears. This was an unexpected but all too familiar occurrence lately. His vision blurred and his throat constricted in bitter pain. He turned away and drew a hand across his eyes in anger. Usually he was alone when this happened, but the sight of those wings and the emotions they'd opened within him had caught him by surprise, like the yawning of a mighty sinkhole. Bobby bit back the sadness which ballooned in his heart.

Unaware of Bobby's inner turmoil, the rest of the class moved on to the next exhibit. Clearly none of that which had affected Bobby had touched them, for their eyes remained glazed with boredom, their faces painted with apathy. It took Bobby a few moments to get himself under control, and once he did he rejoined the other children alongside the next dreary item.

Yet he didn't remember anything else they saw after that, for his entire mind was completely, utterly fixated on those beautiful wings.

He remembered her voice, soft and low, as she read to him each night when he was younger. The smell of her skin: fresh, warm and soft, not long from the bath. Her hair tickling the sides of his face as she bent close to kiss his forehead goodnight. Warm breath as she whispered, "Sweet dreams".

He also remembered the ache of loss as her weight left his bed, the hollowness left by her departure a lament in his heart. The swish of the door as it pulled closed across the threadbare carpet. Muffled voices through walls as arguments began. Father growling with anger, mother pleading in cowed supplication. And, on occasion, the dull slap of flesh against flesh, followed by the suppressed choke of sobs.

He remembered how he'd muffle his own tearful sobs with his pillow, trying to ignore the gaping hole within him as he slipped into a shallow, restless sleep.

The next day at school, Bobby found his classmates lounging on the steps outside of school, discussing the previous day's trip, each trying to outdo the other with how dreary they'd found it all. Each statement was clearly an attempt to impress the *really* cool kids, those who were so cool they didn't even mention the visit as they passed cigarettes back and forth in cupped hands and affected nonchalance.

Bobby sat apart from them all on a small grassy hill at the back of the schoolyard, trying to read a book in the ever-shifting shadow of a big oak tree. It was another day of crushing heat as the sun beat down without mercy. His skin was greasy inside his uncomfortable and worn charity-store clothes, sweat prickling across his back and trickling down his forehead. His lungs felt compressed, preventing him from taking a proper breath. Through his discomfort, the rising and falling drone of the other children's voices buzzed around his head like annoying insects.

"Did you see the *cat*? The one with six legs? Oh my *GOD*, that was dis-*gus*-ting!" The shrill tone cut through the air, slicing straight into Bobby's skull, making him wince. The voice belonged to Terri Brasseaux, a gawky-looking girl nearly two years older than the other kids on account of being kept back. She tended to be obnoxious, and tried to dominate the other children via the status she thought her age conferred upon her.

Bobby didn't mind her, usually. She wasn't especially nasty, and could often be maternal to some of the younger kids. He also felt a little sorry for her. He sensed insecurity behind her forceful personality, a strong desire to be liked and accepted.

But at that moment Bobby's sympathy for Terri was at an all-time low. The oppressive heat, the inane chatter of the other kids, and Terri's high-pitched voice all conspired against him, drawing his attention to their discussion when all he wanted was to read, to get lost in fantasy.

"That was nothing. It was the stupid religious things that pissed *me* off. Bunch of boring old garbage. Only *idiots* think that crap is real." Bobby tensed at the condescending drawl. Its owner, Dylan McKendrick, *was* someone Bobby wasn't especially fond of, someone whose attention he tried to avoid. Not quite a bully, Dylan was a nevertheless a menace to his classmates. The boy was sly with it, never going too far or allowing himself to be caught by the teachers. To Bobby, he seemed like a snake that had learned to talk and wear human clothes.

Bobby gritted his teeth as Dylan continued. "I mean, imagine believing there's a special place you go when you're dead. Only fairies and lunatics think heaven is real."

Bobby clenched the pages of his book. He could no longer read the words, his vision constricting to a point of incandescent white light. He didn't know if Dylan was deliberately mocking him, but it made no difference. His anger had risen unbidden and blazing like it so often did these days. He had no control over its appearance. All he could do was hold himself rigid lest it consume him, cause him to have an involuntary outburst.

Carl Taylor decided to chip in. "Yeah, those animals in the cases looked terrible. My dad says they're not even real stuffed animals. They're fake, made of cloth and plastic. He says the guy that owns the place is a fraudt . . . a frids . . . a con-man!"

"Oh, shut up, Taylor; what would *your* dad know? He spends all day with his hands shoved inside dead animals. You ask me, *he's* a freak." Even without looking, Bobby knew Dylan was smiling, heard it in his voice, pictured Carl dipping his head in apology though he had absolutely nothing to apologize for.

Bobby's fury ratcheted up another notch. He was angry at Dylan, at Carl, at the whole conversation.

"But still . . . he might have a point . . . "

Now Bobby was sure, utterly positive that Dylan intended his words for him. There was a creeping note of cunning in the boy's voice, a knowing lilt that sounded to Bobby like a warning.

"I mean, those things *were* all utter trash. Especially . . . those big wings. Who did that guy think we were? A bunch of kids from the 'special school', dribbling and crapping ourselves and believing everything we're told? Nah, those wings were the worst thing in the whole place. You'd have to be a total *retard* to think they came from an actual *angel*."

Before the boy had even finished talking, Bobby was moving, anger propelling him to his feet.

"You shut your mouth. You just shut your damn mouth, Dylan McKendrick!"

His breaths came fast and hard, sucked into a chest that felt as though it was being crushed. Color and light danced before his eyes, the scene before him playing out in hyper-detail.

Most of the other kids stepped back out of surprise and maybe a little fear, though they would never admit to it. But Dylan stayed seated, a snake-like smile on his face.

"What's got up your butt, Granger? Did you think those wings were real . . . were actual angel wings? Surely not, Bobby. Why would you think that?"

That was when it hit Bobby, the certainty Dylan knew about his reaction to the wings, how they'd affected him. The boy wasn't stupid. Mean, yes, but not stupid, and in a way that was worse, made him more dangerous. If he was dumb, he'd be predictable, manageable.

Instead of being calmed by that thought and becoming more cautious, that realization made Bobby even angrier.

Now he knew exactly why Dylan was baiting him.

"Maybe . . . maybe if you thought those wings really *were* from an angel, you could believe your mom isn't *really* gone. That she isn't just a rotting corpse in the ground."

Those words served as a starting pistol for Bobby. He launched himself at Dylan, taking fierce delight in the look of astonishment that appeared on the other boy's face. He screamed in rage, swinging his arms wildly as the other kids scattered in panic.

Later that night, Bobby sat in an uncomfortably silent den with his father. Cold television light flickered across the room as a show played out its inconsequential and meaningless plot.

His outburst at school had gotten him suspended. Dylan had played the part of the innocent, feigning surprise at Bobby's actions. The other kids had backed Dylan's story, although reluctantly. It seemed to Bobby as if they'd known they were doing something fundamentally wrong.

Bobby had protested his punishment, but no one at school would listen. Phrases such as *'disruptive behavior'*, *'deteriorating attitude'*, and *'emotional distress'* were mumbled with little sympathy. He sensed they'd already made up their minds about the situation as soon as they discovered he was involved.

Bobby knew he was viewed as a troubled child, and he agreed that his personality had significantly changed since his mother's passing. Surely that was understandable. The death of a loved one was bound to cause emotional instability, was it not?

Even at the age of eleven, Bobby understood what he was experiencing, even if he wasn't dealing with it particularly well. Having a taciturn father whose emotions were locked away—at least the more tender ones—didn't help.

He looked at his father, who sat upon his chair in the living room as though it was his throne, as though he reigned over some remote kingdom of old. The man's craggy face changed expression rarely, usually to show disappointment in Bobby, as it had done when he'd been informed of the suspension. It also changed when roused to anger, a thankfully rare occurrence as far as Bobby was concerned, though much too frequent when mother had been alive.

Back then his father's skin used to twist like a scrunched

paper bag and his eyes would glow with fire. In those moments Bobby knew his father had been replaced with a rage-filled monster, a demon in human disguise that subsumed and suppressed his father's aloof personality.

Despite this, despite potentially risking the ire of this man, Bobby needed to ask the question which had been weighing upon his mind since the funeral.

"Um, dad? Dad?" He said.

No reaction.

Bobby cleared his throat, injecting volume into his voice.

"Dad, can I ask you something?"

The way his father turned to face him was ponderous, glacial. Bobby's insides trembled but he held his resolve despite the dead look in those eyes.

"Do you think, I mean, is it possible that mom . . . that she might live on somewhere in spirit? That she might be in heaven or something?"

Bobby dipped his head quickly as if expecting a blow.

His father remained silent, staring at Bobby for what felt like eternity. Eventually he sighed, closing his eyes briefly. His hands became fists where they lay on the chair's arms, clenching and unclenching.

"No Bobby, she ain't. Your mother is dead and in the ground and that's all there is to it. There's no such thing as heaven, no ghosts, spirits or souls. We're just dirt and that's what we return to. Now stop asking childish questions and let me watch my show in peace."

With that, Bobby's father turned back to the TV and spoke no more.

Bobby's guts churned, the strength draining from him. If he hadn't been sitting he might have collapsed to the floor. Tears pinched the back of his eyeballs and his throat closed over a bitter lump.

Yet beneath his grief, still fresh as ever, was a spark of anger, a kernel of fire which fiercely resisted what his father claimed. It whispered to him: *it's not true, she is in heaven; or somewhere like that. Her spirit still goes on.* The image of the angel wings crept back into his mind, expanding their hold on him.

Bobby waited until he was sure his departure wouldn't be remarked upon before slipping away to his room, climbing into a comfortless bed.

"Momma, when people die do they really go to heaven?"

Though only six, he was already well acquainted with death and its trappings, though until recently it had remained a mostly abstract concept.

Both grandparents on his mother's side—his father's lost before he was born—an aunt, and several pets had given him an almost blasé approach where the demise of loved ones was concerned.

That didn't mean he didn't feel the pangs of loss whenever it happened, but he was old enough now to begin more philosophical questioning.

His mother had pulled him close, smoothed her hand through his hair—it was always messy, sticking up in random clumps—and kissed his forehead.

"Well, you know that's what we believe to be true, and what the pastor tells us when we go to church. Remember?"

He'd nodded, feeling her chin rise up and down with the movement of his skull.

"If people just ceased existing, don't you think that would be an awful waste of all that life? All those memories and thoughts and ideas and personalities? If all that simply disappeared wouldn't that be the saddest thing? Hmmm?"

What she'd said had made sense to his little mind, though he'd felt he didn't quite grasp the full implication. It was as if the thought was too big for him to contain, at least at the time.

Something had occurred to him back then, his thoughts jumping around as they often do in the very young.

"How do people get to heaven, Mommy? I saw Grammy. She was just lying in the coffin and then they put it in the ground. When did she go to heaven? How did she get there? Did God come and dig her up?"

His mother's arms had wrapped around him again. She'd made a strange sound, halfway between a cough and a swallow, but when she spoke her voice was light and sweet as always and he'd heard the smile in it, with only a tinge of sadness.

"That's because the part of people that goes to heaven is invisible, Bobby. It's called the soul. The soul has their essence which lives on for eternity. You can't see it, but if you close your eyes and listen hard enough, you might hear it as it departs. It sounds like a hushed chorus singing one continuous, beautiful note. Those who've passed on are guided into heaven by angels. Now, isn't that better than simply ceasing to exist?"

He'd agreed that it was, but by then his mind had begun to drift onto some unrelated subject.

Many years later he'd closed his eyes and listened as she'd instructed. All he'd heard was the dull pulse of his own pained heart, the sound of blood rushing through his ears like a lonely, mournful surf washing over him as his mother's coffin was lowered into the dirt.

A few days had passed since the stilted conversation with his father. In that time the misery and bitterness at his young life had grown in tandem with his obsession regarding the angel wings.

He'd decided he had to see them again, and had snuck out into the night once his father was fully preoccupied with the TV.

The museum wasn't too far from his house. He'd arrived to find the building shrouded in darkness, but still waited behind a bush for an hour or so to make sure it was empty.

When his impatience could be held in check no longer Bobby circled the building, keeping low to the ground like Special Forces soldiers he'd seen in the movies.

Eventually he found a museum window that had been left unsecured. Heart thumping in his chest, Bobby eased the window open, tensing in expectation of it screeching on rusty mountings or getting stuck on a warped frame. But it slid up easily, without breaking the hush of night.

He hoisted himself up and through, landing on silent feet, crouching as he wrestled to control his breathing. After a moment, Bobby stood up, fairly sure he was alone in the huge, dark building.

The thought brought him little comfort. Now that he was here he felt afraid, and not just because he was trespassing. The deep gloom of the museum's interior was relieved only here and there by a small measure of ambient light from outside.

The exhibits he'd seen only a few days before had transformed from the ordinary to extraordinary, taking on a sinister appearance in the darkness. The two-headed snake looked as though it might strike at any moment, glinting eyes keeping watch on Bobby as he walked past. The pig with five legs appeared ready to bolt from its pedestal. A three foot tall figurine of the Virgin Mary now wrapped herself in shadow, taking on an unholy aspect.

Nevertheless, beneath his fear was a growing certainty, a calm reassurance that he was in the presence of something unearthly and wonderful. There was a hum deep within him, a buzz which soothed his nerves and released the tightness in his chest.

Despite the darkness and clutter of displays, it took Bobby mere seconds to find the angel wings. They emitted a subtle glow, a golden sheen which was only barely discernible. If he turned his head, it made the merest impression on his periphery, the barest suggestion of light.

But when he looked directly at the wings, focusing entirely on them, he discovered that all his sadness, anger, fear, and anxiety melted away. Peace and serenity consumed him.

Searching around the case, he quickly found the door at the back and unclasped it. He reached inside and pulled the wings from their display stand, handling them with reverence.

They were far lighter than he'd imagined, lighter than he thought they had any right to be. He nearly fell backwards as he lifted them up, braced as he'd been to take on a weight they failed to possess.

He turned them around in his hands, examining every inch of their fascinating detail. He still could not perceive the frayed stitching, the faded and discolored feathers or the threadbare gaps. The wings were perfect to him, without flaw or need for improvement. How could it be otherwise? They'd come from a divine being, though he had no idea in what manner an angel might be separated from its wings.

His nose failed to detect the dry, musty odor wafting from them. Instead, Bobby breathed in glorious fragrances, faint yet partly recognizable—sandalwood and cypress were words that came to mind. The sweetness filled his head with images and colors too, blooms of purple and crystalline yellow. He began to feel as though he was floating in the depths of space, as though some massive, unseen planetary body gently pulled at him.

He could have stood there basking in the glory of those heavenly wings forever, but then an idea occurred to him. Although it seemed to arrive fully formed, he guessed it had been growing in his subconscious ever since he'd first seen the wings.

So alluring was this idea, he shook off his pleasant stupor and carefully slipped the wings onto his back.

The harness was constructed of stiff plastic bands with canvas straps to secure it, and had obviously been added to the wings at some point in the not too distant past. Bobby was surprised to find how easily they slipped into place, lying snug against his back. His body adjusted quickly to the wings, as though they had always been meant for him, as if they were molding themselves to his form.

He cinched the straps tight as he looked around for a way to get onto the roof.

He found a doorway on the upper level which led to stairs. He climbed them only to find himself in a cramped attic space. Then he spotted his opportunity: a fire escape that led outside was to his right.

Bobby climbed carefully out onto a small metal landing, making sure the wings didn't get caught. Then he clambered up the fire escape ladder and onto the roof.

As Bobby made his way across the flat roof, he fully believed that if he were to hop into the air, he would be carried away on the wind.

Atop the building a slight breeze rustled through the warm night, so faint it was barely a breath. But the wings caught hold of this slight current, weak as it was, seemed to grab onto the wind and begin to move. Bobby thought he felt them flexing, as if they were now part of him, alive, not simply some contraption strapped to his back.

Bobby made his way to the far end of the roof.

Looking over the edge, he felt vertigo. From up here, the building appeared far taller than it had seemed when he was on the ground. The drop before him certainly looked like far more than the two stories he knew it was, even allowing for the attic space.

He stepped back from the edge, startled by a sudden urge to step off the roof into thin air.

He knew he shouldn't have been surprised. That was precisely why he was here. His belief in the power of the wings had compelled him to this point, an odd mixture of fear and excitement sweeping him along, never allowing him to contemplate the final outcome.

As he considered what he was about to do, his confidence faltered. He stared up at the dark sky, into unfathomable measures of distance and time, as stars shone pinpricks of light at him from above. Their seemingly eternal presence calmed him. He took a deep breath.

He thought about his life. The warmest light in his world had been extinguished with his mother's death, leaving him with a father who showed nothing but contempt and dismissal. How long would it be before that turned into anger and violence? Bobby was certain his father had loved his mother, but that hadn't stopped the arguments, the beatings, the cruelty.

He was bereft of friends, either due to his own doing or because they'd given up on him. Thanks to his suspension, he wouldn't be returning to school any time soon. Even the teachers had largely cast him aside as a lost cause.

The future loomed before him like an insurmountable black wall, oppressive and bleak. What else could there ever be for him except more pain, more misery?

Bobby stepped forward once again to the edge of the roof, tears dripping down his face. He reached over his shoulder to touch the wings for comfort, as he looked back up to the stars.

I'm coming, Momma, coming to be with you. I hope you're waiting for me.

As he launched himself from the roof into the night sky, Bobby thought he heard a soft chorus of gentle voices welcoming him into their ranks, as the wings on his back spread wide in exultation.

RUN RABBIT RUN

Andrew Lennon

MASTERS OF MIDNIGHT

TOMMY KICKED a hardened lump of mud as he walked along the trail through the woods. It broke into tiny pieces and flew in all different directions. He didn't pay any attention to this, continuing to walk, kicking a discarded Coke can instead. His head stayed drooped between his shoulders and his eyes stayed fixed on the ground, although his focus was elsewhere. His thoughts were still in school. How could one day have gotten so bad so quickly?

He'd been having a good day. Tommy and his friend, Alex had been planning their weekend. Alex was to come to Tommy's house, and then it would be a night of Pepsi, pizza and *Splatterhouse* on the NES. Tommy did have a PS4 but he wasn't the biggest fan of modern games, they were all graphics and no content. He had a love for retro gaming, a love that Alex shared. Friday night NES gaming at Tommy's house had become a regular thing. If they were able to convince their parents enough to let them, then they'd make it last the whole weekend. This weekend was supposed to be one of those times. Alex had gotten permission to stay over and Tommy's mother had informed him that she was fine with it, as long as they looked after themselves. She didn't want to have to worry about cooking for them as she had her own plans this weekend.

At fifteen this was no big deal. Tommy could cook—well, pizza at least. And they had more than enough cereal, so they'd live on pizza, cereal and snacks for the weekend. It sounded like heaven.

Over recent weekends they'd worked their way through quite a lot of the classic titles: *Super Mario Bros, the Legend of Zelda, Mega Man, Castlevania,* the list went on and on. The joy that those pixelated games gave those boys was unmatched by anything else. They'd never been great with girls, so they chose to ignore that quest for now, perhaps give it another shot when they reached college. Right now, games were the answer.

Alex had never heard of *Splatterhouse.* Tommy couldn't believe it. How could someone who loved games as much as Alex not know about that game? Tommy got far too excited while explaining the basics of the game.

"You look like Jason, right?" he said as he climbed onto the bench in the school yard. "And you get different weapons. It could be a machete, or a plank of wood, or an axe and then you . . . "

And that's when it happened. It was at that moment that Tommy's day took a drastic change in course. Tommy was demonstrating the game action to Alex. He stood on the bench and cupped his hands together, as though he were holding a baseball bat or something like that. In his excitement, he swung his clubbed hands and took a spin anti-clockwise. He hadn't seen anyone coming in his direction. He didn't know there was anyone there at all, until his double fist connected with the nose of Zak Marlow.

Zak was a monster of a boy. Still only fifteen, he towered over Tommy, Alex and every other boy at the school. In fact, the only person who was taller than him was Mr. Davies, the P.E. teacher. Zak was around six foot five, and weighed the equivalent of a rugby team. At least that's the joke that was told when he wasn't around to hear it. No one would dare say anything like that to his face, or else they'd be facing severe repercussions. Repercussions that Tommy was about to face himself.

Zak's face was an explosion of red. Tommy looked down at his hands in a daze. They matched the color of Zak's face. Tommy stood slack jawed and in shock, his eyes flitting back and forth between the two red patches. Blood continued to pour from the giant kid's nose. He cupped his hands over his face in a failed attempt to catch the bleeding. It just trickled through his fingers and dripped to the floor. His eyes widened with rage and he glared at Tommy.

"I'm going to fucking kill you." It came out muffled.

"Z-Z-Zak, I-I-I . . . " Tommy stuttered.

"You are dead." Zak stormed off towards the bathroom to clean himself up.

Tommy looked to his friend, his eyes almost filled with tears from the dread that bubbled inside him. His knees were shaking. He struggled to climb down from the bench and then sat and put his head in his hands.

"Dude, why did you do that?" Alex asked.

"I didn't fucking mean it!" Tommy screamed. "He's going to kill me."

"It'll be okay, man. I mean, at least it's Friday. He's got the weekend to cool down."

"Are you kidding me? It's Zak fucking Marlow. He doesn't cool down." The tears were now running down Tommy's cheeks. He had given up trying to fight them back.

"Dude, don't let everyone see you cry." Alex's eyes darted around hoping that no one could see. "Don't make it worse."

"I don't see how it could get worse." Tommy wiped his tears away.

"I'll meet you at yours later, okay?"

"You're not walking home with me now?"

"Erm, no." Alex bit his lip. "I need to go to my house to grab some things first. I'll see you there."

"Thanks, friend," Tommy spat.

73

He continued to kick the can along the mud trail through the woods. He just hoped that Alex was right. They could enjoy the weekend and fingers crossed by Monda, Zak would be over it, at least calm enough for Tommy to explain that it was an accident. No one in their right mind would take that guy on.

Tommy's gaze remained on the can as it rolled along the floor. He hadn't even noticed Zak waiting for him at the clearing on the edge of the woods. He hadn't seen the sinister smile that Zak wore, or the thick branch he held in his hand.

The can made a clank and rattled as it rolled along the ground, the bits of mud and stone inside jumping around and clattering within the tinny sides. Tommy kicked the can again, watching it roll along the dirt path until it came to a stop against a large black Dr. Martens boot. Tommy's eyes slowly began to rise from the boot, up along the blue denim jeans, past the faded *Metallica* print T-shirt, until he reached Zak's face. His nose was bright purple and still had specks of dried blood scattered around it. His smile grew until teeth showed, transforming it into a snarl.

"Hey there, tough guy."

"Zak, I swear I didn't mean to hit you," Tommy begged.

"Well, you did." Zak swung the branch from one hand to the other.

"I . . . " Tommy faltered. "Please, Zak."

"Shut the fuck up, you little shit. Come here and get what's coming to you."

Tommy turned on his heels and started running. Zak knew that he couldn't catch him, speed had never been his forte. Instead, he planted his feet and launched the heavy branch as hard as he could. It flew through the air, turning top over bottom, until it made impact with Tommy's back, causing him to fall to the floor. The impact was so hard that Tommy actually flew forward a little bit, like a scene from an action movie when one of the guys gets shot in the back. His arms and legs spread like a starfish, his back goes in and his chest goes out, his face holding a grimace as he flies through the air. If someone had taken a picture of Tommy when he reacted to the impact of that branch, he would've been suitable for a movie poster. *Tommy: Death in the Woods.*

He landed on the floor with a thud, his face connecting with the dirt. Mud and dust rushed into his mouth. He lay on the floor for a moment, feeling where his cheek had grazed on the hardened, soil path. He spat sand from his mouth and tried to get back to his feet. He pushed himself up, realizing at that moment he must've cut his hands as well, because they were stinging when he pressed them into the dirt.

Before he was able to get to his feet, a boot connected with his back and pushed him down to the floor.

"Where'd you think you're going?"

Tommy rolled to his back and faced the looming threat above him.

"Not nice being hit, is it?" Zak smirked.

"It was an accident," Tommy screamed, his voice breaking with fear.

"Woah, why are you shouting?" Zak looked around. "There's no one who can hear you here."

"Leave me alone."

"Fuck you."

Zak raised his boot and attempted to stomp on Tommy's stomach. Tommy raised his knees and managed to block it, but the impact on his legs still hurt badly. The block made Zak lose his balance. He didn't fall, but he did teeter to one side, giving just enough time for Tommy to get to his feet.

Tommy turned and ran off the path and into the trees. Zak started his pursuit, but Tommy was much quicker than him. Both boys knew that.

"You know you're gonna get it eventually, Tommy. So you may as well quit now," Zak panted.

Tommy turned to look at the giant that bounded behind him. Zak's face had turned crimson, Tommy didn't know if that was due to his anger or his lack of fitness. Regardless, he wasn't going to wait and find out. He pushed his legs harder, harder than he'd ever pushed before and somehow drove himself to increase his speed. He managed to see a glimpse of the dark brown trunk as he turned around—just a quick flash of bark before his face and chest felt the impact of it.

Feeling dizzy from the blow to the head and unable to breathe properly due to being winded, Tommy stumbled backward. His arms reaching out in front of him, trying to grab something, trying to grab anything, but there was nothing there. He fell and landed on his back, luckily the ground had been smothered by leaves from the trees. It managed to cushion his fall just a little bit. He didn't notice the sharp, jagged rock that was right next to his head. He had no idea how lucky he'd been not to land on that.

As Tommy's vision began to clear, a large shadow loomed over him.

"I hope that fucking hurt." Zak laughed.

The shadow slowly transformed into the image of Tommy's fearless predator. Zak sat atop the smaller boy, hammering his large fist into the nose of his prey.

Tommy's head bounced off the floor beneath him. He tried to fight back, but he was too weak. It was like Zak couldn't even feel his punches. He tried to roll away, but his attacker was too large, Tommy was pinned. He wasn't going anywhere.

Another fist connected with his face. He heard something crack. Possibly his jaw, he didn't know, but he was pretty sure that something had just broken. Tommy lay on the floor and wailed in pain. He thrashed from side to side trying to get free, but it didn't do a thing. If anything it seemed to make Zak's hold on him even stronger.

"Help." Tommy screamed a horrific, howling scream.

"Shut the fuck up." Zak slammed his knuckles into Tommy's cheek.

"Please. He's going to kill me." His were the guttural cries of a trapped animal.

Zak punched again and Tommy's head felt as if it were filling with air. His vision pixelated. It wouldn't be long until he passed out. He flung his arms around, trying to find some way to get out of the death hold the giant teenager had on him.

His hand touched something cold and hard. It was a rock. Tommy wrapped his fingers around it and then with the last bit of strength he had left in him, he swung his arm around and walloped the rock into the side of his attackers head.

A blanket of confusion covered Zak's face. His eyes widened with shock. Slowly, he slumped to the side like an overbalancing rucksack. Tommy rolled out from underneath him and managed to climb to his feet.

"Fuck you!" Tommy screamed.

Zak lay on the floor. He didn't respond. His eyes still held the shocked expression, not looking at anything, staring straight ahead. Suddenly the large body began to shake and convulse. Red, foamy liquid began to bubble and erupt from between his lips.

"What are you doing?" Tommy cried.

Zak continued to jerk on the floor.

"What the fuck are you doing?"

Suddenly the shaking stopped. It was then Tommy noticed the growing red circle on the side of Zak's head. It continued to widen as he watched. He looked to the rock that he still clenched tight in his hand. The sharp, jagged edge was covered in blood. A droplet fell from the tip, Tommy's eyes watched as it fell to the ground, everything slowing down. That tiny red blob slowly dropped lower until it eventually landed on one of the brown leaves below. The splash was miniscule, but the impact was infinite.

"Oh shit." The weapon fell from his hand and Tommy lowered to the floor and knelt next to Zak.

"Wake up." His eyes began to leak tears. "Wake up. I can't be a murderer."

Zak answered him with nothing but the stare of dead eyes.

"Oh shit, oh shit, oh shit."

Tommy circled the spot as if looking for some kind of answer to his problem. He faced the body again.

"Shit!" His voice filled the woods.

With nothing else left inside him but panic, he ran home.

When Tommy arrived home his mother was in the kitchen. He scurried up the stairs quickly taking them two at a time and rushed straight into the bathroom, slamming and locking the door behind him. He climbed into the tub and took a shower in a panicked attempt to scrub this nightmare away.

The water was hot, which stung his face, but soothed his body. After his attempt at scalding this experience from his body, he inspected his wounds in the mirror. Already he had signs of two black eyes coming through. His mouth was split and bloodied, his cheek swollen so much on one side that it looked like he had a golf ball embedded underneath the skin.

He knew that he should really go to the hospital, as he felt pretty sure that his cheekbone was broken. That would've been what the cracking sound was before. Luckily, he was still able to open and shut his mouth without too much pain, so he felt sure that his jaw wasn't broken. Although he was such a mess that it wouldn't surprise him. He was surprised that he was still alive at all, not like Zak. *Oh God, Zak.*

Tears began to stream down his bruised and swollen cheeks. His lip quivered and his body shook as he tried his best to not give an audible cry. He ran the tap from the faucet, repeatedly throwing water onto his face, as though it would somehow make him feel better, wash those memories away.

"Tommy is that you?" his mother called from downstairs.

"Hey. I'm just getting a quick shower and then heading straight down to the basement. Alex is due over soon."

"Okay, and have you organized dinner like we discussed?"

"Yeah, we're ordering pizza." He shouted from the bathroom.

"Okay then. Well I'm going out for a bit. Keep the place tidy, please."

"Will do. Bye."

"Love you, bye." His mother left and shut the front door behind her.

He didn't reply. For the first time ever when his mother had told him that she loved him, he didn't say it back. He couldn't, he felt that when she discovered what he'd done, she wouldn't even want to know him anymore, let alone love him. He had destroyed his life, and hers. He had killed someone. Self-defense, sure you could argue that, but who would believe it really? Even if found innocent, there would always be that doubt in the back of people's mind. No one would look at him in the same way again. He dropped to the floor and curled into a fetal position on the cold bathroom tiles where he lay hugging himself, crying.

Eventually, when the tears dried up, he put on some fresh clothes and stashed his torn and dirty clothes in the back of his wardrobe. He then went down to the basement and turned on the NES, holding a vain hope that it would somehow distract him from the situation.

After around half an hour of attempted play, Tommy's phone

buzzed and made a *ping* sound. He looked at the display. A text from Alex.

I'M HERE. OPEN THE DOOR, DUDE.

Tommy sighed, placed the controller on the couch and slowly rose to his feet. Everything in his body hurt. His knees felt like they would snap if he tried to bend them any further. Gradually, he made his way to the front door. When he answered with his back arched over, he resembled something of an old man.

"Holy shit." Alex's mouth gaped open. "What happened to your face?"

"Don't ask." Tommy left the door open and walked away.

Alex followed his friend into the house and downstairs to the basement. He just stared as Tommy struggled to get down to the couch.

"Seriously, you get hit by a car or something?"

"Yeah, a 2001 Zak Marlow." Tommy smiled with cracked, bloody lips.

"Shit. Zak did that to you?"

"Yep. That's not the worst of it though." Tommy could feel his eyes filling again.

"How could it be worse?" Alex leaned down now, inspecting his friend's face like it were a puzzle box or something. Tommy flinched away when Alex attempted to poke his swollen cheek. "What did your mum say?"

"She hasn't seen me yet."

"So how could it be worse? You look lucky to be alive if I'm being honest."

"I killed him," Tommy said, bursting into tears.

What he said next was unintelligible. Alex didn't say anything, simply stared as Tommy broke down before him. After a while, not knowing what else to do, he wrapped his arms around his friend and held him in a hug.

"It'll be okay, dude. We'll sort this," Alex whispered.

"Huh, how?"

"You're not fucking with me, right?"

"Are you serious?" Tommy screamed. "Do I look like I'm fucking making this up?"

"Okay, okay. Calm down." Alex stood up and paced back and forth in front of the TV. "Listen, Zak was a dick. Everyone knows that. It was self-defense, right?"

"Right. I thought he was gonna kill me."

"Right, and let's be honest. This guy has had it coming for years."

"Are you fucking serious?"

"Just hear me out."

"Alex, I killed him. I fucking killed him," Tommy bawled. "I don't want to go to jail."

"Okay first thing we'll do. We gotta hide that body."

"What?"

"Stay with me. Next thing. You're not gonna like it. We're gonna steal my dad's car and crash it. That'll explain your wounds."

"You're joking, right? Who the hell will believe that?" Tommy almost laughed for a split second, until he started blubbering again.

"Why would anyone question it? Two stupid kids go on a joy ride?"

"And why do only I have injuries?"

"Hey, I'm gonna be in the car when it crashes." Alex smiled. "I'll probably get something too, might even get off school for a bit."

"You're fucking crazy."

"You already knew that, dude. First things first. Put your shoes on. We need to sort out this body."

"Okay, enough fun and games, Alex."

"I'm fucking serious, Tommy," Alex screamed. "You wanna go to prison? You're young, and small. You wanna be someone's bitch?"

"Alex, I . . . "

"Put your fucking shoes on."

The walk to the woods took a lot longer than usual. Tommy struggled to keep pace, every step sending excruciating pain through his body. Alex had to help him along the way. It was dusk when they finally reached the tree line. As they walked farther into the woods, the blanket above from the trees started to block out what little light was left. Alex turned on the flashlight app on his phone and used that to guide them.

"Okay which way?" Alex asked.

"Just over there." Tommy pointed. "It wasn't far from the path. I was running and hit a tree and that's when he. . ."

"It's okay." Alex stopped his friend from talking before he started crying again. He could hear the break in his voice. "Come on."

They crept along through the fluffy pile of leaves, invading the woods with a rustling sound as the debris moved around their feet. Alex flashed the light from right to left, the beam catching something.

"There," Tommy said.

"What?"

"That's the rock."

Alex shined the light at the sharp-looking rock. About two inches on the end of the rock looked to be a dark brown color, but it wasn't very clear in this light.

"Oh shit," Alex gasped.

"I know," Tommy blubbered.

"Okay so where is he?"

"Huh?"

"Where is he?" Alex pointed the light at his friend.

"He should be here." Tommy looked dazed. He turned on the spot, looking for the body.

"Where is he, Tommy? Are you sure he was dead?"

"Yes I'm sure he's dead!" Tommy screamed. "I watched him fucking die."

"Where the hell is he then?"

"I don't know. I left the rock right next to . . . "

Tommy's phone started to ring in his pocket. He retrieved it and looked at the display.

MUM

He pressed the green "answer" button and put the phone to his ear.

"Tommy?" she asked.

"Hey," he replied, trying to sound like he hadn't been crying.

"Where are you?"

"Um. Me and Alex have gone for a walk. I thought you were out."

"Well I was. I just got back and one of your friends is here waiting for you."

"Huh?" Tommy gestured to Alex that he had no idea what she was talking about. "Who is it?"

"What's your name, dear," he heard his mother asking on the other end of the line.

"Mum?"

"Zak," she said. "Zak is here waiting for you."

KRUZE NIGHT

Lisa Lepovetsky

MASTERS OF MIDNIGHT

W HEN H UGH S PAFFORD SAW the poster for "Kruze Nite," he stopped his BMW so fast the bus behind him nearly crumpled his fender. As it was, the bus driver blared the horn the whole time Hugh took to jump out the door, run through a curbside puddle in his Italian loafers and tear the neon-orange poster from the light pole.

Hugh didn't care. He barely heard the nasal blast at his back. This was just the thing he'd been looking for recently—since his fifty-fifth birthday last month, to be exact. He pulled into a convenient parking space, and examined the poster more closely:

KRUZE NITE!!!
All '50s and '60s vintage vehicles welcome
Meet at sundown
at the old Dairee Kreme Drive-In
on SR 17
for the ride of your life!
Be there or be square!

And at the bottom of the poster was Friday's date, over a sketch of Hugh's car. Not the stupid black Beemer everybody at the bank expected him to drive, but the candy-apple red fifty-seven T-bird stored under a tarp in his garage. His car. For years Hugh had saved all the money his father paid him in the Harrod's Run hardware store, and bought the T-bird as soon as he got his driver's license. Of course, it was white when he first got it, but a few years later, Hugh had painted it himself—the brightest, hottest red he could find.

Even when he'd gone away to college and then a stint in Nam, he'd kept the T-bird. When he couldn't have it with him, he stored it on cement blocks behind his parents' house. They'd threatened to get rid of it when he and Lauren finally bought a house on the Main Line in Philadelphia—Lauren's dream, not his. And in spite of her glares and pouts and veiled threats, he'd towed it the seventy-five miles from his hometown, only to park it in the unused third stall of their new garage. He'd gently draped a canvas tarp over the still-bright paint and had nearly forgotten about it—except when Lauren complained each spring about the storage room it ate up in the three-stall garage. They needed the room for the kids' toys, and later for the kids' cars. Hugh ignored her comments, and eventually the kids were both gone to their own homes in distant states. And only the T-bird was left.

Now, sitting in the steamy BMW, listening to the hot summer rain batter against the metal roof, Hugh realized why he'd kept the Thunderbird. He'd known that someday, when he really needed it, he'd be given a chance to return to those innocent, simple days of his youth, even if it was for only one night. He wiped the moisture from his face and carefully rolled up the poster before driving home.

"You must be kidding." Lauren slowly put her fork down on the woven placemat and stared across the table at him. "Don't you think this male menopause thing has gone far enough?"

With some effort, Hugh swallowed another bite of grilled chicken. Usually, he changed into his sweat pants before dinner, but he had decided to keep the jeans on for a little longer this evening, even though the fabric cut uncomfortably into his thighs. At least Lauren couldn't comment about his waistline.

"I wish you wouldn't use that term," he said. "It's impossible for men to pause something they don't have."

"I've told you, it's a psychological thing," Lauren said patiently. "What do *you* call it when a middle-aged man suddenly decides to grow his hair long and wear blue jeans and cowboy boots to work in a bank?"

Hugh forced himself not to touch the graying ponytail dangling over his left shoulder. "I'm a vice-president," he said between clenched teeth. "I can wear what I want. And these are designer jeans. Anyway," he muttered, hating the way Lauren always put him on the defensive, "I'm sitting most of the day, so people only see my coat and tie."

Lauren just shook her head and continued eating in silence. After a few minutes, she said, "You don't even know it'll run."

"Of course it runs," he snapped. Lauren frowned, but said nothing more about the car during dinner. Hugh felt he'd lost an important battle, but couldn't quite put his finger on the turning point.

As he helped her load the dishwasher later, Hugh tried a new tactic. "You know, you could come with me."

She looked at him blankly. "Come with you where?"

Hugh wanted to slap her. How could she forget something so important so easily? "Friday," he sighed, "to that Kruze Nite thing. It might be fun."

"Fun?" Lauren peered at him incredulously, as though he'd just told a joke at a funeral.

"Sure." Hugh felt his armpits grow damp. He wished he could just shut up, but somehow he felt it was important to convince Lauren. "We could dress up in fifties duds. I'd wear a tee shirt with cigarettes rolled into the sleeve, and you could get a poodle skirt and a tight button-down sweater. You'd still look pretty foxy, babe."

He moved closer to her, and bent to kiss her neck. She moved away a step, still staring at him. But now her look was softer, a little sad. She ran her fingers through her short hair, and Hugh was startled by how many silver strands were mixed in with the dark ones. He hadn't noticed them before.

"I don't think so," she said quietly. Then she turned back to the dishwasher. "But you go ahead, if you need to."

Hugh felt a wave of relief, and realized he had secretly hoped Lauren would decline. For some reason, he wanted to do this alone. He tried to sound disappointed.

"If you're sure."

She didn't turn around. "I'm sure."

She pressed the buttons on the dishwasher, and it hummed and sloshed in the evening light glowing through the kitchen window. The rain had stopped, and bands of gold streamed from between the purple clouds. When Lauren turned toward him again, her face was indistinct in the dying sunlight. Hugh saw again the young woman he'd first asked out during his senior year in college, and suddenly he wished he'd known Lauren earlier, during those bright high school years in Harrod's Run, when the world was still crisp and new and she was just budding into womanhood. Regret and loss stabbed through his chest, and for a moment he couldn't breathe. He turned away, unable to look at her any longer.

Hugh went to the garage. He wanted to check out the T-bird, but instead of using the door from inside the house, he grabbed the remote control and went out the front door. He stood for a long time, staring at the square panels of the garage door. What if Lauren was right, and the car wouldn't run? He hadn't really driven it since he'd put it up on blocks—what? Thirty years ago? More? His jaw ached as he ground his teeth. Hugh pressed the button to open the garage door. The car hunched under the heavy tarp, barely visible in the dim light. Hugh pulled the tarp off.

And there she was—the symbol of his youth, gleaming cool

and crimson, like Sleeping Beauty's apple. He inhaled the metal-and-leather smell of her, laced with a musky underlying scent of petroleum. He ran his fingertips gently along the chrome edging the windows and sighed heavily. He looked out the open garage door into the pale purple air. Wisps of fog drifted along the driveway, undulating in the pink light from the street lamp.

And suddenly they were there, waiting for him. All the boys and girls he'd loved back at Harrod's Run High: Johnny Brazos, the handsome star quarterback who'd been killed by a sniper's bullet in Vietnam. Blond prom queen Jill Wallace hung on his arm. She'd dreamed of going to Hollywood, but became a teen mother instead, and drank herself into an early grave.

Shirley Todd and her twin brother Stan were there, too, though Shirley had been killed in a plane crash on her way to serve in the Peace Corps three years after graduation. Stan had hanged himself three months later. And Hugh's best friend, Frank Lucas, sat grinning behind the wheel of his baby blue Chevy. Good old Frank, who'd retired early to Florida last December, only to have a fatal heart attack while moving furniture into his new apartment.

But here they were in Hugh's driveway, laughing to each other and hanging out in saddle shoes and ponytails, just the way they had back in the school parking lot. The light was bad, and he couldn't see them clearly, but well enough to know they were teenagers again. No grey hair, no wrinkles or scars, no grief or fear or disillusionment. Just the enthusiasm and beauty of youth, their whole lives ahead of them.

As Hugh watched, stunned, they waved at him. Frank motioned for Hugh to come over, still grinning his famous lopsided grin. But Hugh hesitated. Was there something dark at the edges of that grin, something a little too enthusiastic about those waves?

Then Lauren opened the door from the house, startling him.

He whirled, his heart beating wildly with fear and anger. When he turned back to the driveway, his friends were gone.

"What do you want?" he asked, still facing the driveway.

"Do you think the car will still run?"

"Of course she'll run," he said.

He was sure she would. But he'd have to put the tires back on first, and check under the hood. There was a lot of work to be done in the next couple of days. He'd have to call in sick tomorrow. Without rolling up the sleeves of his blue silk shirt or even removing his sport coat, Hugh set to work.

By Friday evening, the T-bird was ready for action—and so was Hugh. Often Lauren had watched him from the doorway as he worked feverishly for two days—polishing, draining, tightening, greasing—all the things old cars needed. She'd said nothing, but her face had spoken loudly enough. The spidery creases at the corners of her eyes and around her lips deepened as the worried frown became permanent. No matter how he tried, Hugh could no longer find in her the young woman he'd once loved.

He'd bought a black leather jacket Friday morning, and pulled it on over his white tee shirt, though the late afternoon was quite warm. He'd even gotten his hair cut, and smoothed the sides with his palms. He liked the feel of the slick hair, curling at the nape of his neck, though he wondered whether he should have touched up the grey. He shrugged: too late now.

Lauren was at her usual post, standing in the open door leading from the garage to the house, arms folded across her chest.

"What do you think, babe?" Hugh asked brightly.

"Please don't call me babe."

"Sorry." Hugh sighed. Why did she always have to rain on

his parade? He unfolded a road map, and began studying it. "Where's Route 17?"

After a moment, Lauren came down into the garage. She leaned against the side of the car, and held out her hand for the map. Hugh gritted his teeth. He knew she'd never understand, but couldn't hold the words back.

"Please don't lean on the car."

Lauren straightened and moved away from the car, but she said nothing. Hugh resisted the impulse to run a rag along the hood where she'd been leaning.

"Thanks," he muttered, then pointed at the map again. "I can't find 17 anywhere around here."

Lauren stared at him for a long moment, then said, "Route 17. Isn't that the little road between Harrod's Run and Willow Hollow, where you and your buddies used to drag race? I remember you always joked about Route 17 being lucky, because that's how old you were when you got this car."

Hugh slapped the map. "Of course!" he cried. "That's why the Dairee Kreme sounded so familiar. They served the best chili dogs in the whole state. God, I'm such an idiot. How could I have forgotten?"

He tried folding the map, but suddenly the creases all seemed to run the wrong direction. Cursing, he threw it to the ground. "Forget it. I've got to get going."

"Willow Hollow's nearly sixty miles from here," Lauren protested. "You'll never make it in time."

"Sure I will," Hugh smiled, peering at the cloudless sky. "Kruze Nite doesn't start until sundown. I still have a good two hours 'til then, plenty of time if I put the pedal to the metal."

The now-familiar frown clouded Lauren's face again, but she said nothing about not driving too fast. Instead, she came past the front of the car, careful not to touch the red metal, and put her hand on his cheek. Then she kissed him softly on the lips.

"I wish you didn't have to do this," she said.

He opened the door and slid onto the white leather seat. "I don't *have* to," he protested.

"Don't you?"

"Of course not. I just think it'll be fun, that's all."

Hugh slammed the door—a bit harder than necessary—and started the engine. Lauren stepped away as the car roared. Hugh backed out of the drive and squealed away, glancing only once into the rearview mirror as he approached the stop sign at the end of their block. Waving from the drive, Lauren seemed less real, like a character in an old movie. Then he turned the corner and she was gone.

Hugh eased down the ramp onto the turnpike and drove west, into the sun, toward his hometown, toward Willow Hollow, toward Kruze Nite. His hair whipped around his face and the combination of wind and sunlight reflecting off the hood made his eyes water, but he refused to allow himself the luxury of prescription sunglasses. Bifocals simply were not cool. They were for old people.

As the trees and farmlands flew by, Hugh felt as though the years were being torn from him by the wind, like tattered clothes. He turned on the radio, found a "golden oldies" station, and sang along with his favorites at the top of his voice: Buddy Holly, The Big Bopper, Richie Valens. *Where were they all now?* he asked himself. When Hugh couldn't remember the words, he just made them up. As the turnpike disappeared beneath his tires, the sun dropped until it glittered behind the hemlocks. The air turned a bit cooler.

Finally, he found the exit that would take him through the hills to Route 17 and the Dairee Kreme Drive-In, where he'd meet with other classic car owners and cruise the local towns in a rock 'n' roll caravan. Hugh felt his stomach tighten in anticipation, and turned off the radio so he could concentrate on his driving.

The two-lane road snaked through the woods, and traffic trickled down to the occasional rusty pickup truck. He nearly missed the turn-off to Route 17, the sign partially hidden by leaves. The sky to the west was a deep magenta, and the air streaming past was dampening as the dew point approached, but he knew he must be almost there.

"Please," he murmured to the darkening woods, "don't leave without me."

At last, he rounded a sharp bend, and there it was—the Dairee Kreme Drive-In, at the far side of a rutted, overgrown dirt parking lot. The old wooden building huddled in the light from his headlamps like some angular animal, frozen with fear. The sign still dangled dangerously from its metal post by one chain, swaying slowly in the gentle breeze. There were no other cars, no signs of life. Venetian blinds shielded the large front windows from prying eyes.

Hugh cranked up his windows against the encroaching dampness and climbed stiffly from the T-bird. The damp air made him shiver, and he was glad for the leather jacket. He stopped and gazed around him in the dim light, afraid they'd left early. But there were no tire marks in the surrounding dirt, none but his own, no crushed tall grass other than what he'd just driven over. Nobody else had been here yet.

Hugh headed toward the dark building. Perhaps someone was waiting inside or around the back to greet the drivers, to let them know what was going on. High grasses whispered against his blue jeans, and he slapped at mosquitoes and gnats, roused from their nests by the scent of warm flesh and blood. He found a door at the side of the building, but it was bolted with a heavy padlock.

Hugh continued around toward the back, where the purple shadows faded to black among the trees and dense underbrush. He found another door, and this one opened when he turned the knob. Rusty hinges screamed loudly, and a bird answered in the distance. He went inside.

"Anybody here?" he called, though he didn't really expect an answer. The air inside the diner had the neglected, motionless feeling of long-deserted buildings everywhere.

He had entered through the small kitchen. A door into the main serving area was barely visible in the gloom, and he headed that way. The front of the building was dark, as well, except for the glow from his headlamps pinstriping the windows through the venetian blinds. Hugh pulled the filthy, frayed cord, raising the thin metal strips of the blinds until the center window was clear.

He looked around. To his left was the familiar sliding window and counter for the drive-up customers. He ran his fingers across the top of one of the round metal tables, for the few older customers who didn't care to eat in their cars. The old Coca-Cola clock had stopped at two-fifteen. The whole place was silent, as though it were waiting for something, listening for something.

Then Hugh heard it. Very faint at first, then gradually louder—the rumble of tires and deep thrum of motors. He squinted through the dusty glass, shielding his eyes with one hand. Behind the T-bird, he could barely make out a long line of classic cars driving past the overgrown Dairee Kreme parking lot. Three of the cars pulled out of the line and drew up beside Hugh's car, engines idling, headlamps burning through the grimy panes. The others pulled onto the shoulder of the road.

The doors of the three cars opened simultaneously, as if on cue, and the occupants emerged. The figures moved a few steps toward the diner, until they were silhouetted by the bright lights from the cars. Hugh couldn't see their faces, but he'd known who they were even before they got out of their cars.

Jill waved first. Her charm bracelet glittered on her wrist, and Hugh remembered when Johnny had given her the bracelet for her 'sweet sixteen' birthday party. Then they were all waving at him, looping their arms in big circles, motioning for him to come with them. He rubbed at the window, trying to see them better, but the dirt only smeared, creating odd distortions in the bodies of the five teenagers.

"Wait up," Hugh called to them. "I'm coming." His voice seemed unnaturally loud, and seemed to bounce around the empty room, frightening him a little.

He pushed through the kitchen door, his eyes straining to adjust to the darkness. As he stepped out into the cool damp air, a voice in the back of his mind—a grown-up, serious voice— reminded him that the people he'd seen out front couldn't possibly have been the friends of his youth. Those friends were all dead.

But Hugh pushed that voice away. He didn't want to hear it. Because there was another voice, a younger, desperate voice shouting how it didn't matter. Either these people looked very much like his friends, or he was hallucinating them there because he wanted it so much. And either way, he didn't care. Hugh was going back tonight, back to a better time, a younger time, and it didn't matter to him how he got there. It was just for one night, after all.

He stumbled around the corner of the diner, terrified that they'd have left, gone on without him. But they were still there, five young dark figures outlined in the glare from eight headlights. As Hugh approached, they all turned back to their cars: Johnny and Jill got into his black M.G. convertible, Stan helped Shirley into their dad's Desoto, and Frank opened the door of his blue Chevy.

"Wait," Hugh called to them. He couldn't think of what else to say, but he didn't want them to just leave like that. There should be more.

Frank shook his head as though he'd heard Hugh's thoughts.

He motioned for Hugh to get into his own car, then slid behind the Chevy's wheel. After a moment, Hugh climbed reluctantly into the T-bird. He closed the door behind him and removed the emergency brake. The smell inside the car seemed musty now and cloying, the fumes a little too strong. Hugh wanted to roll down his windows, but the cars on either side of him were moving now, circling around him to join the long line of old cars waiting at the side of the road.

Frank drove past him first. Hugh smiled and lifted his hand to wave. But in that moment, Frank's face was illuminated by Hugh's headlights, and Hugh saw it clearly. It was not, as Hugh had first assumed, the face of vibrant youth. Frank's skin was pale grey, mottled with purple blotches under the colorless eyes. His mouth drooped sharply, in a death rictus, a bizarre imitation of the familiar lopsided grin. Something crawled from the corner of his lips, and Hugh gagged.

Then Stan and Shirley rolled by in the Desoto. Shirley was mercifully hidden behind her brother, but Stan's head lolled to one side at an impossible angle, flopping loosely as the car bounced over a pothole. His hands were clasped to the steering wheel, but he couldn't have been controlling the Desoto's movement. Hugh tried to scream, but didn't have enough air in his lungs.

Suddenly, Hugh knew with an awful certainty what he'd see when Johnny and Jill joined the procession. Johnny's head would be blown open in the back, and Jill's peaches-and-cream complexion would now be bloated and pasty, like the flesh of some pickled animal. He pounded his foot onto the clutch and grabbed the gearshift, desperate to get far away from the Dairee Kreme Drive-In and its terrible customers.

But when he wrenched it toward him, nothing happened. The stick wouldn't move. He pulled again, with both hands, but to no avail. He tried to yank it in different directions, but nothing worked. Panting, Hugh wiped sweat from his eyes. The car wouldn't respond, no matter what he did. Panic gripped him.

Hugh bit hard into his lower lip, hoping the pain would help bring some clarity to his mind. It did. The grown-up voice returned, reassuring him that even if the people in those cars were really the specters of his long-dead friends, they couldn't hurt him.

Just wait for them to go away, it said. Then you can relax and figure out what's wrong with the T-bird. And you can go home. Hugh clenched his teeth and closed his eyes, and waited. His tee shirt felt clammy beneath the leather jacket, and he could smell the ripe, metallic odor of his own fear.

Suddenly, he felt something move in his right hand. He realized he was still holding on to the gearshift. The knob was moving by itself, putting the T-bird into first gear. And the car lurched forward.

Hugh jammed his right foot onto the brake until his leg ached. But nothing happened, the pedal never moved. The car continued forward until it was moving slowly behind Johnny Brazo's black M.G. Hugh yanked at the door handle. It remained locked in place, as though welded there. As did the window cranks. Hugh began crying, pounding at the windows.

"Let me go," he shouted against the glass. "I've changed my mind. I want to go home." But the pale young faces in the other cars never wavered, dead eyes fixed on the long journey ahead.

Hugh screamed. And the candy-apple red T-bird moved quietly into place at the end of an unending line of shiny old cars.

THE RULES OF LEAP YEAR

Monique Youzwa

MASTERS OF MIDNIGHT

IT WAS FEBRUARY TWENTY-NINTH AGAIN.

Over the next 24 hours, one of my family members would try to kill me. After six leap years, there weren't that many of us left. I had made all the proper preparations. The alarms were all set, ready to blare out their warnings the second someone stepped onto the property. The secret passageways were all sealed, except for one, but this was a new addition only I knew about. The contractor who installed it had known about it, but he won't be telling anyone. I made sure of that.

I sat at the bank of screens, watching feeds from two dozen cameras. A pistol was holstered at my side and a shotgun rested on my lap. Though it was just after midnight, the screens were lit up like noon, with floodlights keeping shadows to a minimum. No one was going to set foot on my property without my knowledge.

And it *was* my property, regardless of what my extended family believed. I earned it twenty-four years ago when I killed my father and claimed the land for my own. It was his fault, really. Grandfather had been very specific about the rules, as stated in the private video will his executer had played for us. No law would allow such a will to stand, but our family had no use for the laws of society. We made our own laws, and had the money to keep the law off our backs.

An alarm sounded at 12:07 A.M.. I sat up, checking the location. It was the back gate. I brought it up on the main screen, watching for any movement. The gate was open, swinging in the breeze, but nothing else moved. Since I had locked it myself less than an hour ago, I knew this wasn't an accident. I checked the feeds from the surrounding area. Nothing else moved.

"Bait?" I asked the screen. It wouldn't be the first time someone tried to lure me out of the house in the hopes of an easy kill. Gregory had lost that night. He hadn't expected my decoy or my skill with a sniper rifle. No one had tried such uninspired tactics again in the last sixteen years.

Until now.

I watched the gate swing for a few minutes, wondering who was on the other side of the fence. Laurence, perhaps? He refused to go by Larry, felt it was beneath him. Apparently, his career as a sandwich maker elevated him above such a common name. He seemed like the type to think such a silly tactic as opening a gate was brilliant.

Draw me out and kill me in the yard? Imbecile.

Karen would also resort to such juvenile measures. Not because she was young, but because laziness was her major flaw. The other five I wasn't so sure about, but I wouldn't put it past any of them.

Another alarm went off, this one at the front of the house. The cameras there showed another wide-open gate.

"Hmm. Fast one," I murmured. It was a long way from the back of the property to the front, especially if you had to take the long route outside the high stone wall. I glanced at the family photos displayed on the wall beside me, wondering which one of them could have trained enough to reach it at such speeds. None seemed likely to me, but I had to admit I didn't know any of them terribly well. My private detectives kept tabs on all of them, but those details showed more about their marital status, working habits, hobbies, things of that nature. Their personalities were of no interest and may have changed over the years. None of them had gym memberships, or I would have heard about it. But there was nothing to stop them from working out in their own homes.

I turned back to the cameras. A figure moved by the front

gate. The person didn't enter the property, just walked by. Whoever it was went to great lengths to hide their identity. The hood of a plain black sweatshirt blocked their face from view. Black pants and boots completed the outfit. The hands were covered in black gloves. I couldn't even tell the gender. The person disappeared behind the wall again.

Alarms sounded moments later, this time on the north side of the house. There was no gate there, only the 8-foot wall that surrounded my property. I stared at the camera, a thin finger of fear tracing its way down my spine.

"That can't be," I told the screen. The figure had crossed the other way by the gate, from north to south. How could they have crossed back without me seeing? Perhaps they had moved farther back before heading north again.

There was no movement on the north wall cameras. Perhaps whoever was out there had thrown something to distract me. I quickly scanned the rest of the images but saw nothing out of place. I leaned back in my chair, checking the time. 12:32 A.M.. The 29th had barely begun and already I was under attack, seemingly from all sides.

I sat up in my chair again, clutching the shotgun to my chest. All sides? Could all of them really be out there? All seven remaining members of the family?

"Why would they work together?" I asked the cameras. "Only one of them can claim the property."

Another alarm, this time on the south side.

Again, no movement that I could see.

Moments later, a figure by the back gate stopped in the center of the opening. They turned and faced the house. Another figure appeared by the front gate, repeating the gesture. A third person scaled the fence on the south side, perching on top of the rock wall. A fourth did the same on the north wall. None had actually set foot on the property yet, but it was coming. I knew it.

The question was, which one would it be?

Another thought suddenly hit me. What about the other three? Why had they not been included in this silly plan? Had they not been trusted enough by these four? Or were they out there somewhere as well, hiding in the shadows, waiting for their turn in this game?

The two on the fence dropped down again, out of sight on the far side of the wall. The two at the gates also disappeared behind the wall. I stared at the screens, waiting for them to reappear.

Two hours later, there had been no sign of any of my unwanted visitors. I knew they were trying to confuse and frighten me. Get me worked up so I would panic and make a mistake. It had almost worked for a moment when I saw that there was more than one of them. But they couldn't all claim the prize, and would turn on each other long before they found me. I was sure of it.

After so long without any action, my eyes began to get heavy, my body sore from sitting in front of the screens for so long. The bed in the corner of my little sanctuary beckoned with its softness and comfort, but I knew lying down was a terrible idea. Especially when I knew four of them were out there. Instead, I stood up, stretching my arms, legs, and back. I took my time, watching the screens as I did it. When the stiffness eased, I stepped over to the table beneath the family photos. A coffee maker sat there, along with a couple of mugs and a sugar bowl, already filled with my favorite blend. All I had to do now is turn it on and wait.

Within a minute, a heavenly scent filled the room.

I was pouring my first cup when the alarms blared again, four at once this time. The noise startled me and I spilled coffee on my hand as I jerked towards the screens. I saw two figures strolling through the front gate. Two more entered at the back. Another two had scaled the south wall, and the last one dropped down on the north side. I wondered if the three new ones had been there the whole time, hiding in the shadows while the other four played their little game. Or had they just shown up?

Not that it mattered either way. What did matter was that all seven of my relatives were now here, on my property. They spread out when they reached the house, and I watched as they tested windows and door handles, attempting to enter my home.

After a couple of minutes of knob twisting and window rattling, one of the potential intruders grew bolder. The gloved hand found a rock in the flower bed he was trampling and used it to smash the big picture window in the dining room. Then the devil waved his companion over, helping them through.

The companion wasn't too careful, though. I smiled as I watched the idiot boldly grab the sill and then suddenly pull back, falling out of the window.

"Hmm, did you get cut? How sad for you."

The glove was yanked away from the wounded hand. The blood on the palm looked black in the floodlights, and I smiled at the sheer quantity of it.

"Serves you right," I said. "That window's going to cost a fortune to replace."

The wounded one climbed through the window again, favoring their cut hand. Once inside, they grabbed a napkin off my dining room table and wrapped it around the wound. I saw the white fabric darken immediately and cursed them for ruining it. Those had been Grandmother's and I had kept them in pristine condition until now. The other member of this particular duo stepped through the window, much more carefully than their companion. The two of them stood together, bobbing their heads and making small gestures with their hands. Then they split up, one creeping to the front of the house. The injured one headed to the back, wrapped hand clutched to their chest.

I watched as they opened doors, letting the other members of my family into my house. On another screen, the lone member of the group smashed a hole in my patio doors, reaching through the glass to unlock it. This one crept inside, stepping carefully over the broken glass on the floor, and I cursed whichever family member it was. Another expensive repair was in my future. This was going to be the most costly leap year I'd ever had, especially when considering the renovations I'd made to create my current hiding place.

All seven of them gathered in the main hall. By their nods and gestures, I assumed they were making plans to find me. One of them turned, staring up at the camera. I sat up, disturbed by this. None of them could possibly know the locations of the cameras. Every one had been installed after I'd taken possession of the property. Since I'd done all the work myself, there had been no one else to give out the location of my cameras.

But here was someone, staring right at it, as if he or she wanted me to know they knew it was there.

"You can't know that!" I yelled at the staring figure.

Their hand slowly lifted, waving back and forth, countering my statement without knowing I had made it. Then the fingers folded in, all but one. The bastard was flipping me off.

One of the other members of the group pushed the hand down, gesturing to the stairs. The bold one nodded. Then the group dispersed, all heading in different directions.

I sat back, the heat of my anger dying away. I helped it along with a smile, knowing that there was little chance they would find me. This room hadn't existed when Grandfather was alive, and Father hadn't had the time to make any changes after Grandfather's will had been read.

I often wonder if the old man had known that he would die

on February 29ᵗʰ, had somehow planned the reading of the will on that particular day? Had he known that chaos would follow?

His executor had been present, as had the rest of the family. The moment the old man had been declared dead, he had asked us to join him in Grandfather's study. There were some protests from the overwrought members, but the man had insisted. When the will was mentioned, family greed took over, and everyone followed him willingly.

When we had all settled in the large room and the door had been locked behind us, the executor had opened Grandfather's safe and pulled out a folder and a disc. We'd waited impatiently while he slid that most important document out and began to read what was written there.

"Cornelius Garrison has created a video that explains the details of the will. I will confirm the funeral arrangements as you watch it. When it has finished, the paperwork will be signed." The man peered at us with cold, unfeeling blue eyes, then placed the disc in the laptop on the desk. He turned it towards us, clicked the mouse to play the video, and strode out of the room, closing the door behind him.

Grandfather appeared on the screen, sitting behind the desk before us, his wrinkled hands folded on the blotter.

"If you are watching this, then I am no longer with you. I have lived a long life, a hard life, fighting in three wars, risking my life for my country so my children could be free. But along with that freedom, you have learned complacency and greed. You come to me, one at a time, begging for the money I worked hard to earn over the years so you don't have to earn your own. I have helped where I can, but no longer will I give you what you haven't earned. I killed men in the wars I fought, to save myself and my friends so I could come home to my family. But my family has no understanding of what that means: to have to kill in order to stay alive. But now you will, if you want what you feel is yours, to possess the estate you believe you are owed for sharing my genes.

"But there are rules to be followed, just like I had during my service. All I have will be left to Gerald Garrison, my eldest son. The house, the land, the stocks, the money, all now belong to you. No one may take them from you, and you are not to give anything to your undeserving relatives. If you pass away, you may set the new will as you see fit, though I hope you are heeding my words and considering whether or not your family deserves your generosity.

"As for the rest of you, you can obtain the wealth Gerald now possesses if you have the stomach for it. For every four years, on February 29th, you can attempt to take the wealth for yourself. You must kill Gerald to do so, at which point everything he has passes to you. Whoever claims his life will gain the entire estate. No other killings are allowed that day, or any other until the next leap year. This will teach you patience, which is another quality most of you lack.

"The process will continue each and every leap year until this family learns what it means to earn the things you desire in life, or until you're all dead. If it is the latter, then the world is better off without you."

We all stared at the screen, even when the video ended and only blackness remained. A few moments later, the door opened and the executor entered. He crossed to the desk, opening the folder and pulling out the paperwork. He held out a pen to Gerald, my father. Gerald stared at the pen in stunned silence, then grasped it in his shaking hand, and signed the papers where the executor indicated. The man handed a copy to Father, took the disc out of the laptop, nodded to us once, and left the room.

"This is insane. We are to kill each other for this? For a house and some money?" Aunt Ether exclaimed.

"Grandfather can't be serious. This must be a joke," said Cousin Timothy.

"How can we do this?" cried Uncle Will.

"Obviously, we can't," Father said.

That was when I grabbed the silver letter opener off Grandfather's desk. I had stabbed my father through the heart before he had even realized I'd moved. He'd grabbed at me, clutching my shirt as the blood drained from his body.

"James, no," he moaned. Then he had slumped to the floor. Everyone stared at me in horror, backing away from the bloody corpse. Some fainted on the floor. A few screamed.

"How could you?" Laurence had gasped.

"It's February 29th," was my reply. "Now get out of my house."

That was twenty-four years ago.

I glanced at the screen showing the back of the property. Father's was the first unmarked grave I had dug there. Six more family members followed, one every four years. There was a seventh grave there as well, dug for the contractor who had built my current sanctuary. Information could be bought and I couldn't risk certain blueprints falling into the wrong hands.

On the screens, my family roamed throughout the house, searching for me room by room. They opened closet doors, peered behind furniture, even ventured into the dusty attic trying to find where I was hiding.

One of them stopped in the middle of my bedroom, covering one ear with a gloved hand. The figure prowling around the basement did the same. Two others cocked their heads on two different screens as if listening to something.

"What do you hear?" I asked them.

One more alarm went off. Though I had installed it myself, it was one I never expected to hear.

"No!" I cried, spinning around in my chair to face the door of my hidden room. It was locked from the inside, so even if someone had found the hidden passageway, there was no way they could get in.

"But no one knows about this room. No one knows about the passage!" I yelled at the door.

"Someone does," said a voice behind me.

I swung around in my chair, lifting my shotgun. A masked figure rose from behind the screens. The pistol in their hands gleamed silver as they pointed it at my chest. I fumbled for the trigger, but the pistol fired first. As the bullet rammed its way through my shoulder, I cursed myself for being unprepared at this most critical moment. I had not expected to have to defend myself here and it was going to cost me my life. After more than two decades, I should have known better.

I struggled with the shotgun, trying to lift it up and pull the trigger, but the damage to my shoulder slowed me down. The figure came around the desk and plucked it from my hands. A knee dropped on my chest, pinning me to the floor as my attacker pulled my pistol from its holster at my waist. Taking all three weapons with him, the figure strode over to the door of my sanctuary, unlocking it and swinging it wide open.

"You can't do this."

"Yes, I can," he replied, removing his mask. I recognized the face, though it couldn't have been him. I'd killed him two years ago.

"You're dead," I moaned.

"Obviously not."

"You are. I killed you myself."

"Thank you for admitting it so easily," said Laurence, stepping into the room.

The other six members of my family filed in after him, all staring down at me with cold contempt in their eyes.

112

"You've broken the rules," I spat. "You've included an outsider. He can't kill me. Only one of you can. You all forfeit everything."

"No, cousin, you are the one who broke Grandfather's rules," said Kaitlin, stepping forward, a thin smile on her face.

"Never."

"Such a death can only occur on February 29th," she replied. "And you just admitted to killing one of us two years ago."

"I didn't! He wasn't one of us!"

"Oh, but he was." The contractor's lookalike crouched down before me, his pistol pointed at my face.

"You never met my sons," said Cousin Justin.

"You have no children. I'd have known. You're not married or in a relationship of any kind."

"Don't have to be. But there was a girl I met on vacation, not long after you slaughtered your own father right in front of us. Long before your investigators began following us. She got pregnant and I convinced her to keep it a secret. I was afraid of what you might do."

I stared at the young man in front of me, who glared with hard, hate-filled eyes.

"We spent years trying to hatch a plan to find a way into my Great Grandfather's house," he said.

"My house!" I screamed, but the lookalike ignored my interruption

"Then you started hunting for a contractor. As luck would have it, my brother worked in that exact profession. He had no legal link to this family, not on paper anyway. He had no family you knew of, either, no one to tell your secrets to. And you left him alone long enough to create this passage into your little cell, tucked away behind your screens. Luckily, he passed all the information on to me so we could plan your death together. He never expected that you would kill him."

The twin shook his head slowly, eyes brimming with tears for his lost brother. "All we wanted was a chance to take back what you stole all those years ago."

"I stole nothing."

"You stole your father's life," said Laurence. "Not that you would ever see it that way."

"It doesn't matter. You have forfeited everything for killing a member of this family outside of Grandfather's guidelines," Justin added, placing a hand on Laurence's arm. Laurence nodded and turned back to me.

"Then let me leave. If I am truly forfeit, then I will go without a fight."

The seven of them glanced back and forth at each other before smiling down at the contractor's twin.

"Would you give any of us the same courtesy?" he asked.

"But Grandfather's will . . . "

"Stated nothing about dealing with such an infraction."

The twin smiled, his white teeth shining in the light of the video screens, and pulled the trigger.

LETTERS

Michael Bray

MASTERS OF MIDNIGHT

HE NEVER SAW IT coming. That was the part that hurt the most. Miles thought they were happy. Their friends always said they were attached at the hip. Miles and Bronwyn (or Bronnie, as he called her), the couple who had outlasted every other relationship in their circle of friends. They were making plans for the future. An around the world cruise. Having kids, a boy and a girl, was the hope. There were no warning signs or at least none he remembered until it was too late.

Those times, when he would walk into the room and catch her staring off into space or wearing a frown which didn't suit her delicate features, he would ask her what was wrong and she would smile at him and tell him everything was fine.

He thought about times like that a lot now. Especially at night when he lay in bed, sleep a distant luxury to which he rarely had access to. Those long nights spent awake, listening to cars passing or airliners rumbling in the distance as they ferried their passengers to and from their holiday destinations, were the worst. They were long and frustrating, the ceiling above the bed which was far too big for him alone making a perfect screen for him to review those memories and situations and play through all the things he should have done differently.

You couldn't have done anything. You had no way of knowing.

He hated that voice. The one that tried to fix him from within. He knew it was wrong. There were signs that could have made the difference, he just missed them. He lay there in the dark, staring at that canvas, exhausted but knowing he was destined to spend the rest of the night awake. He closed his eyes and tried to force the issue, but that was worse. He saw it in flashes.

The note she had left on the table.

The second note on the bathroom door telling him not to go in and to call the police.

He ignored that of course and broke in, splintering the lock. He thought there might be time to save her, but it was obvious she had been there for some time, swinging from the wooden beam, the length of blue washing line embedded deep in her neck.

Miles snapped his eyes opened and groaned to the empty house.

Why?

That was the question that appeared the most and one he knew would never be answered.

Things will get better with time. Just wait and see.

He hated the way the voice in his head patronized him. It had already been six weeks and it was just as raw now as when it first happened.

Things can't go on like this.

On that, at least, he agreed. He needed help, and even if his pride baulked at the idea, he wasn't stupid enough to fumble through on his own and hope for the best. He would call the number he had been given for the grief counselor. Maybe they could prescribe him something to help him sleep and get some respite from the incessant misery.

The office was too bright. Sun blazed in from the window at the back of the hulking man who sat opposite Miles, who tried not to stare at the man's bulbous nose upon which his glasses were perched. "Mr. Dickinson," the man said as he shifted position, chair creaking in protest. "I understand you have been through an incredibly traumatic experience. Spousal suicide is growing nationwide, sadly. It's a real issue."

Miles nodded, regretting ever coming. He made a mental note

to ignore the so-called voice of reason next time it made a suggestion. "It's bright in here." he muttered.

The man, who went by the name of Crawford, frowned and smiled.

Smoker's teeth.

"It's a bright day, Mr. Dickinson."

Not when you've hardly slept in weeks, asshole.

Miles kept the response to himself and decided to move on. Desperate to get out of the office and breathe in some fresh air. "I hoped you might be able to give me something to help. With the lack of sleep, I mean."

Crawford folded his plump hands on the desk. "Well, to tell you the truth, I try not to prescribe medication in the first instance."

"I thought you were supposed to help me."

"Please, hear me out." Crawford said. Miles got the impression he was enjoying the position of power he felt he held, but said nothing.

"Now, Mr. Dickinson, you've experienced a terrible loss. An unexpected loss. In my experience, those are the hardest to recover from as it leaves more questions than answers."

Miles nodded. He couldn't argue with the assessment"

'That, in my opinion, is the reason for your ability to move on and seek the closure you need. I assume you have questions you wish to have answered, things you wish you had said to your late wife?"

"Actually, that's exactly it."

Crawford shifted again, causing his overloaded chair to emit another groan. "I want to suggest something to you. A method which may help. Granted, it's unorthodox, but there has been some success with it."

"Alright, tell me about it," Miles said, more confident that the therapist seemed to know what he was doing.

"I want you to write your wife a letter. Hear me out before

119

you protest. I want you to write her a letter and say all the things you wish you had said, all the things that are troubling you. Get them all down on paper, then put the letter away somewhere. A drawer or a safe place. Some people prefer to burn them. The idea is that you get to ask those personal questions and at least unburden yourself so the healing process can begin."

"A letter?" Miles said, unsure if Crawford was serious. "Your answer is to write a letter? I thought you could help me."

"I know it sounds strange, but just try it. You might find yourself surprised."

"No, I don't think so. Thanks anyway though." Miles said, standing and walking to the door.

"It's just one of many options, Mr. Dickinson. If you come back we can discuss alternatives."

Miles heard him but didn't turn back. If that was the best grief therapy could offer, he had no interest in pursuing it further.

Instead of taking the pain away, the bottle of vodka had only made him feel sick. Worse, it didn't even make him forget.

He lay in the dark on his side of the bed, Bronnie's side cold and unruffled. He badly wanted to sleep, yet every time he closed his eyes those images came. The two notes. The discovery in the bathroom. He forced them away, wanting them out of his head.

For a while he lay there, listening to the world pass by, his eyes drifting over the ceiling when his mind returned to the meeting with the grief counselor and the whole letter writing idea. It was still ridiculous, of course, but the little voice deep inside was suggesting to him that maybe, just maybe, it was worth a try. The only alternative was to lie there staring into space feeling sorry for himself.

Decision made, he got up, considered finishing the last

quarter of the bottle of vodka then thought better of it, instead, he powered up the laptop and settled down to write.

For a while, he stared at the screen, the text cursor blinking at him with impatience. He moved his fingers towards the keys, then pulled away again. He could think of nothing to say, or even how to begin. He tried to imagine she was there in the room, back when things were good before everything changed forever and asked himself what he would have said to her.

Just start with the basics. Tell her you love her and miss her.

He moved his fingers back into position over the keyboard, alive with adrenaline as he started to type, tentative at first, then his tempo increasing as the emotions he had held onto for so long were finally free.

He paid no attention to typos or spelling. He just wrote.

He couldn't bring himself to write about how her life had ended. He still wasn't ready for that. He did, however talk about how he missed her, how much he loved her. All the things he should have said more often when she were still alive.

When he had finished, the room had taken on the pink orange glow of pre-dawn and his entire body ached, but it was done. It still didn't feel real until he printed it and held the eight pages in his hands. He read through, the feeling he was seeing them for the first time and they had been written by someone else was hard to shake.

He folded the letter and put it into an envelope, sealing it. The therapist had suggested he burn it, but he didn't want to do that. He wanted to do it right, to burn it at the park by the bench where they used to stop and sit during their long Sunday morning walks in winter, her pulling close to him as their breath plumed in the chill air.

He loved those moments when it was just them. No work, no phones, just the two of them enjoying each other's company.

That's where he would do it.

In her favorite place.

That was for later, though. First he needed to rest.

He went back to the bedroom, a place which had become a prison, a place of misery. He lay on the bed, hands folded behind his pillow and had every intention of thinking about Bronnie, but he was asleep within seconds, for the first time his slumber without interruption or nightmares.

The park was quiet aside from a couple of mid-afternoon dog walkers and an enthusiastic older man completing laps of the park somewhere between a brisk walk and a slow jog. After a fitful sleep, Miles had expected the process of destroying the letter at the bench would be a smooth one. Just those few hours of rest had made all the difference, and for the first time in weeks, he felt almost human again.

That all changed when he saw the bench and recalled the things associated with it. rather than bring him joy, seeing it again only reminded him they would never sit on it as a couple again and that every memory the two of them would ever share had already happened. It was because of this, that he couldn't bring himself to sit there. He knew Bronnie would have laughed at him and told him he was stupid, yet it didn't change anything. He knew if he sat there alone, it would somehow destroy the special feeling the bench had.

Jesus, it's just a bench. Get a grip and do what you came here to do.

Miles stared at the letter and knew he couldn't do it. He couldn't destroy it, at least not there. Instead, he shoved the letter back into his jacket pocket and started to walk back to the house, a place which was rapidly starting to feel more like a prison. His work had told him to take as long as he needed. Although he wasn't in any way ready to face the constant whispers and false concern thrown in his direction from people he had never spoken to before—anything had to be better than the perpetual misery.

Just be rid of it. Just writing the letter isn't enough. You need to destroy it.

He was just a few streets from home now and knew the sleep which had come the night before was likely a one-off. There was a post box on the corner, one he had walked past hundreds of times and never noticed. In an age of instant messaging and emails, there was little use for actual letters.

Without thinking, he took the letter out of his pocket. There were no details that could be traced back to him and it was easier than burning it. Whoever found the blank envelope at the sorting office would dispose of it and that suited him fine.

There was no thought, no hesitation. He barely broke stride as he slipped the letter into the post-box. He didn't even look back.

He did, however, make one final stop before heading home. He was out of vodka and knew the night was going to be long.

As hangovers went, Miles was confident this one was in the top three worst ones he had ever experienced. He had been woken by a combination of sunlight streaming through the window and someone close by mowing their lawn, the incessant drone of the mower not helping the raging headache which pulsed in his skull.

He didn't notice the letter on the doormat until later when he was making coffee. Confused, he picked it up, wondering if it was another belated condolence or well wishes from one of his neighbors who for some reason had only just found out about what had happened.

He tore open the envelope, wishing the headache would give him a little respite. That and everything else ceased to matter when his eyes drifted over the words.

Unlike the letter he had sent this was handwritten and a single sheet with three short sentences written on it. He read them again and again, the world around him ceasing to exist.

He finally exhaled, realizing only then he had been holding his breath. It was too much for him to process and he emitted a short bark of laughter at the sheer absurdity of the situation as he scanned the words on the letter.

Miles,
This is what I wanted and I'm happy now. You have to move on and let me go.
*It was never a case of not loving **you**, I didn't love **me** anymore.*

Bronnie

His stomach tightened into a hot ball of something he had never felt before. A cocktail of fear, elation, disbelief and happiness. The words on the paper blurred as he blinked through a film of tears. It was the first time he had cried since the day it happened. He touched the paper, letting his fingers glide over the words.

Wait, don't get carried away. You know this isn't possible. It could be a sick prank. It's not what you think.

He dismissed the voice in his head immediately. It was her. Somehow, some way he knew it was Bronnie. It was written the way she would have worded it. Short and to the point, a no-bullshit response as was her way. He could imagine her saying it, standing in front of her, not realizing how her being angry

124

made her all the more attractive. Miles didn't believe in miracles or the supernatural, but supposed those things by definition were only believed by those who experienced them. There was more he wanted to say, he wanted to keep these lines of communication open, so rushed to the laptop and powered it up, unsure what he was doing or why, just knowing it felt right.

You're setting yourself up for disappointment. This can't be what you think it is. Be rational.

Fuck rational.

This was the exact thing he had been hoping for, the chance to talk to Bronnie. He didn't know how it was possible, and he didn't care. He just knew he had to act on it and deal with the consequences later.

He wrote to her, begging her to speak to him, asking for answers, knowing he was rambling, but it didn't matter. He had to get it out and prove it wasn't a one-off or some kind of twisted coincidence.

When he was finished, unable to stop his hands from shaking, he sealed the envelope. It was the most alive he had felt in weeks.

Not sure what had triggered the response, he repeated his route. Went to the park, stood by the bench, held the letter then posted it in the same post-box on the way home.

On arriving home, he was full of energy, anxious and excited, nervous and afraid. The biggest high he had ever experienced. Miles dragged a chair from the sitting room to the hallway, positioning it opposite the door. He wanted to be there when his reply arrived, no matter how long he would have to wait.

You realize it's the middle of the day. The post won't be here until early tomorrow morning at the earliest. Stop torturing yourself. You know this isn't real.

Ignoring his inner voice, he focused on Bronnie and what she might say in her response. It wasn't even odd to him how quickly the situation had become completely normal. He knew it was insanity, and yet, he had the physical evidence.

125

You don't have any evidence. This could be a sick prank and then what?

He'd thought of that, too. He'd asked her in his letter to prove it was her in a way only the two of them would know. That is how he would get his proof. That is how he would know. He waited to see if his increasingly annoying inner self had any further comment to make but for now it was silent. He was glad and settled in to wait for the letter to arrive.

At some point, he realized he must have dozed off. Miles snapped awake, the first hues of his third day of waiting filling the room suggesting he had missed a large chunk of the night to the micro-naps he had been having as he waited for his reply. The stiff neck and discomfort were forgotten when he saw the letter on the doormat. His exhaustion must have been deeper than he anticipated, as he didn't even hear the letterbox flip closed when it was deposited. He lurched out of the chair and rushed down the hall, snatching up the letter.

Before he even opened it, there was no doubt. As he tore the plain white envelope open he smelled her perfume, the one she always said was her favorite so he would buy her a bottle every year for her birthday.

The heady mix of nervous excitement radiated through him as he scanned the letter.

Miles,
I can't answer all the questions you have, it's simply not possible. Just know that I'm happy now and this is a better place. It's important for you to move on and forget about me. I know it will be hard, but you have to. I didn't want to be in this world anymore, but I would hate to think you are wasting your

life on my account. I know you might not believe this is me, and that is one assurance I can give you if only to help you move on. To answer your question, I had salmon on our first date, although it was you who had ordered it. I didn't like the steak I'd ordered as it had mushrooms on it so you gave me your meal instead.

I hope this helps to convince you this is really me. You need to pull yourself together, Miles, and move on. As horrible as it was, this is what I wanted. You deserve happiness too. Remember, I'll always love you.

Bronnie.

Miles slumped against the wall and slid to a sitting position, sobbing and unsure how he felt. It was all so overwhelming that he simply had no idea how to process what had happened. He read the letter over and over again. The magnitude of it hit him then. He knew the answer to the greatest unanswered question of all time. He knew now life went on, and there was something else, a better place beyond the cruel and violent world he had come to hate.

Don't get any stupid ideas. She wouldn't want you to follow her. It says so in the letter. She wants you to live.

Miles moved the letter closer to his face and inhaled, the scent of her perfume igniting memories which somehow were even more painful. He didn't know what to do, how he could possibly go on without her. He badly wanted to be with her but at the same time didn't want to go against her wishes. It was this impossible conundrum that was rattling around his brain without any sign of being solved when there was a knock at the door.

It was her.

He knew it. Some instinct deep within him knew she had come to him in person. Still, he couldn't move. He sat on the floor, clutching the letter and staring down the hall as another knock came.

127

Go on then. Answer it. This is what you wanted. Be done with it.

He knew that, for once, the inner voice was right, yet he was frozen. Even breathing seemed difficult, like something he had to give conscious effort to do. He imagined getting the courage to stand and open the door, only to see that Bronnie wasn't how he imagined. That she was, in fact, a horror movie cliché, a banshee from beyond, washing line noose still embedded into her neck, tongue bloated and protruding as she glared at him with milky hatred filled eyes.

Don't be stupid. Just answer the fucking door.

A third, less patient knock roused him to action. He didn't want her to go away if this was his one chance to finally see her again. There was no sense trying to explain it. Maybe it was some kind of bond built by his love for her or some other kind of supernatural explanation beyond the knowledge of mankind. All he knew was it was real and happening to him.

On trembling legs, he pulled himself to his feet and towards the door. He had never felt such fear, such anticipation. It was so overwhelming he could feel himself trembling as if his body couldn't handle the potent euphoria and terror combination. Even as he reached out to open the door, he felt detached, as if he were watching someone else through a fisheye lens.

There were three men on the other side of the door. Miles stood for a moment, confusion taking over. One of the men he recognized. The other two he didn't.

"Dr Crawford? What are you doing here?"

Crawford shuffled his feet and cleared his throat. "Mr. Dickinson, I . . . we need to speak to you."

"I think I know what this is about. Actually, I was planning on calling you today to thank you. The whole writing a letter idea you had was genius. It works. Look, see for yourself. She replied. Bronnie replied."

He was crying again but didn't care. He thrust the letter towards Crawford, who glanced at it but didn't take it.

"Mr. Dickinson, I think you should come with us so we can help you."

"I don't need help anymore, Dr Crawford. Thanks to you, I can finally move on. Bronnie and I are in touch and communicating."

Crawford again shuffled his feet and flicked a nervous glance towards one of his colleagues. "Mr. Dickinson, I don't think you understand the . . . severity of your situation. Please, just come with us and everything will be alright."

Miles looked at Crawford then at the two men, they looked official, both burly men who looked like they wouldn't take no for an answer. Fear knotted his gut.

"I'm not going anywhere until you tell me what this is about."

"You're ill, Mr. Dickinson. You and I have discussed this many times."

"Many times? I've only been in your office once."

Crawford shook his head. "No, Miles, that isn't true. You and I have been having regular appointments twice a week for the last six weeks. You were referred to me by your grief counselor."

"You are my grief counselor. What are you even saying?" Miles said, growing agitated and angry.

"I'm your doctor. You need to come with me now to the hospital. We'll take care of you."

Miles barked a laugh and knew it would sound as insane to them as it felt to him.

"Hospital? I'm not sick. Don't you understand? For the first time ever I actually feel well. I know it sounds inane but Bronnie replied to my letters. We're communicating, just look."

Crawford looked at the letter as Miles thrust it towards him again. That paper is blank, Miles. There is nothing there to see."

"Are you insane? It's right there"' His words trailed off as he looked at the paper in his hand. Crawford was right. It was blank. "I don't . . . I don't understand this."

"It's actually not uncommon with couples where an unexpected death occurs. In this instance, where not only was the death unexpected, but with a suicide, the mental toll on the spouse can be devastating if left untreated."

Miles hardly heard a word. He couldn't take his eyes off the letter. "It's real. I read it," he mumbled.

"Unfortunately, I suspected this would be the outcome when you came to me with this whole letter writing idea."

"But it was *your* idea," he whispered as he retreated into the apartment. He rushed to the table and picked up the previous letter he had received from the desk, but it too was blank. Beside it sat the bottle of perfume he had taken from Bronnie's dresser, an accusing piece of evidence against him.

"I don't know what's going on," Miles said as he slumped in the chair, letting the two blank pieces of paper fall to the ground at his feet. Crawford and the two orderlies entered the apartment.

"Your neighbors alerted us, Miles. Said they were concerned about you. At first, they said they could just hear you talking to yourself. Then things escalated. They said they saw you walking the halls wearing your wife's clothes and talking to her as if she were there with you."

He was about to deny it as ludicrous when a flash of memory came to him of stumbling past Mr. and Mrs. Brenton in the hall, struggling to walk in Bronnie's shoes which were far too small for his feet. The look of revulsion on their faces as he smiled at them, the taste of Bronnie's badly applied lipstick returning with disturbing familiarity.

"I left my number and they called me. They say you've been walking the hallways, coming in and out of your own apartment and posting the same letter over and over again. They said this happens all night."

"They're wrong. I wouldn't do that. I don't understand."

"Have you been taking your medication? The one to help with the voices you hear?"

No, he hasn't. We put a stop to that straight away, didn't we? Thought we could fix it ourselves, that we didn't need help.

Miles shook his head. "I don't understand this."

"We'll help you, Miles, but you have to come with us now."

"I'm going nowhere with you. Just leave me alone and let me think. You hear me? Get out of here."

Crawford stood firm, whatever initial nerves that were showing when he arrived were now long gone. "I'm afraid you don't have a choice. You are in no fit state to make your own decisions Miles, so we spoke to your sister. She has assumed responsibility for you and agreed to have you brought to the hospital for a time for your own good, just until we can help you."

Miles lurched out of the chair, trying to skirt around Crawford to the door, but the two orderlies were waiting for it, and moved to restrain him, one pinning him against the wall as the other prepared a syringe. Miles screamed and kicked, desperate to be free.

"Let me go, you don't understand. Bronnie is out there. I need to talk to her. You can't do this to me."

Crawford remained stony-faced as Miles was injected with the sedative.

"You don't understand now Miles, but we all have your best interests at heart. This is the first step to recovery."

Miles didn't hear it. He was already slipping away. He was in a dream inside a dream. A dream with a door and someone knocking. A door which, despite the inner warnings not to, he opened, and there she was. Bronnie. A horror movie cliché, a banshee from beyond, washing line noose still embedded into her neck, tongue bloated and protruding as she glared at him with milky hatred filled eyes.

131

ONE MILLION HITS

Evans Light

MASTERS OF MIDNIGHT

"CANDY BUCKETS TIMES FOUR?"

"Check."

"Gorilla Mask?"

"Check."

"Can we speed this up, Trevor?" Eighteen-year old Demarco Hansen checked his watch as he examined the assortment of Halloween costumes and other holiday gear spread out across the garage floor.

" ... And we've got the whoopee cushion and mobile shower costume, a green stretch suit, foil-covered robot boxes and the hockey mask, all ready to go," Trevor continued. "Kurt, you gonna rock Frankenstein on round one?"

Kurt slipped the foot-tall green latex mask over his head and gave two thumbs-up, one for each bolt protruding from his neck.

"Cool. We're all set. 'Operation: Halloween Shakedown' is ready to commence. Now where the fuck is Austin?"

As if waiting for his cue, Austin Taylor jumped around the corner into the open garage door. He was a lanky boy, tall, and his entire face and head were coated in thick bright red greasepaint, hair included. He cocked his head to one side like a human-rooster hybrid.

"Oh yeah!" he shouted, waving his arms back and forth wildly, a crazy smile plastered on his face.

Trevor and Demarco stared at him in bewilderment. Kurtis took off the Frankenstein mask to get a better look.

"What the fuck is that supposed to be?" Demarco was not in the mood for silliness that didn't involve filling a dozen buckets to the brim with free candy.

135

"Aw, c'mon, guys—you know what I am! Guess!" Austin demanded.

The boys circled him. "Hellboy's retarded nephew?" Demarco asked.

"Ha. The sad part is that you think you're funny."

"I know! I know what you are," Kurtis shouted. "A used tampon!"

Demarco and Trevor erupted with laughter.

Austin frowned. "Oh yeah!" he shouted again, waving his arms emphatically.

"*Oh yeah*," repeated Trevor, mocking him. "You're a used tampon all the way. Nice costume. It suits you."

"It's obvious what I'm dressed up as, so you can all drop the act," said Austin. "The Kool-Aid Man. You know—he screams 'Oh yeah!' when he breaks through walls. Tonight when people open their door, instead of saying 'trick or treat' I'm going to shout 'Oh yeah!'"

Skeptical looks were tossed in his direction.

"Based on that statement, I'd like to revise my previous guess," Demarco said. "You're a retarded used tampon, and that's my final offer."

"Well fuck you, Demarco, who cares what you think? You're just a jealous douche who didn't come up with it first. Admit it, my Kool-Aid Man rocks."

"Fine, Austin—you're the Kool-Aid Man for the first neighborhood run-through, but after that you're going to have to wear a mask," Trevor said. "The plan is to shake down every house several times, and having an unforgettable costume kind of misses the point."

Demarco couldn't resist one final jab. "Yeah, I don't think anyone will ever forget that time a giant bloody tampon rang their doorbell and asked for candy. That's the kind of thing a person can never forget, no matter how hard they try or how much counseling they get."

Kurtis chuckled as he put the Frankenstein mask back on.

"You guys ready? If we're going to make the big score, we've got to get moving. Suit up!" Demarco ordered.

So the boys got to it and within minutes were ringing doorbells up and down both sides of the street, plastic buckets in hand. For the first of many planned trips through the neighborhood, Demarco wore the robot costume, Trevor carried the shower rod encircled by a plastic curtain, Kurtis had the Frankenstein's monster mask and Austin was the bloody red Kool-Aid Man-tampon head.

They were well beyond even the borderline age for trick-or-treating, not simply too old for Halloween, but *way* too old. Regardless, they'd gone trick-or-treating together every year for as long as they could remember, since elementary school.

This was going to be their last ever trick-or-treating experience. They'd graduate from high school in a few months and likely go their separate ways after that. They were determined to make the most out of their final Halloween together.

The plan worked perfectly. Quickly changing costumes between rounds, they'd made at least three visits to every house in the neighborhood by the time porch lights started going dark.

Every house that was, except the one that belonged to Mr. Copeland, a grumpy old codger who thought Halloween was the work of the devil and didn't hesitate to preach about it to anyone who'd listen. Rather than hand out candy, each year he erected a giant cross in the middle of his front yard wound with white lights, completely indifferent to the complaints of racist symbolism associated with his alternative "Christian" decoration for the holiday.

As ten o'clock approached, the boys found themselves in a desperate race against time. Unwilling to end the night while there were still houses willing to give a final dump of the bucket, they decided to split up and spread out to cover more ground.

Demarco swapped costumes one last time, changing into the green stretch suit, covering his face and body. He headed deep into the neighborhood as houses with porch lights rapidly became few and far between.

It quickly became evident that his endeavor was futile and decided it was time to head back. On his way home he was surprised to find a house several doors down from his own with the porch light still burning bright. He'd already stopped there several times that evening and couldn't remember what costume he'd been wearing on the last visit.

Screw it, it's worth a shot. He ran up the steps and rang the bell.

The man who opened the door wore an expression that said he'd had just about enough of Halloween.

"Goddammit, Demarco. You again?" Maurice Harris shook his head in disbelief at the teen standing before him dressed head to toe in a stretchy green suit. "I can see your face through that thing, you know. How many times have you already been here this evening? You're taller than me now—get a job and buy your own goddamned candy. Halloween is for kids."

"Aw, c'mon, Mr. Harris. I'm looking out for your health. Don't want you to get diabetes from eating all that leftover candy. Tell you what, give me whatever you've got left, and I'll forget to tell Mrs. Harris about how you go for a smoke behind the shed every time she leaves for work? What do you say? Deal?"

Maurice frowned, but gave the half-full bowl of fun-sized snickers on the table by the door a glance anyway.

"Who's at the door, Maurice?" Mrs. Harris called from inside.

"Hi, Mrs. Harris! It's me, Demarco," the boy shouted enthusiastically over the man's shoulder. He held out his candy bucket and shook it, giving the man an "or else" look.

"Don't worry, honey. Demarco stopped by to take the leftover Halloween candy off our hands so we don't get diabetes," Maurice said sarcastically while reluctantly dumping the remaining candy into the boy's bucket. "Wasn't that thoughtful of him?"

"Gee, thanks, Mr. Harris," Demarco said with mocking gratitude.

"Come back here next year, boy, and I'll have a whole box of treats waiting on your ass," Mr. Harris growled, whispering so his wife wouldn't hear. "Twelve gauge buckshot treats."

Demarco mimicked smoking a cigarette. "Smoke 'em if you got 'em, old man."

With that, Mr. Harris slammed the door in his face and flipped off the light, leaving the boy standing on a dark porch. Laughing, Demarco ran home to join the others, eager to count the evening's spoils.

The others had already gathered in the garage and shed their costumes. After chucking their gear back into the Halloween storage box, they chased each other up the stairs to the rec room, their favorite hangout for playing video games and watching movies.

With the precision of accountants, they separated the candy into piles laid out on the floor all around the room, one each for the Runts, Nerds, Tootsie Pops, Fun Dip, Laffy Taffy, Pixie Sticks, Fun Size candy bars, Whoppers, M&Ms, and the rest of their favorites. In the center of it all, they tossed the candies they'd never dream of eating: Tootsie Rolls (both regular and assorted flavors), Squirrel Nut Zippers, Mary Janes, Chick-O-Sticks, candy corn and circus peanuts. On top of the discard pile perched a shiny red apple, the solitary piece of fruit they'd received that evening.

They took turns choosing what they wanted until the candy was fairly divided between them. Satisfied with how things had gone, the four nearly-adult boys lay scattered around the room eating candy, exactly as they'd done when they were still in elementary school.

Demarco's mom called to them from the kitchen downstairs. "Demarco, are you and your friends hungry? Since they're spending the night, I can make sandwiches if you want." She paused. "Demarco, can you hear me?"

"Yeah, Mom, I'll ask them." he shouted back. "You guys want anything to eat?"

"Nah," Kurtis said. "I feel sick already."

"Me too," said Austin.

Trevor shook his head.

"All right, I'll tell her."

"Wait!" Trevor said, eyes suddenly brimming with mischief. He picked up the apple from the discard pile as a dastardly smile spread across his face.

"Do you still have those fake blood capsules?"

"Yeah, they're in my room," Demarco said. "Why?"

"Tell your mom we *do* want sandwiches. I've got a great idea."

Several minutes later the quartet was lined up at the bar in the kitchen, behaving like perfect gentleman as Demarco's mom prepared a generous stack of ham and cheese sandwiches. Kurtis fiddled with his phone as they waited, but the other boys talked and laughed about their evening. Mrs. Hansen was happy to see them present in the moment instead of snapchatting or taking selfies or whatever it was they were always doing online.

Trevor placed a candy bucket in front of him on the counter, smiling like a little kid.

"So . . . did you boys get a lot of candy?"

"Oh wow, you wouldn't believe how much, Mrs. Hansen," Austin said. "Probably the most ever."

"I don't want to lecture, but you boys make sure to check the wrapper before you eat anything, and throw away anything that looks like it's been tampered with," she said, setting a sandwich in front of Kurtis and Austin. "Better get off that phone and eat, Kurtis," she urged, turning back to the counter by the stove to make a sandwich for Demarco and Trevor.

"Yes ma'am, Mrs. Hanson. Just finishing up something real quick."

Once her back was turned, Trevor nodded. Kurtis pressed the 'record' button on his phone's camera and Trevor picked up the bucket of candy and walked over to where Mrs. Hansen was preparing to make more sandwiches.

"Look, Mrs. Hansen!" The instant she turned Trevor thrust the bucket into her hands. "Look how much candy I got! Can you believe it?"

The bucket was halfway full of assorted sweets. Perched atop it all, right in the middle, was the shiny red apple.

"Oh, my goodness," Mrs. Hansen laughed nervously, taken aback by the boy's sudden display of youthful exuberance. "That *is* a lot of candy. Better keep your toothbrush handy or else you'll be paying for your dentist's new boat next summer."

"You know how I can tell I'm growing up, Mrs. Hanson?" Trevor said, still smiling wide. He snatched the apple from the bucket holding it up in wide-eyed admiration.

"We got so much candy, but for some reason the only thing I want is this apple. It *was* a little weird that some guys were handing out apples from the back of a van, but they looked so friggin' delish, I couldn't say no."

He brought the apple to his lips, opening wide for a bite.

A horrified expression spread across Mrs. Hansen's face. "Wait, you need to check—"

Before Mrs. Hanson finished the sentence, Trevor chomped down hard, ripping off half the apple in a single mighty bite. As he began to chew his face twisted into a painful grimace. He dropped the apple, clutching his mouth with both hands.

Mrs. Hanson shrieked and dropped the bucket of candy, scattering sweets across the kitchen floor. "Trevor, what's wrong?" she cried, grabbing the boy by the shoulders, trying to examine him. "Look at me, open your mouth!"

The boy trembled as his eyes rolled back in their sockets, as white as Mrs. Hanson's face.

The rest of the crew leaned forward, watching with keen interest. Even as Trevor began to gurgle, Kurtis' eyes remained fixed on the screen of his phone. Bright crimson streams spurted out from between Trevor's fingers.

"What's wrong with you, Kurtis? Stop playing on your phone and call 9-1-1!" Mrs. Hansen screamed as Trevor pulled his hands away to reveal a mouth absolutely brimming with blood, jaw quivering.

The boys stifled their laughter as long as they could bear, but Trevor's Oscar-worthy performance got the better of them. Austin was the first to snicker, and that triggered Demarco to erupt with full-blown laughter.

"Why are you laughing? Can't you see he's hurt? Help him!" Mrs. Hansen shrieked, dismayed to discover what cold-hearted monsters the next generation had become.

Trevor shook and gurgled as though in the throes of a seizure. He stumbled towards his friends, clutching the edge of the counter until his knuckles shone pearly white. "Help me!" he wailed, spewing blood onto his friends as he spoke. The boys *ewwwed* and *awwwed* as they wiped the red goo from their faces, smearing it on their clothes.

Mrs. Hansen staggered back from the hideous scene until she bumped up against the stove, aghast.

Kurtis looked up from his phone for the first time since the show began. "And . . . cut!" he commanded, like a director on set. "Got it. That's a wrap. Good job!"

"What? What are you talking about?"

"Sorry, Mom—but it was too perfect an opportunity to pass up," Demarco smirked. "We couldn't help ourselves."

Mrs. Hanson's fearfulness flipped into burning anger in the blink of an eye. "Shame on you, shame on all of you! Almost gave me a heart attack, and for what? Look at this mess!" The woman was clearly bewildered by the spattered blood all over her kitchen.

She kicked indignantly at the heaps of candy scattered across the floor. "I'm not cleaning any of this up, not one thing. This kitchen had better be sparkling by the next time I come in here. You'll be washing your own clothes, too. If I find even a single speck of fake blood that's not cleaned up, I'm calling everyone's parents and you can all go home. I don't care how late it is."

Kurtis, Austin and Trevor exchanged sheepish grins as she stomped off in a huff.

"But Mom . . . " Demarco called to her.

She stopped dead in her tracks. "What?" she snapped, not even bothering to turn around.

"What about my sandwich?"

She did not dignify his insolence with a response and resumed her march down the hall, slamming the bedroom door behind her.

An awkward silence was left in her wake.

"Did you see the look on her face?" Austin whispered. "I thought you were a goner, Demarco. You know she was wishing she'd had an abortion just then—probably close to coming back in here and performing one herself, very late term."

"Yeah, whatever. She'll get over it. Kurtis, let's see that video."

Kurtis shook his head and slipped the phone into his pocket.

"No way, man, not until we clean up this mess. If I'm spending the night here I don't want to wake up dead, you know what I mean?"

143

After fifteen minutes of scrubbing and sweeping, rinsing and stacking and putting stuff away, they had the kitchen clean and their fake-blood splattered shirts churning in the washing machine. Satisfied that everything was put sufficiently back into place, they headed upstairs to Demarco's room, eager to check out their prank video.

Kurtis hooked his phone up to the computer as the boys huddled around. A few button clicks later, they were laughing like drunken monkeys all over again.

"Look at your mom's face!" Austin said. "No wonder she rushed off to her room, probably had to clean crap out of her britches."

"I bet this one gets ten-thousand hits before the weekend's over. We might actually make a little green, if you know what I mean," Kurtis said, rubbing his fingers together.

As soon as the video reached the end, they restarted it, playing it over and over, pausing at exquisitely perfect moments to better appreciate the hilarious expressions on Mrs. Hansen's face.

"Right there—*stop*—look at that! Her face looks like a dog bit 'er right in the crotch," Trevor laughed. "Classic!"

"You really nailed that performance, Trevor. For a second there I wondered if that apple had a razor blade in it, for real," said Demarco.

"Why spank you very much!"

"Definitely need to add a slo-mo replay at the end of this video before we post it online," Austin said. "Let me see that first reaction again. That was the absolute best."

Kurtis clicked the progress bar back to where Trevor took the first bite and Mrs. Hansen dropped the candy bucket.

"Wait, go back. Stop. Did you see that?" Trevor yelled.

Kurtis clicked pause, freeze-framing the video.

"What? Yeah, that's the money shot, the best reaction in the whole thing. Late to the party much?"

"No, not that. Before. I thought I saw something," Trevor said, his face intently examining the computer monitor. "Scroll it back, one frame at a time."

Kurtis clicked the single-frame rewind button until Trevor motioned for him to stop.

"Holy shit! No fuckin' way."

The screen was frozen during a momentary pan of the camera across the floor. Spilled candy filled the frame.

"Right there. See it? Zoom in on the upper right corner," Trevor ordered.

With several clicks of the mouse Kurtis did as asked, zooming in on the candy spilled across the floor.

"See it now?"

"No way!" the other three boys said, almost in unison.

Kurtis let out a low whistle. "Forget ten-thousand. We're gonna get a million hits with this one."

Clear as day, a single word was spelled out by scattered candies on the floor, each individual letter perfectly formed, as though carefully arranged:

"Why didn't we see it before?" Austin asked.

They let the video roll once again. The camera panned up to show Trevor's face and the blood spurting through his fingers. As he spewed all over his friends, the camera dipped towards the floor. The word appeared onscreen again briefly, clear as day, before it was completely destroyed by Mrs. Hansen's retreating feet.

"How in hell did that happen?" said Trevor.

"Woooooooo . . . " Austin mocked, making a ghostly sound.

"Fuck it," Demarco said. "Let's see if we can do it again. Give me that bucket."

Trevor handed him the bucket, the same one that had spilled in the video.

"Want to get your camera ready, Kurt? Just in case?"

"Let's just see if anything cool happens first."

Demarco mimicked his mother's gestures from the video, dropping the bucket onto the floor in the exact same manner. It bounced once and tipped over, scattering candies haphazardly across the floor.

The boys examined the mess from every angle, but no word was to be found. Demarco quickly scooped the candy back into the bucket and tried again.

Still nothing other than a mess appeared on the floor.

Trevor gave it a try, then Austin.

Nothing.

"Oh, well, it was worth a shot," said Kurtis. "We got us one hell of a killer video, though—there's no way anyone's going to think we used special effects. Everything happened way too naturally. Let's get it uploaded. We're going viral, boys. We're breaking the internet tonight!"

Fifteen minutes of editing later, the video was ready for prime time and uploaded to YouTube with the clever title: *MAD MOM GETS HALLOWEEN "TREAT"—FOR REAL!*

"Ready for liftoff, gentlemen," Demarco declared as the video went live. "Let's sit back and watch the view count soar!"

They gathered around the computer, giddy with excitement, refreshing the web page over and over to see how many people were watching the video, hoping to read a never-ending comment scroll full of amazement and praise.

Thirty minutes and exactly three registered views later, the excitement of the evening was officially pronounced dead - time of departure, 11:47 P.M.

Bored of staring at the screen, Austin was the first to bail, flopping down on Demarco's bed to turn on the TV, settling in with Spongebob. Kurtis and Trevor watched random videos on the computer, glazed looks on their faces.

Demarco was disgusted. "What the hell happened to us? It's not even midnight and we're sitting here watching cartoons like we're eight years old," he said. "It's *still* Halloween. We got all the treats—maybe it's time we served up some tricks? What do you guys say?"

Kurtis and Trevor perked up.

"You thinking what I'm thinking?" Kurtis held up his phone, tapping the camera.

"Video pranks!"

"I know the perfect victim," Demarco said, full of excitement once again. "Maurice fuckin' Harris. He leaves the house at five A.M. every morning for work, even on the weekends, so you know he'll be asleep. I bet he'll lose his shit and make one hella funny video."

"One million hits, baby!" Kurtis cried, fist-bumping Trevor.

"One million hits."

"So what should we use? The Frankenstein mask?" Demarco asked. "It's the only sorta-scary thing we've got—unless Austin wants to transform back into bloody tampon-head."

"Ugh. No," said Kurtis. "Frankenstein is good. Austin, you coming?"

"Nah, man, I'm all good. Just gonna chill."

"Oh, okay. That's cool . . . you fuckin' pussy," Demarco said, "but I'm going to need to take this with me." He walked over to the outlet and unplugged the television, holding the cord up in his hand.

147

"Hey! Why'd you do that?" Austin whined. "That was a lost episode."

"Because, Austin, you're going to get your lazy ass out of bed and help us with this prank. Either that or you can start walking home, because my mom for sure isn't going to give you a ride."

"She already gave me a ride. Last night." Austin muttered, tying his shoes. "Juicy."

Trevor dropped the Frankenstein mask into Austin's lap.

"I already gave a performance tonight. Your turn."

They crept down the stairs, out the front door and into the chilly October night, moving silently past darkened driveways. They stopped on the sidewalk in front of Maurice Harris's house, the evening's excitement fully resurrected from the dead.

Austin slipped the Frankenstein mask over his head.

"God damn, it's dark. I can't see shit."

"No worries," said Demarco. "We'll lead you around."

Kurtis reassumed his director duties. "All right Austin, don't forget the plan. We're going to position you outside Maurice's bedroom window and I'll get the camera ready. When you see my flashlight's beam hit the window, do your thing."

"What's my thing?"

"Scratch on the window and growl, I guess. Get him to look outside and then scare the shit out of him. Trust your instincts, you'll be great. C'mon, one million hits, baby!"

With that final pep talk, Austin's friends led him around the side of the house and into the darkness of Maurice's backyard, positioning him beside the bedroom window.

The lights were off, as they'd expected. They held their breath, listening. All was quiet.

Trevor, Demarco and Kurtis shuffled off to the side of the yard so Maurice wouldn't see them when he looked out. A flashlight in the face would kill his night vision, but they weren't in costume and didn't want to end the evening dealing with police. Demarco figured it was better to be safe than sorry, and Kurtis insisted that shooting the scene from the side would be more cinematic anyway.

Once safely out of view, Kurtis held up his phone, adjusted the camera's zoom and started recording. He nodded at Demarco.

It was showtime.

Demarco flicked on the flashlight. A blinding beam of light created a bright circle directly in the center of Maurice's bedroom window, casting an eerie shadow over Austin and his Frankenstein mask as it reflected off the glass.

"Oh man, that looks so awesome," Trevor whispered.

"Shhh!" Kurtis commanded, pointing at the camera's red blinking light.

Austin commenced his performance, moaning loudly while tapping on the glass in a menacing rhythm. The boys waited, expectant. The stillness of the plantation blinds inside silently taunted them.

Austin growled like a bear, slowly pounding his fists against the glass, steadily increasing his rhythm until a manic cadence resonated between the houses.

"Your time is up . . . You can't escape . . . " Austin's voice was deep, unearthly. Demarco was delighted.

The blinds separated, a single pair of white eyes appearing in the rift for a moment before they dropped back into place. The sudden appearance of Maurice's peering peepers gave Austin the very scare he was trying his hardest to give. Startled, he ran from the window into the yard, but quickly regained his composure.

The plantation blinds jumped upwards once more, all the way open this time, making the window look like the opening eye of a giant awakened from slumber. The flashlight's beam streamed through the glass to reveal Maurice's boxer-clad, pot-bellied figure standing inside.

Kurtis adjusted the camera to perfectly capture Maurice's reaction.

Time for the money shot, thought Demarco.

Arms outstretched, Austin took off on a stiff-legged charge towards the bedroom window. The October night shattered with a deafening roar, taking the bedroom window along with it. An angry orange flash sliced through the gloom, then another, before the world plunged back into darkness. An image was seared onto Demarco's retinas: his friend hovering above the ground, feet kicked forward, Frankenstein mask tumbling away from his bewildered face.

Austin's body hit the ground with a meaty squish and a gurgle. The other boys stood dumbfounded as the camera continued recording the scene from its perch at the end of Kurtis' arm. Trevor swung the flashlight towards where Austin lay and immediately regretted it.

Their friend was on his back, head unnaturally twisted to one side. His mouth opened and closed like a newborn searching for its mother's nipple while his hands pawed at the bloody mess that had recently been his torso.

Trevor flipped off the flashlight, hiding the grisly scene. The instant his light went out it was replaced by another, from the bedroom inside. A terrified duet rang out.

"Oh my God! Maurice! What did you do?" a high-pitched feminine voice wailed.

"He had a gun, Mary, was trying to break in. What was I supposed to do?"

"Call the police, Maurice, call the police. We *have* to."

"Goddammit, Mary, shut up and let me think! You know I've got priors, you know what that means if they find me with a gun. We'll go bankrupt trying to plead my case in court. We'd be ruined, you *know* that. There's got to be another way."

The arguing continued as the boys gradually recovered from

their momentary paralysis. Kurtis stopped recording, slipping his phone back into his pocket.

"Fuck, fuck, fuck!" Demarco clutched his head, bending forward as though about to hurl.

"Let's run," said Trevor. "Let's get the fuck out of here. It's too late for Austin. The three of us didn't hurt anybody."

"We can't just leave Austin," Kurtis protested. "We put him up to it, he didn't even want to come. We can call an ambulance, maybe there's still time."

Trevor grabbed Kurtis by the shoulders.

"Dude, Austin's dead. If we don't get the fuck out of here we'll end up wishing we were, too."

"No, Kurtis is right," Demarco stated firmly, drawing himself upright, trying to regain his composure. "We shouldn't leave him, but we can't stay here. We've got futures, we're about to go to college. We can say we were cutting through the yard on our way home from trick or treating and Maurice shot him and we freaked out. You heard him talking, he's got priors. We can say the rest of us took off before he shot us, too."

Demarco knelt down beside Austin in the wet grass. The boy's motionless eyes were glossy orbs in the wan light from the bedroom window.

"Is he alive?" Kurtis whispered.

Demarco touched his friend's forearm. It was already cool, much cooler than it should have been, even considering the chilly October night.

"C'mon, let's get him out of here."

Demarco lifted Austin under his armpits, while the other boys each grabbed a thigh. The stench of blood and shit filled the air as they hoisted him. As they hustled away with their friend, a debate was breaking out inside the house between Maurice and his wife.

"Get dressed, Mary. We're leaving."

"Maurice, you fired twice. Somebody had to call the police."

"You don't know that. Maybe everybody thinks someone else called and nobody does. Maybe people thought it was only kids shooting off fireworks. It *is* Halloween."

"What if you killed somebody? What then? Maurice, please. We have to call . . . "

The angst-filled voices faded away as the three boys fled with their dead friend into the night, stumbling through a sparse patch of woods behind the house. Brambles pulled at their legs as they heaved towards a grassy area that lay not far beyond.

The boys placed their friend's body down onto the manicured strip of soft rye grass that ran behind the houses. Hearts racing, they collapsed beside him, out of breath and trembling from adrenaline and exertion.

They waited, panting, listening for approaching sirens, watching for flashing blue-and-red lights to come racing down their street, for Maurice's house to be surrounded by policemen with guns drawn, for barking dogs to track them down.

Minutes passed by one after the other yet the night remained silent. A solitary flashlight made a quick sweep through Maurice's back yard, followed by the screech of tires on pavement and red tail lights departing his driveway. Clearly he'd decided against calling the police himself.

As minutes threatened to become an hour, the boys realized no one was coming. As far as anyone knew, Demarco's mom included, they were all upstairs watching a movie.

Demarco wished that was the case. "There's no reason any of us have to get nailed for this if we play our cards right. Maurice doesn't know who was in his backyard or what happened—if this whole thing gets pinned on somebody else, you think he's going to squeal? I don't."

"What are you thinking?" Kurtis asked.

Demarco pulled the boys in close and whispered the plan.

Mr. Copeland's Halloween cross was the real deal, over six feet tall and constructed of wooden beams five inches thick, long strands of white LED lights wrapped neatly from top to bottom. Since Mr. Copeland used it to decorate his yard every Christmas, Easter and Halloween, he'd installed a permanent concrete mount that held the cross firmly in place.

Kurtis followed the electrical cord from the cross's base to an outlet beside the front porch. He unplugged the lights and the yard fell dark.

Trevor and Demarco set to work, hastily unwinding the lights from around the cross, laying the strands out neatly beside it.

Once the cross was stripped bare, Demarco took charge.

"Grab him under the arms," he whispered, sternly. "Like that, that's good . . . a little higher. Pin his shoulders against the crossbeam."

"Fuck. He's fucking heavy as shit. I can't hold him very long," Trevor said, gasping in effort.

"Me either." Kurtis strained.

Demarco didn't waste time with a response. He wrapped the cords around Austin's thighs and waist, several times around to hold him tight. Congealed blood and viscera squished out as the strand of lights dug into lacerated flesh.

Having relieved some of the load for Trevor and Kurtis, Demarco carefully wound the other strand of lights down the crossbeam, starting at Austin's left wrist. He wrapped the cord all the way down one arm, several times around the neck at the upright, and then continued down the other arm, tying it off at the other wrist.

Kurtis and Trevor slowly released their hold, afraid that the cords might break under the weight. As the lights slipped snugly into place they removed their hands completely. Austin stayed put, hung up like Christ on a crucifix, head bowed forward.

With the single leftover strand of lights, Demarco tied Austin's forehead to the upright, the jutting bulbs resembling a crown of thorns.

"It is finished," Kurtis whispered.

"People might think it's a fake body, a prank on Mr. Copeland," Trevor offered.

"He's a total whackjob anyway," Demarco said. "Hopefully they'll lock the old nut away, and that will be the end of it. One thing is certain, though: we gotta get outta here. Trevor, plug the lights back in to make it look like Copeland went completely batshit."

Once the lights on the cross were back on, the boys dashed across the street. Demarco carefully opened the still-unlocked front door and stuck his head inside, fearing that his mother may have detected their absence and be waiting for them, even more furious than before.

He saw no sign of her. The house remained dark and still. The boys removed their shoes so they wouldn't track mud into the house. Carrying their sneakers, they slipped inside and tiptoed up the stairs to the bedroom, closing the door behind them.

Unable to deny his curiosity, Demarco headed straight for the window and pulled the blinds apart to see the cross in Mr. Copeland's yard. Austin's corpse still hung there, crucified by his friends.

He knew it was real, but it did *look* like a Halloween decoration. Maybe nobody would notice, at least for a while. Maybe they'd have time to come up with a more convincing story to fool everyone into believing they'd had nothing to do with it, that they'd been here sleeping the whole time with no idea anything had happened to Austin.

As he gazed out the window plotting their alibi, Trevor flipped on the bedroom light, blinding them momentarily. Demarco quickly dropped the blind back into place, hoping no one had seen him.

"Holy shit," he blurted as he turned around.

The room was as they had left it earlier, strewn with assorted costumes, the floor littered with buckets full of candy. Trevor and Kurtis, however, appeared considerably different from the last time he'd seen them in a brightly lit room. Smeared with dried blood and shit from their knees to armpits, they looked as though they'd been mud wrestling on a slaughterhouse floor.

Demarco looked down at himself to find the same.

The boys spent the next hour getting cleaned up, showering first, then scrubbing their clothes until a red ring circled the tub. Realizing that they'd never get the clothes fully clean, they settled on wringing them out and wrapping them up in a garbage bag, which Demarco hid in the attic beneath a loose strip of fiberglass insulation. Kurtis scrubbed the bloody tub until it sparkled white once again, using up an entire roll of paper towels in the process.

The first light of dawn was peeking through the blinds by the time they were done. Exhausted from stress and a night without sleeping, the boys flopped across the bed, knowing full well that they should be working on their plan, but too delirious to discuss anything coherently.

Blessed sleep was about to overtake Demarco when a loud metallic clang snatched him from the edge of slumber. Something large rumbled outside in front of the house. A series of loud beeping noises followed by the heavy thump of plastic on asphalt reminded him that it was garbage day.

Suddenly wide awake, the boys tumbled towards the window. Lifting the blind ever so slightly, they huddled in horror as the garbage truck moved relentlessly towards Mr. Copeland's house, the mechanical arm swinging down to grab and dump one trashcan after another. It stopped in front of Demarco's house and took care of business.

Then pulled up in front of the house next door.

It advanced to the next house after that, the one directly across the street from Mr. Copeland's. The mechanical arm began to descend but stopped, frozen midair.

A large man in a jumpsuit and ball cap appeared in the street, walking towards Mr. Copeland's house, away from his garbage truck towards the cross. He stopped on the sidewalk and examined it, shaking his head in apparent disapproval. The boys held their breath in nervous anticipation, the man's every move commanding their rapt attention.

The garbage man fished a phone from his pocket and appeared to take photographs of the dead boy on the cross. Evidently satisfied, he returned the phone to his pocket and headed back to the truck.

"He thinks it's a decoration!" Demarco said.

"I think I'd rather he went ahead and reported Mr. Copeland," Trevor said. "I'm ready to get this over with one way or the other."

No sooner had he spoken the words, the garbage man halted in his tracks, scratching his chin as if mulling something over. The boys watched in dread as the man turned and strode straight into Mr. Copeland's yard, headed directly towards the cross.

"Fuck, fuck, fuck." Trevor's words sounded like a stabbing knife to the heart, over and over.

The man stopped at the foot of the cross, staring up at the dead boy before he reaching up to gingerly touch a dangling hand. He jumped back, clearly startled, whipping his phone out once again, dialing, the alarm on his face a flaming beacon even from a hundred yards away. The man brought the phone up to his ear.

On the dresser behind the boys, a shrill tone rang out. They spun about. On the dresser, a glowing cell phone screen announced an incoming call.

"What the fuck?" they said in unison, exchanging confounded looks.

"How did he know who to call?" Kurtis asked.

Demarco snatched the phone from the dresser. Beneath the flashing "incoming call" was the word "Dad".

"Oh shit—this is Austin's phone."

"Should we answer it?"

"Fuck no."

"What's the garbage man doing?"

"Talking to somebody on the phone, he looks freaked the fuck out."

"This is not good."

Austin's phone abruptly fell silent in Demarco's hand. A few seconds later a text message notification popped onto the screen: "On my way. Be ready to go."

Demarco showed it to the others.

In the distance rose the wail of sirens.

"Remember, we don't know anything," Demarco instructed. "Austin was here when we went to bed last night. We'll pretend to be asleep if anyone shows up asking questions. They wake us up and we're shocked and confused. Got it?"

Within minutes several police cars descended upon Mr. Copeland's house, setting up a perimeter as one pulled into the driveway to block the garage, lights flashing, sirens screaming. The garbage man gestured wildly as an officer pulled him away from the scene. Two policemen closed in on the house, guns drawn, while two others assumed a defensive position behind the vehicle.

The policemen knocked on the front door, and the boys watched in stunned silence as old man Copeland casually swung it open. He wore a white bathrobe with a matching tuft of chest hair poking out over the top. He exhibited the demeanor of someone awoken by the sudden commotion, groggy and confused.

The officers didn't hesitate, grabbing the old man by his terrycloth lapels, yanking him onto the porch as though he was as light as *papier-mâché*. They dragged him down the stairs, Copeland losing both slippers before being planted face-down in the yard at the foot of the cross. Guns at the ready, the other officers stepped out from behind the car as the old man was cuffed.

The boys remained hushed as the whole affair unfolded on the other side of the window. Kurtis absently grabbed a bucket of candy and started eating one piece after the other as he looked out upon the scene. The officers snatched Mr. Copeland back up to his feet as a black Dodge Charger pulled up in front of Demarco's house.

Mr. Taylor, Austin's dad, was a tall man, lanky like his son. He stepped out of the car, watching with fascination as policemen shoved an old man towards what appeared to be a crucified zombie decoration. The officers gestured towards it, their faces red and shouting, as if attempting to extract a confession of murder there on the spot. The entire spectacle was absurd, unreal. Demarco's gaze shifted back and forth from Mr. Copeland's front lawn to their dead friend's dad, who appeared to be momentarily mesmerized.

Whatever spell Mr. Taylor was under broke the moment he recognized his son. The man burst into action, dashing across the street, charging up the sidewalk, straight into Mr. Copeland's yard. Fists clenched, he lunged at the bedraggled hand-cuffed man beside his son's body. Thunderous screams of fury rattled the glass of the window through which Demarco watched in astonishment of the drama unfolding below.

Two policemen quickly holstered their weapons and grabbed

hold of Mr. Taylor's arms before he tore the old man apart. They pulled the distraught father towards the street, attempting to calm him. Mr. Taylor argued for a few minutes before relenting. Dejected, he headed back to his car.

Remorse gnawed at Demarco's insides as he looked upon Mr. Taylor's anguish, the man's face a demonic amalgam of rage and sorrow. Stark tears streamed down the man's face, each runnel perfectly visible from Demarco's second-story perch. Mr. Taylor wiped the wetness away with the back of his hand as he sat back down in the driver's seat of his car, vacantly staring into the distance.

The police had abandoned their attempts to elicit a confession at the scene and appeared to be reading Mr. Copeland his rights. The back door of the cruiser in the driveway stood open, ready to transport the prime suspect to the station.

Not knowing what else to do and having nothing at all to say, Kurtis handed a piece of candy to each of his friends. They unwrapped the candies in silence, popping them into their mouths as Mr. Copeland was thrust towards the cruiser.

A sudden blur of motion below drew Demarco's attention. Mr. Taylor was out of his car, charging up the street towards the crime scene once again, wailing like a banshee as he ran. In his hand was a small black pistol.

The officers released Mr. Copeland, instinctively drawing their weapons, training them on the dead boy's father as he approached. Mr. Taylor didn't hesitate. The instant the police pointed their guns in his direction he planted his feet, locked his elbows and fired—once, twice, three times. The cracking gunshots rattled both the windows and the three boys hiding behind it.

His aim was true. Mr. Copeland danced a little jig, hands cuffed behind his back, as bullets burst into his chest, instantly turning the front of his bathrobe and chest hair from white to bright red. The old man took three feeble steps towards his house, as though he wanted nothing more than to crawl back into bed and start this whole blasted day over again. He never made it, collapsing into a heap right there on the driveway instead.

"Oh shit!" The word was spoken in perfect harmony, as though Demarco and his friends had planned to say it at this exact moment all along.

A second barrage of gunfire convulsed through the neighborhood, as the barrels at the end of every policeman's arm spit fire back at Mr. Taylor.

Austin's dad didn't dance as the bullets punctured his forehead and abdomen. Instead, he fell flat onto his back, sprawled motionless on the sidewalk. The cops stood tense, guns directed towards Mr. Taylor's motionless body.

Yet another gunshot reverberated from down the street, its thunderclap deeper, louder than the ones before. A policeman's head exploded. One moment it was there, the next it was not, replaced by a fine mist suspended in the air above the set of shoulders where it used to reside.

A stout middle-aged man with a bushy black beard appeared on the sidewalk further down the street, shotgun raised as he advanced towards the remaining policemen. Demarco recognized the man as Richard McNealy, Mr. Copeland's next door neighbor and lifelong best friend.

Additional gunfire shattered the silence of the early November morning, one shot after the other in rapid succession. By the time the ringing echoes fell silent, Richard McNealy and a second policeman lay dead on the ground.

The three boys turned towards each other, each with their own unique look of unbelieving, of hoping that someone, anyone would say something, something that would change everything, that would take it all back, would make it all go away.

Kurtis was the first to step back from the window, ashen-faced and quivering. Lost in a daze, the bucket of candy he clutched for comfort slipped from his hand and tumbled across the floor, spilling candies as it bounced.

The boys gaped, incredulous, as they read the single word spelled out by scattered candies on the floor, each individual letter perfectly formed, as though carefully arranged:

VIOLET

Jason Parent

"COME HERE, GIRL."

Ed patted his thigh as he stared at the fourteen-year-old corgi struggling to shimmy out of her crate. The dog stared back, eyes swelling with excitement, big dumb smile on her face as if she didn't have a care in the world, her back legs hardly working, just par for the course.

She fell flat on her belly halfway out of the crate, still smiling, still staring up at him with her big beautiful doe eyes. Eyes full of ignorant happiness. Eyes that caused Ed's own to fill with tears.

The dog, Violet, was old. Ed was old too. He'd named the dog after his daughter, who'd passed away some thirty years ago in a car accident. Nobody's fault, just bad weather and bad luck. He and his wife, Mara, had no other children. After his daughter had passed, then a few years later, their golden retriever, and another decade after that, Mara herself from cancer, Ed had spent so many years alone.

Struggling to live.

His daughter had clung to life for days after the accident, his wife for years after her diagnosis. Hell, even the golden had fought to live every day it could. He figured he'd owed it to all of them to keep on keeping on for as long as he could, no matter how much it pained him, missing them every day.

So he got himself a dog, and he named her Violet. The corgi hadn't replaced his daughter, but she had certainly and quickly become another daughter. And she was all he had.

Fourteen years. He smiled wanly. *That's like damn near a hundred in dog years.* He went to Violet and hefted her into his arms. The corgi licked his cheek once then rested her head against his shoulder.

165

He stroked the back of her neck. "Why do you even go into that crate anymore? Huh? I haven't shut the door to it since you were a pup."

Ed held her close. He knew the answer. The crate was her home, just as beside him on the couch was her home when he watched television and curled against his hip was her home when he went to bed. The one-bedroom, one-bathroom apartment wasn't much, but it was enough for the two of them.

But Violet had severe arthritis, and she was suffering. She was lucky if she could walk more than a few steps without her back legs splaying, her belly plopping against the ground. Every time it happened, she looked up at Ed with those unassuming, apologetic eyes as if she might have done something wrong. That guilt—projection, he knew, but that did nothing to soften it—burned hot in his chest, the pain deep and pure, his breath hitching in response to any inclination concerning the battle Violet was losing.

He reached for her leash then shook his head, scolding himself for his gaff. The dog hadn't needed the leash for months. She wasn't running anywhere.

With a heavy sigh, he picked up his keys and went out into the hallway. He didn't bother locking his door, the average age of his neighbors being close to eighty. He carried Violet down the three flights of stairs that led to the complex's front doors. From there, it was a short walk to the pet area, where Violet could do her business.

He placed her on the grassy earth with all the caution of a man balancing an egg on a spoon. Once she seemed to be standing firmly, he gently held her just above her hips so she could walk without fear of falling.

Violet took a few steps then spread her legs to pee. Her legs kept slipping, but Ed caught and held her as urine trickled onto the grass.

166

"You really need to put her down," someone said from behind him.

Ed felt heat rising in his face, some from anger and some from shame. He knew the dog's quality of life had been on a drastic decline and had battled the idea of putting her down. But every time he turned it over in his head, he wanted to scream and sob and shake his fists at the heavens for the cruelty of life's feeble condition.

It was his decision to make, though, and he didn't care for busybody neighbors butting their goddamn noses into his business. He whirled around, ready to lash out, but checked his temper and donned a phony smile before it was too late.

"Hi, Gladys." Ed hoped his face wasn't as red as it felt, though he could always blame it on the strain of bending over and carrying the dog, burdens he'd undertake for another fourteen years if it meant being with Violet all that time. "How's Kirk? Any change?"

Gladys was a hospice nurse who worked double duty, after hours caring for her husband, Kirk, who was suffering from ALS in an apartment down the hall from Ed. He didn't mean the question to sound callous and hoped it hadn't, for he was genuinely concerned about Kirk's well-being. Kirk had always been a fine neighbor and, had his disease not debilitated him so early on in Ed's tenure at the complex, might have made a decent friend.

Gladys, on the other hand, was a bitch—a nosy, gossipy troublemaker that never knew how to leave well enough alone. A week didn't go by when she wasn't fighting with someone in the building. Ed did his best to excuse it. The woman lived a hard life made harder by unfortunate and undeserved conditions, something he knew a little about himself.

"No change," Gladys said, her mouth a thin line. "At least he didn't poop himself today."

Ed didn't know what to say to that, so he said nothing.

A gnarled finger extended, she pointed at Violet, who was now lying against Ed's sneaker. "You need to put that thing down and soon." She snarled. "If you don't, I'm calling animal control." With that, she turned to leave.

Ed clenched his teeth as he watched her go. He glanced down at his girl, who was looking up at him with tongue lolling, big dumb smile returned. He couldn't help but smile back. Like swaddling a baby, he wrapped Violet in his arms and headed inside.

Gladys's comment festered like a wound that wouldn't heal. After giving Violet some fresh water and helping her into her crate, he decided he needed some fresh air. He stepped back out of his apartment, once again leaving it unlocked, and headed for a lap around the block to clear his head.

When he got back, his front door was ajar.

His body screamed trouble. Without thinking, he ran through the door. There, Gladys stood over his dog, a long needle in her hand. In the crate, Violet's eyes were closed. Her side rose and fell rapidly as a purplish liquid ran from her mouth.

"It's for her own good," Gladys said, her mouth tight. If she felt anything for what she'd done, it didn't show. "It's mercy."

Crying, Ed pushed Gladys aside, ran to his dog, and pulled her from the crate. He raced down the stairs, taking them two or three at a time, putting tremendous strain on his own aching joints. But the pain was a distant echo, the worry and maddening dread spurring him forward at a pace he had no longer thought himself capable.

He placed his girl on the passenger seat of his car and slid behind the wheel. He drove as fast as he was able, swerving through traffic and blowing through red lights, barely able to see through the tears in his eyes.

When he screeched to a halt outside the animal hospital's entrance, Violet was already dead. Ed broke down. He didn't bother going inside.

A week passed, and Ed was no better off than he had been at the time of Violet's death. That night, he caught Gladys leaving on an errand. Once she was clear of the hallway, he hurried down it to her apartment, shimmied open the door, and stepped inside.

"It's for his own good," he said, almost snarling as he smothered Kirk with a pillow. "It's mercy."

THE DOGSHIT GAUNTLET

John McNee

PAUL WAS IN THE MIDST of cleaning excrement from his shoe when he met Maddy. He was at the bus stop, leaning against the shelter, daintily using an old ticket receipt to attack the orange-brown muck on his heel that had refused to dislodge when he'd scraped it against the curb.

Then he heard a voice. "Here." A hand appeared in front of him, clutching a packet of tissues.

"Thanks." He took the tissue first—urgent matters required his attention—then looked up to see who the hand belonged to. When he did, he met the green eyes of a beautiful stranger. Maybe 30 years old. Slim and fair, with a dusting of freckles across snow-white skin and chestnut hair tied back behind pink ears, she wore a friendly smile and an emerald raincoat, with a red leather satchel slung over her shoulder. "Thanks," he repeated, somehow meaning it more the second time around.

"Don't tell me," she said. "The alley."

"What?"

She nodded across the road to the housing estate, and the narrow alleyway that ran between the gardens, joining their street to the next one over.

"Oh yes," he said, letting out a dry, cynical laugh while he wiped his loafer clean—or clean enough. "The Gauntlet, that's what I call it."

Her laugh was much better than his. Genuine. "That's a good name for it," she said. "The Dogshit Gauntlet."

"It's always the same." He sighed. "Take your life in your hands coming that way. I'd never chance it unless I was running late. And then today I was running late, took my chances, the worst happened and—best of all—my bus didn't even show up on time."

173

"You have to be focused if you're running the Gauntlet," she chided him, chatting away like she'd known him all her life. "Concentration is paramount. You can't afford to take your eyes off the ground for a second."

"Yeah, well, I got distracted, didn't I? A moment's weakness . . . "

And what was it that had distracted him?

Oh yes, the woman at the window.

In the faded robe. With the wide, flat face and the staring eyes. The same woman who was always standing at her bedroom window, staring down at him whenever he came past. Staring down from her window in the house in the middle of the row. In the middle of the Gauntlet.

He knew he needed to watch his step. He needed to beware. The people who lived on that estate treated the alleyway like a personal puppy latrine. He had to be careful. He knew he shouldn't look up. However much the woman at the window unnerved and unsettled him. He shouldn't look back at her.

But he couldn't help it. He looked. And he paid the price.

Well . . . he wasn't about to tell the girl all that.

"I, uh . . . I think you got it," she told him, nodding to his shoe, wrinkling her nose in only mild disgust.

"I hope so," he said, putting his foot down and scanning the area for a bin, the shit-stained tissues still between his fingers. There was no bin.

"Just drop it," she said. "It's not as if anyone who lives around here cares."

He did and, even though she was right, still felt a twinge of guilt about littering. A quick scan of the nearby hedges and gutters revealed dozens of cigarette butts, empty bottles, crushed cans, crisp packets and takeaway containers. "I take it you're not a local?"

"Christ, no," she said, practically spitting the words. "I'd sooner slit my wrists than live here surrounded by those kind of people. I must sound like a snob, but I don't care how much money anyone has, I honestly don't. You can be poor and still take pride in your home, you know? In your community. Poverty's no excuse for anti-social behavior. Don't shit where you eat, as they say."

He looked at her and caught her struggling not to smile at her own joke. He hoped, by the expression on his own face, he didn't appear too bemused. And then, over her shoulder, he saw his bus approaching. "Are you getting the 38?"

She shook her head and gave a little look like disappointment. "The 15."

"Ah." He glanced again at the shitty tissue, rolling down the road on the breeze. "Well, thanks again." He smiled at her. "I won't shake your hand."

"No, better not," she replied, instinctively folding her arms even as she returned the smile.

The bus pulled up and he hopped on. It moved away and he gave her a little wave out the window. She waved back.

Then he sat down and replayed the whole scene in his head, from start to finish. It couldn't have lasted more than five minutes, but by the time he reached his stop he would conclude it to be the most exciting, invigorating encounter he'd had all year. In several years, in fact.

There wasn't much competition in Paul's life. He worked a boring job and lived a lonely existence. His love and social lives had been dead for so long he'd given up any effort to revive them. Being lonely was easier and more comfortable. Not that he was any uglier, meaner or more socially awkward than the average man. It just didn't seem to happen for him, that was all. No chemistry, with anyone. Among all the relationships in his life, there wasn't one he felt went more than skin deep. No profound connections. No love. Nothing *real*.

But there was something with her. Something different. As

inane as their chat had been, he could still feel the lingering crackle of its electricity within his veins.

And he hadn't even asked her name. Odds were he'd never get the chance. She'd probably never be back at that bus stop.

Oh well, he told himself, ever the pragmatist. *No sense getting your hopes up.*

And yet . . .

"Well if it isn't Mr. 38!" She shouted to him as she crossed the street from the alleyway. He looked up from his paperback to see her—a grinning vision in the same emerald raincoat from the day before. Her walk was all swagger and made her pony-tail bounce at her back.

He wondered where she got all that confidence. If only she could bottle and sell it she'd make a fortune. "Miss 15. Good morning to you. Braved the Gauntlet, I see?"

"And emerged unscathed." She beamed. "Nothing for an old pro like me." She thrust out her hand. "How about that handshake?"

He obliged, unable to keep from grinning himself. "I'm Paul."

"Maddy."

"I have to ask. Are you always so bright and breezy in the morning?"

"Oh yes. I always take a little bump of speed just to get myself out of bed. But I won't crash for another half an hour. Or maybe I'm just a morning person."

"Either way, you're doing something right."

She smiled, nodded, tucked a lock of hair behind her ear, and for a few mildly painful seconds, nobody said anything.

Then he asked: "So where does the number 15 go?"

"Riverside Business Park," she answered quickly.

"You work there?"

"Melrose Media." An award-winning television production office. "I'm a producer."

"Wow," he said, genuinely impressed. "How long have you been doing that?"

"Just started. They hired me onto their formats team. At the moment I'm spending most of my time in pitch meetings, coming up with new ideas for dating shows for millennials. Or coming up with ways to make old ideas sound new."

"Sounds like fun."

She made a face like she wasn't sure, but didn't want to complain. "Yeah, it can be, sometimes. What about you?"

"I'm the database manager for a bathroom wholesaler. Not very glamorous, I'm afraid."

"No, that's important work. Think about where we'd be in a world without bathrooms."

He laughed. "Yeah, I guess you're right."

"So what are you reading?" She nodded to the book in his hand, but before he could answer, raised a finger. "Hold that thought."

It was his bus. She'd heard it before he did. He couldn't remember ever being so disappointed to see it.

"You can tell me tomorrow," she told him.

Tell me tomorrow. He clung to that on the bus ride, hearing it echo in his head. For the rest of the day. A promise. A guarantee. Maybe, just maybe, the start of something.

Tell me tomorrow.

He didn't tell her. Not tomorrow or the day after that or the day after that. There was no chance. They had so many other things to talk about. All kinds of subjects to cover. Musings on work and relationships, travel and entertainment, good food and bad manners. Even a little politics. And at no point did the conversation ever lag. At no point did he spoil everything by making some stupid comment that ground things to a halt.

If only talking to everyone could be as easy as talking to her, he thought.

And there was always so much left unsaid, because he always had a bus to catch. By the end of the first week he was firmly convinced that he should ask her out. That didn't mean he could. He'd spent so long in the depths of loneliness and self-pity that the idea of asking anyone out—even someone who seemed like she would be receptive to the idea—was terrifying.

What made it doubly difficult was that he was getting less time to speak to her each morning and so less time to build up to asking the question. Every day she was getting to the bus stop slightly later than the day before.

His immediate suspicion was that she was setting out later each morning so she wouldn't have to spend so long talking to him, but that was just his own insecurities talking. The way she spoke to him, the smile she showed him, told a different story. Of more concern was the expression she wore immediately on emerging from the alley. A dazed, haunted look of confusion and alarm, as though she didn't know where she was or what was happening to her. It melted away when she saw him, but for the brief moment it was on her face, it was deeply unnerving.

Finally, towards the end of the second week, came the day she failed to beat the bus. Paul had stood in the shelter, psyching himself up to ask her out.

But then the 38 arrived and she was nowhere to be seen. Reluctantly, he stepped aboard and took his seat, staring out the window at the Gauntlet, waiting for her to appear.

When she did, the sight filled him with deep concern. She looked more lost and panicked than before. Frightened, even. And she didn't see him. She stood, shaking, glancing up and down the street, then back over her shoulder, into the alley. She looked mad.

But then his bus turned a corner and he couldn't see her any more.

The following day was Friday. The cap on two solid weeks of flirting and fretting. And he was determined that he wouldn't spend his weekend having the same internal dialogue with himself. He'd ask her out today. He didn't care how long he had to wait. He'd miss his bus if he had to.

Which he did. Then the 15 came and left, but Maddy still hadn't appeared.

Most likely because it was her day off. Or she was sick. Or had a meeting somewhere else or was filming on location or any number of other perfectly good reasons that weren't his business to know. But he stood there a couple minutes longer, eyes fixed on the entrance to the Gauntlet. And then he went looking for her.

He crossed the street to the alley and stared all the way down it. Running straight across the middle of the Madras Quadrant housing estate, it was a horrible path to walk. A narrow, forty yard stretch of potholed tarmac and gravel, sprouting weeds, all manner of litter and dark, deep puddles. And the dogshit. Always.

Watch your step, he told himself, as if he needed telling.

Maddy was nowhere to be seen, but he wanted to be thorough. He kept his eyes on the ground ahead of him as he went, ignoring the back gardens and windows of the houses at either side. It was tempting to look. The scheme had a reputation as the place in which the local authority dumped all its most problematic tenants. Ex-cons, drug dealers, perverts, complex

179

mental health cases, the works. So he couldn't help the nagging feeling that he could steal a glance at any one of the pebble-dashed properties and catch sight of something truly reprehensible.

But he kept his head down. At least, until he got to the house he always looked at. The one halfway along the row. Halfway to the end of the Gauntlet. The house with the woman in the window, who always, always, *always* stared back. And because he always, always, *always* did, Paul lifted his head and looked.

And then he stopped. Because, while the woman in the faded robe, for the first time in all the occasions he'd looked, was not at her window, Maddy was in the garden. She stood, hunched, against the wall of the building, at the corner where it met the garden fence. Her hands roved its surface like she was scratching, searching.

"Maddy?" When she didn't answer, he approached, keeping an eye out for anyone who might notice him. "Maddy!"

Her head was tilted, turned away from him, facing the wall. As he watched, she shifted sideways, hands continuing to move in slow patterns. The property's back door was a few feet to her left. The kitchen window was directly above her. But if she was hunting for a way in, then for some reason she couldn't see them. If that's what she was after.

"Maddy?" Drawing closer, he placed a hand on her shoulder and slowly turned her around to face him.

Her eyes were glazed and wouldn't meet his. Her mouth was open, lips moving slowly, but no sound coming out. She was squinting, brow furrowed, like she was trying to solve a riddle.

Paul spoke her name again, asked her what she was doing, but got no reply. When he took her hand in his and tried to lead her away, she followed, but dragging her feet, leaning back, like she was reluctant to leave.

Only when they were out in the alley did she speak. "There." Muttering, like she was talking in her sleep. "I know it's there."

"What's there?" he asked.

Her answer was a hiss, full of anger. "*Secret.*"

Paul was leading her away, back to the alley's entrance. "I think we need to get you home," he told her. "Do you know where you live?"

"Templeton Mews," she muttered, irritably. It wasn't clear if she was aware who she was talking to, but Paul recognized the address. A highly desirable block of luxury flats just a few minutes along the road from him. All this time she'd been living around the corner.

"We'll pop into mine first," he said, not that she seemed to be listening. "It's on the way."

He cast a quick glance back to the house before they reached the street. And saw her. The woman in the faded robe. At her bedroom window. Face pale and round. Eyes wide, mouth open.

She stared back.

"If you're hoping for an explanation, you can flat-out forget it," she told him, when she was sitting on his couch, a mug of chamomile tea in her hands. "I don't have one."

"How are you feeling?" he asked. He was standing against the kitchen counter, not too far away, but maintaining a reasonable distance. His flat didn't allow for much else. Only three rooms. A kitchen and living space, a bedroom and a small bathroom.

"Normal," she answered. "Like myself."

"Do you remember what you were doing? How you were acting?"

She nodded. "Kind of. It's like remembering a dream. I get a vague sense of it, but if I think about it too much, it all unravels in my head. I was searching for something, I think."

"Something secret, you said."

"Yeah. That sounds about right." She stared into her tea while she spoke, her voice flat. "The key to mysteries of the universe."

"Has it happened to you before?"

Again, she nodded. "But only there. Only in the Gauntlet. At that house. It's like I cross an invisible boundary and suddenly a switch flips in my head. I black out. Wake up on the other side. Strange that I didn't think anything of it, before. Funny how the brain works." She tapped a fingernail against the rim of the mug and turned to look at him. "Are you gay?"

He straightened, immediately defensive. "What?"

"This flat is *insanely* clean. I've never known a straight man with a place this tidy. And you didn't even know I would be coming round."

"I'm not gay."

"Chamomile tea, Paul." She raised her mug. "Chamomile?"

He laughed. "Straight men can drink chamomile tea. There's no law that says we can't."

She raised an eyebrow. "I've never met anyone quite like you. You know what I mean?"

"Yeah, I do."

She took a deep breath and slapped a hand against her thigh. "Right. I need to call work, let them know I won't be in today."

"That might be a good idea." He had already sent a message of his own.

Maddy put down her tea, stood and took her phone out of her coat pocket. "Afterwards, do you want to . . . I don't know . . . watch a film or something? If you're not doing anything else?"

His stomach did a somersault. "Yes. Absolutely."

She nodded and pointed to his bedroom. "Do you mind if I . . . ?"

"Sure," he said, ushering her though so she could make the call in private.

"Try and find a film a film we can watch," she said, closing the door behind her.

He did his best, taking a seat on the couch, turning on the TV and scrolling through the available options, but it was hard to concentrate. He was a little preoccupied by the thought that the woman of his dreams was in his home, in his bedroom and didn't seem in a hurry to leave. He knew he needed to relax, but he also needed to figure out how to proceed, how to navigate this situation without totally screwing things up.

"Paul?" She called to him from the bedroom.

"Yeah?" He was immediately on his feet.

"Can you come here please?"

He went. He opened the door. And before he could say another word to her, she pounced. Her arms went around his shoulders. Her lips locked against his. Taken by surprise, he flinched, but quickly recovered, returning the kiss, putting his hands around her waist, squeezing her close.

As elation and lust flooded his veins, she began to pull him towards the bed.

He followed.

They remained in that room for most of the weekend, sprawled out in bed, limbs entwined, in one state of post-coital bliss or another. Once or twice they left the flat, to go for a walk or to grab breakfast at a local coffee shop, but mostly they stayed indoors, migrating between the bedroom and the living room. They watched films, ate takeaway food, drank wine, had sex.

And they talked. Talked and talked and talked.

One thing they never talked about was Maddy's transformation in the Gauntlet. It lingered in the background, a subtext to their conversations, but never brought forth. It hardly seemed relevant anyway, when stacked against what else was happening. Paul had never been in love before, so didn't want to admit to himself that was what this was. It seemed too soon to call it that. But he had never felt anything like this. If it wasn't love, if it wasn't *real* love, he couldn't even begin to conceive what such a feeling must actually be like.

Maddy never went back to her own flat during the three days and Paul didn't want her to. He wanted them both to stay where they were, continuing their lovers' lifestyle forever.

Of course, they couldn't. Monday had to come around, and with it, the start of another working week.

"I could call in sick again," she said, her head on the pillow next to his, face so close it appeared distorted in his vision. "So could you."

"We have to face the real world eventually," he said, though his heart wasn't in the argument.

She was silent for a long time before replying. "I suppose so."

They awoke to his phone's alarm at 7am, both burning with desire. And though they really didn't have time for it, love-making was their first priority.

When they finally left the flat, they were washed, dressed and running very late.

"Come on," Paul urged as he hurried her down the street towards the Madras Quadrant estate, far more concerned for her than he was for himself. "I'm definitely missing my bus, but you can still catch yours."

"It's okay, really," she said. "I can get the next one."

"You've had this job two weeks. I'm not having you absent and then late because of me." He checked his watch. Just two minutes till the 15 was due. "Ah, shit."

And when he looked up, they were standing right in front of it. The Gauntlet.

"Paul?" When she spoke his name she sounded like a child. Nervous. Afraid. "Let's go around. I can get the next one, really."

He grasped her hand. "It'll be fine. You're with me. Just stay close."

She swallowed and fell in line.

It wasn't far. Just a forty yard stretch of tarmac and gravel. And dogshit. Paul kept his head down, watching his step, ducking as they went under the branches of an overgrown hedge. He squeezed Maddy's hand, pulling her along behind him, keeping his head down. They were nearly halfway there now. A quick glance to the end of the alley and he saw the bus stop, but no bus. They had time. He danced sideways to avoid a large puddle and the suspicious mound of muck at its centre. He kept walking. He kept his head down. He was nearly at the end . . .

And then Maddy's hand was gone.

He halted. Spun about. She wasn't behind him. "Maddy?"

He doubled back. The same house. The same garden. He went in and found her in the same spot, clawed hands roving over the wall, face pressed to the pebble dashing, sniffing for clues.

"Maddy?"

She moved like an animal. Like an insect. A brainless organism, operating entirely on instinct. Paul's own instincts told him to keep his distance. His heart told him he should go to her. He should help. He should be helping. For God's sake, she was the love of his life.

But there was something so, *so* wrong about her.

When he looked up from the snarling, clicking creature his love had become, he saw the face in the window. The woman in the faded robe. She didn't look remotely surprised to see him.

Slowly, while Maddy continued to inch her way back and forth along the wall, he walked towards the house's back door. He climbed the steps and tried the handle, finding it unlocked. He stepped inside and closed the door behind him.

185

He stood in an open-plan kitchen and living room running the length of the house. It was a complete mess. Dirty dishes filled the sink. Pots half-full with remnants of week-old food stood on the cooker. The living room's thick curtains were drawn, but by the flickering light of the mute TV he could see the floor was littered with old takeaway cartons, dishes and dirty mugs. The furniture was piled high with clothes—some clean, most dirty—and old magazines. The air was pungent with the smell of old food, stale smoke and something else underneath, something sour.

And there, moving through the hazy darkness, into the grey light from the kitchen windows, was the woman. He'd seen her a hundred times or more from the alley, but she had never looked so familiar. She was short and round, wearing grey pajamas and a pale green dressing gown. Her greasy chestnut hair was pulled back in an untidy pony-tail. Her wide face was pallid and puffy, delicate features almost lost amid the expanse of pasty flesh.

"I'm sorry," she said.

He frowned. "What for?"

"I know what you're going through." Flat, the way she said it. Tired. Like she was already bored of his ordeal.

"What am I going through?"

"I was in love once. I had a boyfriend. He was perfect. He took care of me, he loved me. He made me feel like the luckiest woman in the world."

Paul flinched at a sound like footsteps from the bedroom over their head.

"Ignore it," she said. "There's no-one else here." Something desperately sad in the way she said it. "We were going to have a baby," she continued. "A little baby boy. We were so happy. But when I went into labor I was in the house on my own. I called an ambulance."

Another sound from elsewhere in the house, close yet distant. The wail of an infant.

"False pregnancy, that's what they called it," she said. "All the physical symptoms of pregnancy, but no baby. It's all in the mind. A kind of psychosis. That's when I found out the truth about myself. No boyfriend. No baby. Just fantasies. I have these dreams. They seem *so real*, but . . . "

"Hold up," Paul said, tired of her babbling. "There's a girl, in your garden, right now. I know that you know her . . . "

"My problem is I can't tell fantasy from reality." Tears in her green eyes. Tears of sadness and frustration. "That's what the doctors tell me. It's a coping mechanism. I get lonely living here. I can't work with my condition. I don't have family or friends. I'm so alone. I get depressed by reality so I escape into the dream. I let it be real. I shouldn't. Every time I go deeper it just gets stronger. I lose control of it. It becomes impossible to make the distinction between the people who are real and the ones from my head. The baby. That should have been a wake-up call. I should have realized then the damage I was doing. It's not right. But instead, I was . . . I was sad. I was so sad. That was my chance to wake up. But instead I just . . . changed the dream. I never imagined I could inflict it on someone else."

Paul was tempted to grab her by the shoulders and shake her. "What are you talking about?" There was an uncomfortable atmosphere in the room, to accompany the smell. Something that irritated his skin, made him sweat, made him itch.

The woman shook her head, shame and sorrow etched in her brow. "I dreamt up a better life for myself. A better version of myself. I dreamed I was tall and slim and beautiful. I dreamed I had all the clothes I could never afford. A gorgeous flat in Templeton Mews and a good job at Melrose Media. I dreamed I had confidence and style. That I could make a man fall in love with me. The man who ran past my window each morning on his way to catch the bus. Even him, why not. I dreamed we could fall in love."

There was a pressure on Neil's brain, like someone had slipped their fingers beneath the skin at the back of his head, taken a hold of his skull and was squeezing.

"I'm sorry," she said. "When I tell people what it's like, how real it is, nobody ever understands. But at least now, maybe you can."

"No." He was aware of a sensation within himself. A physical feeling of plummeting, like everything that made his life worth living had just dropped through a trapdoor. It wasn't real? She wasn't real? Tears sprang to his eyes, but he wiped them away. "No." Insistent. "She's real." He was angry. Hurt. Tricked. He pointed a finger in the woman's face. "You can't do that. You don't get to take this away from me."

"I'm sorry. I truly am. I didn't know it was possible."

"Enough lies. What's happening to her? Tell me!"

The woman was shaking now, panicking in the face of his temper. "I don't know! I don't think we're supposed to be this close to each other. It's unnatural. It all starts to collapse . . . "

"Oh yeah?" He was already moving towards the kitchen door, sickened by her bullshit. "What happens if I let her in?"

"Don't. Please don't do that."

"If she's not real, what harm can she do?" He opened the door and Maddy was there, on the steps. Head cocked to one side, eyes wide, but unseeing, jaw hanging slack. With a caring touch, Paul guided her inside.

The woman in the green robe didn't move. She quivered like a frightened hedgehog in the middle of a road.

"Maddy," he said, as he led her across the room. "This woman seems to think you're a figment of her imagination. What do you think? Does that sound right to you?"

Slowly, so, so slowly, Maddy's eyes rolled round to finally

lock on the face of the woman in front of her. And within them, Paul caught a flash of recognition.

"Hello," the woman squeaked, the word barely escaping her throat.

For a moment, there was silence and the house was still. Then Maddy's jaw closed. Her lips moved. "Found you," she said.

A moment after that, all Paul could see was blood. A spraying, gushing burst that filled the space between Maddy and the woman like a throbbing red cloud. Paul blinked, the cloud dissipated, and he saw a fistful of the woman's flesh was in Maddy's hand.

Blood cascaded down the robe and pajamas. The woman, throwing hands up to the ragged red opening in her neck, staggered backwards through the living room and fell. Maddy chased her down, clawed hands tearing, ripping, shredding with ferocity beyond all reason.

From above came a cacophony. The thunderous pounding of hands and feet on the ceiling. The horrified shriek of a young child. None of it real.

None of this is real.

Paul put his hands over his ears.

None of this is real.

He turned and ran. As he went out the door and down the steps, he glanced back into the house, part of him hoping to catch some small sign that the beautiful girl he'd fallen in love with was more than someone else's dream turned to nightmare.

The dreamer was already a corpse, her body prone on the floor. Maddy, her face a disintegrating mask of pure madness, had torn open a gaping hole in the dead woman's chest. In the last image Paul saw of her before he squeezed his eyes shut and ran blindly into the alley, it looked like she was trying to climb *inside.*

189

He fled. Back to reality. Back to his old, loveless life. Back to the world he knew and understood. It was hopeless and horrible and he despised it but at least it made sense.

He returned to work the following morning, throwing himself back into routine, into the comfort of his old, uncomplicated life. He told himself that the whole episode had been one bad dream. His brain was complicit in his self-deception. When he allowed it, he could forget everything about the woman he'd loved and all she'd meant to him. In those lonely moments when he willed himself to remember, the scenes that played out in his mind didn't feel like real memories. More like fragments of feverish fantasy. Eventually, after a time, he forgot. He didn't return to the house or even to the Gauntlet, but in time, he forgot why.

And then, one morning, he broke a shoelace and made himself late for the bus. Running to catch it, he decided to chance the old shortcut.

And as he hurried along the alleyway, down the centre of the estate, mindful of where he stepped, he felt a pair of eyes staring down at him from a bedroom window.

He put his head down and kept walking.

TATTOOED ALL IN BLACK

Mark Matthews

MASTERS OF MIDNIGHT

"YOUR TIME IS COMING. You'll be leaving soon. Come back to me if you can. Let me know you're okay."

"I'm going nowhere."

"Yes, Lara, you are, but I'll be okay if I can just hear from you. Promise."

Even in these last hours of Lara's life, I was lying. I'll be far from okay.

"I won't leave you. I'll stay here. In this bed. My spirit. Right here, in this house. Look for me in the floating dust when the sunlight slices through the shades. When your foot hangs off the bed and feels a cold caress. I'll slip in and out of your dreams and be with you always."

Closeness to death had sparked her fluid tongue. Words flowed from her lips like secrets she needed to share since any word spoken might be her last. She was propped up by clouds of white pillows. A checkered afghan blanket lay on top of her. Somber light glowed from the lone lamp, and the air filled our lungs with sadness.

Cancer air.

It was there in each breath. She exhaled the cancer, and I inhaled it in, hoping to catch the disease. But no matter how much love exists in your heart, one cannot catch cancer, and she would not be taking me with her into death.

At-home hospice, they called it, and I tended to her needs around the clock where it mattered little if it was day or night. I made grilled cheese, tomato soup, or scrambled eggs, and she took small bites and then pushed the plate aside. Awkward silence filled in the waiting. Our bedroom, with a large king mattress, bedside table, and two dressers had become a funeral parlor. All that was missing was the tall funeral director who was overly-versed in the language of condolence. Lara lay there as if in an open casket, flowers delivered from co-workers and cousins lined the walls.

"Our spirits. They will commune again," she said. I gripped her hand and looked into her hazel eyes. During the first days she had come home to die, her eyes had been red from a constant stream of tears, but today all I saw was a stoic white. Her pupils were tiny black pinholes, her body was so full of death had this been an open casket for the public to see I might have closed it. Her skin was pasty, and her ears looked alien, not human. Her nose as pug-like as the dog we swore we would buy but never did. Not after the diagnosis.

"We'll be together," I said with a squeeze of my hand. "We will. I will look for you all the days until I die, and then after that."

But the emptiness in my gut told me something different. There was no chemotherapy for the sickness I had. At the hour of her death I expected my insides to be gouged out, for our spirits had been fused together. It happened as we walked the Hawaiian beaches on our honeymoon, where the salt of the deepest oceans baptized our feet. When we lay on the surf under the dark Hawaiian sky and the universe peered down. The stars were so vivid it rained in blues and reds. Her flesh pulsed with life then, her spirit as powerful as the cosmos that looked down upon us. Promises of adventures waited on the horizon.

It was on this very bed upon which she lay dying where we'd had sex with such heat and ferocity my soul penetrated hers and melted us together. Both of us cried out for God as if to say his name in thanks. We fit together like lock and key, a testimony to the glory of our creator.

But the glory was now gone.

I watched her chest rise and fall, each breath I expected to be her last. Her hand no longer squeezed back in response to my touch. The blood flow was leaving. The warmth in retreat. When she finally closed her eyes for good I kissed her lips, waiting for the smile to return, for her eyes to twinkle.

But there was nothing. She was gone.

I curled up next to her, wrapping myself around her like a snake, and wept. Her skin grew cold with no spirit to heat it from within. The quiet of the air hung over us. Even the cancer retreated without its host. It had done its job here. Her body was dead, and her spirit set free.

The funeral was merely a series of motions. My hands were in my pockets often, twiddling at a wadded up piece of tissue from the last time I wore this suit. My insides burst on occasion and I doubled over in pain. People rushed to console me, so I feigned togetherness and tried to keep my insides iron. I repeated what I had heard others say at moments like these as I waited to go back home.

Lara's spirit was there waiting for me and I was eager to return.

I controlled what I could in the empty house by cleaning and organizing. I made color coded labels and filed credit card receipts. I cleaned behind the stove and under the fridge. I never stopped, unless I heard something that seemed out of place, in which case I stood completely still listening for whatever tiny messages might be hidden within. When the furnace kicked on and stirred the air, my head jerked towards the noise waiting for more. But it was just the furnace, no voices, no whispers. Cars from the street outside whooshed by full of life, but inside things were dead and lifeless. I wanted to hear Lara's spirit stir in this house, to feel the heat of her flesh next to mine, but it was as if she had never existed.

Days passed, and I kept the house in such order that Lara could have walked inside at any moment and felt at home. I bought cream for her coffee. I scraped the ice off her car.

195

At night, I lay in our bed soaking in whatever physical residue she may have left behind. Her body's dead skin cells still lay beneath me in these unwashed sheets, and I bathed in the remains. I imagined microscopic bugs in the sheets feeding on the last traces of her flesh.

Lara's real ashes sat on the nightstand. I would have kept her body had they let me, but cremation was her wish. All that was left of her was completely trapped inside a metallic box.

But it was her spirit I needed, and I watched and listened, felt and waited, for the spirit to show itself.

At night, I scanned the darkness. A soul as bright as hers could not remain hidden in black. In the light of day things are clear, but in the dark you can see tiny specks of colorful light floating, flickering. They are souls, and they move, they dance, they collide, they try but are unable to make a shape. Still, there is action in the air, I felt it, but it was not her. Not Lara. Night after night, she failed to show up, so I gave in to sleep and woke to a new darkness each day.

I spoke to her inside my head, out loud to a silent room, and in both prayer and meditation asked for a sign. Each day was spent waiting for the night to come so I could lie in the bed where she had died. I wrapped myself in the same afghan checkered blanket, a larva in a cocoon, my foot hung over the edge. Cold air danced around my exposed flesh, teasing the tiny hairs, my limb hanging over the bedside waiting for dead hands to grasp my ankle, but the touch I longed for never came.

There is no afterlife, for if there was a spirit such as Lara could return.

I shaved little. I brushed my teeth only when the grime became too much to bear. I drank Southern Comfort whiskey and waited for the spirits to make her appear. My brain became mushy. Confused. My stomach full of acid.

Hold on. Hold on. I finally left the house to visit our favorite places. First, the coffee shop where local acoustic guitar players sang and sold their homemade CD's for six bucks a piece. Next, I shopped at the thrift store where we'd given each other fist bumps after finding a secret stash.

On All Hallows Eve I went to an orchard where Lara and I used to pick apples each fall. A brilliant yellow sun rained down in the chilly autumn air as I filled two bags with Honey Crisps. I carried the bags back to my car and a tiny dog poked his head out from under the bumper. He had no collar, no marks, a tiny mutt-mix. There was some pug in him, had to be, and we had wanted a pug, so I took him home. Now we had our dog, and I am sure Lara looked on with a smile. The mutt licked my face in the morning to wake me. He waited for me to sit so he could jump on my lap. There he stood guard to gaze about the house as if sensing my mission to see Lara's spirit.

Now I had help.

I set an alarm to wake me at 3:15 A.M. every night, for I've heard that is the hour when spirits safely walk the earth, and I wanted to bear witness. The alarm is cold and cruel at such an hour, ripping me from sleep into a dark world. Still, I woke with hope and looked about the shadows of the room, waiting for her to materialize at the foot of my bed, for her hand to touch mine, for her eyelashes to brush against my cheek. Still nothing. By four a.m., I was back to sleep.

I bought an Ouija board at K-mart for $9.99. I knew it was pathetic, cliché even, to expect a spirit unique as hers to show herself this way. Still, at midnight during a lightning storm (for lightning storms open up the gates of heaven and let the spirits in) I put my fingers on the plastic piece and waited for movement. A lone candle flickered. My fingers hung tense on the board, all ten of them suddenly longer, skinnier, veins bulging, muscles begging to be moved as I asked:

"Lara. I need you. I need you here. Please tell me. Am I alone?

197

Are you here? Tell me." There was no response, just me and the dog on my lap, looking at the candle as it cast shadows upon the wall, wondering what was real and what wasn't.

I was alone.

Except for neighbors. They brought me chocolate chip cookies, spaghetti in Tupperware, always asking, "Is there anything I can do?" One woman, who spoke in mumbles so soft I could not decipher quite what she was saying, listened for hours while I told her stories of Lara over coffee. Some days she wore only her robe, the roundness of her breast teasing me, her warm heart an effective space heater for my cold life. The simple act of watching her fingers wrap around the coffee cup made me long for her touch.

We finally did touch, had sex on a Saturday morning. She understood when I drew the shades, closed the door, and kept us under the covers. I needed darkness thick as ink to turn her into Lara. My eyes stayed closed as I imagined it was Lara who was beneath me. The woman continued to visit with her smiles and indecipherable mumbles, and I cried out for God in moments of ecstasy and prayer.

I was still praying for my Lara back.

Weeks went on. I ate little other than from an old, expired canister of almonds. My skin grew pale and stomach gaunt. I had sex with my neighbor, I fed my dog. I took the phone off the hook and didn't even charge my cell—the 3:15 A.M. alarm was fruitless. Coffee made me nervous. Sweat beads stuck to me.

Without the dog, I may have never left the bed. Without the neighbor, who came over near daily, I wouldn't have talked to anyone.

Forget about her, you have me, she mumbled. *Lara's gone. Be with me. Really with me. Please. Just be with me.*

Her words were spoken in the dark, between the sheets, and under heavy breaths while blood rushed through my head, faint whispers from lips at my ear. The slithering words of a seductress. A temptress. She was both Scylla and Charybdis and I had crashed. Lara was watching, and I had failed my true love.

The kitchen sink was full of dirty dishes, but the steak knife I pulled from the block of wood was clean and made my hand feel powerful. I tilted the metal and watched it sparkle and speak to me. I needed to kill the Scylla. I really did. I made motions with the knife, and practiced sliding it from one side of her jugular across the windpipe to the other. She had sucked my life force away from its soul mate, so it was her who must die. I would do it in the morning.

I practiced as if walking up behind her and then slicing the knife across her throat. I wanted it to be painless, fast, efficient, so I practiced until my muscles remembered the motions and the real thing would simply be a repetition.

But this guaranteed nothing, and the idea that had shined so brightly faded like a drunken promise. I would be back right where I started.

I want to die and be with Lara.

That was it. Why hadn't I think of this earlier? I would either join Lara in the afterlife, or fade away into the same black nothingness that had taken her.

The dog was fed double for breakfast the next morning and gobbled it up eagerly. The unnamed mutt looked at me with suspicious eyes while I drank from the freezer-chilled Southern Comfort bottle. It burned going down, but there was more burning to be had.

I fetched the red gas can from the shed, and the menacing fumes caused the mutt to whimper when I brought it inside. He shouldn't be here for this, I thought, so I opened the back door and he took a few steps outside. I looked into his sad eyes one last time, wishing I had given him a name. *Whoever finds you will care for you,* I whispered before shutting the back door and leaving him safely behind.

The whiskey in my veins made me drunk with the passion to die. I dug out Lara's leftover pills—Xanax, Vicodin, even morphine—from their hiding place deep in the linen closet. I put equal handfuls of all three in my mouth, and washed them down with a river of southern comfort. Gas can in hand, I climbed onto the king mattress with such relief, and it wasn't long until my brain started to swirl downwards.

Consciousness was fading, and I needed to act fast to make sure I didn't wake. I needed a sure death. The gasoline was surprisingly cold when I poured it on my chest, seeming to sizzle before it was even lit. The fumes burned my nostrils and down into my lungs.

When I struck the match, flames followed the fumes, sizzling my skin and burning down into my throat. I've never felt such a rush. My body burst open and my insides were released like an explosion of fireworks. It was painless, orgasmic. My soul was set free from the charred carcass and I was born again.

My spirit soared. Freedom was had. Lara would be near.

But something was wrong. The joy of death turned to pain. I wailed like a wraith with nowhere to go. My body was as burnt as a witch on a stake, and just as dead, but my soul was still aflame. Through the fire, I saw the face of my neighbor, my lover, who had let herself inside as I had planned. Her face contorted with anguish at the sight that confronted her.

I was a body no more but felt lost, adrift in the darkness of an ocean bottom. Black jellyfish were piled on top of each other, squirming, some moaning words I could not decipher, and I feared I had become one of them.

"Lara," I cried out, praying she might hear.

"Lara, come to me."

The blobs began to take shape. Bodies of black, with nooses hung around their necks, foam at their mouths, slices and cuts on their wrists and their necks, some still bleeding, some with dry blood caked all over. One had fractured leg bones that jutted out of its skin, and I saw the marrow inside, as if he had jumped to his death. Another's skull was blown off from a shotgun blast through the roof of her mouth.

Suicidal souls, all of them. I felt it, and I was one of them.

"Lara, Lara."

Yes.

Her voice! I heard her voice.

"Lara, I can hear you, but I cannot see you, cannot feel you, cannot be with you."

My love, you were with me, and I with you. I came to you.

"No. I looked for you. I waited. I tried, Lara, but you were gone."

No. I was there. I was the dog who sat on your lap. I felt every stroke you gave upon my back. I watched as you suffered and wanted you to be in peace. I then visited you and gazed into your eyes over coffee, waiting for life to emerge from the sadness. I came to you like I promised. We were together and I now carry your seed. I am the spirit inside a new body, one that was lifeless and easily occupied. Together we will have a child, so here I shall stay.

Lightning bolt visions flashed and burned inside of me. I remembered the days on the couch petting the stray mutt and feeling the life in his spine. I remembered sex with the neighbor in the darkest of rooms and the sensations of her flesh on my fingers. I had none of that now, and I felt Lara fading.

"Come back."

Silence

"Lara, come back . . . "

I can not.

"Why?"

Your death. Your suicide. You are a murderer now. You are forever tattooed in black. It's all you will ever hear, all you will ever be. I want none of it.

"Come back"

Too late

I would have screamed if I'd had a real voice, but instead, I was a soul forever burning. Lara was alive, somehow, and with child. She would be a shining star in someone else's sky, but mine was forever dark.

I watched as she covered the last bits of flame on my body with a blanket until the fire roared no more, crumbling to the ground next to the charred body I had left behind. My skin was crispy, the scent nauseating, but I refused to accept my mistake. That I had taken my last breath. I prayed that somehow Lara could make my heart beat again and bring me back to life.

But nothing.

Now in darkness I remain. The torment goes on and time passes. I see Lara light up when she smiles at her baby, the way she used to light up for me. She inhabits her new body as though it's a new house, making it her own. Knowing she's happy is sometimes enough to help me endure getting sucked into this black hell.

But my love has its limits. My loneliness burns, my regrets an endless fuel. I beg for mercy from this perpetual pain.

I beg for Lara to come back, even if it means she suffers alongside me.

And I think I've found a way to make it happen.

If I can make her life a living hell, if I can torture her each night with a touch of the darkness that I've come to know so well, if I can cause enough pain, she will no longer want to live. She will take her own life, and join me.

My persistence is one part of me that hasn't died.

I become her new cancer, the disease I once cursed I now embrace, and it will kill her just the same. I infect her dreams with fears. I turn her waking hours into a nightmare. I splash my sea of blackness onto the brilliant star shine of her soul.

Despite how strong Lara is, her shine dims by degrees each day.

Someone else will need to care for the child, Lara can do so no longer. She is back at in-home hospice, rarely leaving her bed. Her pupils have become black holes, her skin pasty and cold. She is unable to withstand the torment.

There is no relief but to join me.

Tattooed all in black.

Every Lucky Penny is Another Drop of Blood

Joanna Koch

MASTERS OF MIDNIGHT

WHEN SHE STARTED, the big coins fell out first. Quarters, the ones that added up to something, followed by mimicking nickels bypassed for dimes. Towards the bottom, there were mostly pennies, diminishing returns, more work for less reward. More dirt and grime and pocket lint to pick from every coin.

Astilbe didn't understand how Andy's throwaway change ended up as her problem, how her needs and desires bowed their humble heads and started rolling. She chopped them off to make ends meet. Bills were due. The account gasped for dollars like a swimmer swept under. Astilbe thought of more exciting reasons to gasp, thought of the currency a woman might wield to escape the waves of monthly payments, balked that it was Andy's fault she was thinking it and shushed the thought and kept on rolling.

Andy hadn't scored a deal in weeks. He wasn't to blame for bad luck. He got out there and hustled every night. A rare species among men, he kept on working, didn't cheat, treated Astilbe's grandma like a queen, and he had that beautiful golden hair like a handsome prince from a fairy tale. Andy was a good guy, a clean guy. But his money was dirty.

Andy always carried cash. Instead of the clean swipe of a card, Andy unfolded bills from his wallet and tucked loose change in the cleft of a pocket. Later, he tossed change into a glass jar where it accumulated until the top rested on nothing but coins. The mountain teetered higher, the top threatened to slide off and break, and Astilbe, who had seen the jar before she moved in, seen it and excused it like so many small things she once excused and no longer deigned to ignore, asked Andy what exactly he planned to do with all that money now that the jar was full.

Andy had shrugged. *Take it to the bank?* He said it as a question. Andy didn't have a bank account. Astilbe wondered if he knew where the nearest bank was. It was as if he'd never encountered this dilemma. As if someone else had always cleaned up after him, sorted his spare change, wiped away his spills and smoothed over his edges so he could sit back and remain rough.

Andy laughed at Astilbe and said his rough edge was part of his charm. Gave her a rough kiss before he left and squeezed her breast just a little too hard and said she could do whatever she liked with the money. *Keep the change,* he said.

The way he laughed made Astilbe furious. It was hours ago. Hours of her life dribbled away counting Andy's discarded cash. At the bottom of the jar, every penny wore a chiaroscuro of deterioration. Deepening levels of decay corroded Lincoln's face. Some turned black or teal, oxidized into fungal white caked with barnacles, etched muddy brown and verdigris or some other sickly combination of crud. Identity eroded where constant fingers rubbed the famous man flat.

Astilbe's hands felt sticky. The smell of copper left a bad taste on her tongue. Coins stuck together, wedded by grime, tarred and feathered with pocket lint and small hairs. The president's profile passed endlessly under Astilbe's fingertips. Suddenly Lincoln changed sex: a crowned Canadian coin was caught amid the rabble of colonists. Astilbe crammed the queen into the paper sleeve and said, "That's democracy, bitch."

The oldest coins jammed. They slid sideways and stuck, tumbled into Astilbe's lap or flew across the floor. She sought out each renegade, grim and determined. Astilbe didn't want the damn things turning up all over the house, sticking to her bare feet or choking the cat.

After a solid day of labor, the jar stood empty. Astilbe slipped the last fifty pennies into the final roll. Her sigh of relief turned to despair as one deviant coin leapt away. It flew and sniggered behind her back, skirting her sight until she fell to her knees, hunting on all fours.

"Hello, what's this then?" said Andy. He popped in the door, smacked Astilbe's backside and skipped up the stairs two at a time. She turned to chide him and caught the fugitive penny winking at her from a nest of cat hair under the loveseat.

Astilbe eyed the shiny coin. She couldn't reach it. She shoved her shoulder under the seat until her arm was engulfed and pressed her cheek against the leather. Andy smattered down the steps like a herd of caribou. He'd donned his best blazer. It was nine o'clock at night.

"Where are you going so fancy?" Astilbe said.

"Meeting a new client at Le Griffon. I'd ask you to join, but . . . "

"I'm almost done."

"Really? Astounding. Are you sure you didn't lose any coins? Bad luck, you know."

Astilbe patted through a clump of dust. "Not one. Well, as soon as I—"

"Fantastic! How fast can you get dressed?"

The coin jumped into Astilbe's hand. She cinched her fist and hauled out her arm, trailing downy fur. "More than a hot minute," she said. "How about I meet you there later?"

Andy cut loose with his most dazzling smile. "Sure. Take your time. It's going to be a late night. Thanks for this," he said. "It means more to me than you can imagine. Strange, really, but there it is. I'm forever in your debt."

Astilbe melted. She said, "That sounds pretty good."

"I won't forget what you've done, believe me. But I may need to negotiate for leniency while I work on paying you back."

"I offer easy terms to the right man. How about a down payment right now?"

"Tempting," Andy said. "But I really must dash."

"Promise you'll take advantage of my offer soon? This interest rate won't last forever."

"I'm your slave as soon as—oh shit." Andy checked the time and made a smoochie noise into the air. "Gotta go. See you there later. Love you!"

"Love you, too!"

Alone, Astilbe looked at the coin.

Well, it wasn't a penny. That was for sure.

It also wasn't dirty. It shone at her with cryptic glee. The coin was inscribed with a backwards looking language of swirls and flourishes. A spray of wheat was on one side, an arabesque design of a butterfly or skull or bear on the other. The butterfly-skull-bear made a laughing face, a primitive mask with gaping, lascivious eyes and wide mouth imprinted on symmetrical, unfurled wings. *Lepidoptera and others use mimicry to outwit predators*, Astilbe thought, quoting a documentary she streamed when she wanted to chill. She'd set it on repeat, entranced by the narrator's soothing tone and the flight of butterflies and moths making hypnotic, threatening faces by spreading their wings. To birds and lizards and snakes, the wingspan looked like the head of a large animal. Astilbe often watched in slow-motion and imagined the three-dimensional forms implied by the flat wings, the terror inspired by an illusion fragile enough to crumble like powder in a child's clumsy fingers. Astilbe wondered if the coin in her hand memorialized an endangered species, or one that was already extinct.

Astilbe tossed the coin thoughtfully. The last rolling sleeve had forty-nine pennies. This final and most unusual discovery must be sacrificed to make it complete. The coin came down heads and grinned at her.

"Screw that," Astilbe said and sealed the last roll one coin short.

She showered. The clatter of water sounded like spilling change. Astilbe considered her wardrobe choices as metallic muck and the taste of corrosion cascaded away. Andy's blazer suggested a serious event. He must be meeting someone big. Astilbe bypassed a sexy mesh top that showed off her belly piercing and a neon strapless that clung to her body in all the right places. Instead, she settled on a darling black dress with a touch of sparkle and a delicious plunging V-neck.

The trick of the diaphanous dress was in its layers. Some genius had designed it to sway and lilt over extra weight as if the body beneath was a delicate fairy, a Tinkerbelle or a butterfly instead of a solid size fourteen with rumblings of cellulite. Astilbe checked the mirror after she put on the dress and said, "Oh yeah. Killing it."

She tucked the coin in her bra for good luck. Sensing that Astilbe was wearing black, the cat came out of hiding. She wanted to complement the evening look with a fur coat, though not the brand Astilbe dreamed of wearing. Astilbe tried to rub Boo's nose at a distance, bending in an awkward stoop and twisting her black dress away. The cat hissed at her cleavage and scampered.

"Aw, little Boo, I'm sorry," Astilbe said.

The cab pulled up. Astilbe felt bad for Boo, but she'd entreat forgiveness later.

Riding through the city, Astilbe felt fortune vibrating in the air like the charge before a storm. Signs flashed by like multicolored lightning. Voices and music crackled from the streets. Things were going to change tonight.

Were they?

Yes, Astilbe answered the thought. *They're going to change. They have to.*

211

Astilbe entered Le Griffon in full sashay. Undaunted by the amphetamine agility of the women onstage, she placed each foot in a stronghold step that solidified the swish of her hips. Her grandma taught her this trick: beauty and confidence send the same message. If you don't have one, fake the other. And girl, soon enough you gonna start believing it. You hold your head up and be proud of what the Good Lord gave you.

Astilbe spotted the bar and her pride stomped to a halt.

She knew the incline of the shoulder too well. The jacket she pressed too often in anticipation of that one big break: the windfall of cash that never came, the deal that always fell through. Astilbe knew the dark slash of an iron burn under his sleeve that only showed when Andy's arm was raised at this particular angle, raised so his palm might cup the cheek of the woman he kissed, a red-haired woman who Andy's mouth engulfed like a drowning man engulfs the last air he swallows before succumbing to the seduction of the undertow. Like a baby engulfs a swollen breast before succumbing to the seduction of sleep.

Astilbe's nostrils flared and her breath hissed in her chest. Andy pulled away from the red-haired woman. Twin faces beamed at each other in profile. When Andy gazed elsewhere, his eyes went straight to Astilbe. He smiled, stood and waved for her to come over.

Galled, Astilbe stood her ground.

Andy waved as if he hadn't been making out with some other woman. He was a boy, a child in a man's body. Using other people was a by-product of Andy's personality. Sure, he was fun. The good times were so good. Astilbe could almost forgive his betrayal because it confirmed his ignorance. But that red-haired bitch: she was a different story.

Splitting the crowd with a tiger's prowl, Astilbe's claws burned to strike the other woman's face. The dance floor opened and closed around her like the Red Sea parting for Moses' staff.

Flouting Andy's expectant smile, Astilbe swept into range of the red-haired woman and raised a righteous fist.

The woman turned her head and Astilbe almost gagged.

What little there was to the other side of the woman's face looked like a painting by Picasso, and yet it was live flesh. Extra eyes blinked where there should have been one. A nose that angled in all the wrong directions gnarled into a laugh as Astilbe's fist flagged in midair. The red-haired woman placed a gentle hand to her chest and coughed with delicate mirth. "Oh, darling," she said. "Please, no hysteria. You will take my seat, no? Please now, you must sit."

Andy's brilliant teeth clenched and he muttered in Astilbe's ear: "Have you lost your bloody mind? Sit down and stop gaping like a rube."

The red-haired woman flitted upward and lilted over to the next seat allowing Astilbe room at the bar beside Andy. She turned, and held her head at an obtuse angle so Astilbe saw only her good features in the dappled disco-ball light.

From this perspective she appeared to be a stunning beauty, though no longer young by the look of her décolletage. The line of her strong jaw ended in a perfect rounded point where her chin seemed to support an eternal smirk on lips that bloomed with rich color. Her nose appeared petite and sloped up slightly at the delicate end in view. Her cheekbones sank to charming depths and framed her one visible luminous eye. Lashes lent an innocence to the cyclopean monolith, though when she spoke, dark glances fluttered beneath a demure fringe.

"Deformity is to be all the rage next season," the red-haired woman said to Astilbe. Her good eye gleamed.

Astilbe couldn't place the accent. It seeped with culture. Her pronunciation mistakes cut her words into discreet morsels and exotic eruptions, filling her mouth with strange delicacies.

Unusual sounds peppered the mundane English she misused. Her imperfections made her all the more beguiling.

"So you drink with me now," she said. "To prosper."

"Drinks, that's more like it," Andy said. He ordered shots and gripped Astilbe's shoulders, swinging her around. "Introductions! Astilbe, this is Elliane Elias. The House of Elias collection promises to be the break out sensation next fashion week. You're not going to believe it. I'm her representative in the states, right? We're recruiting models. You two ladies are going to be fast friends. Here we go. I'll drink to that."

The server served and Andy raised a glass and they all drank. Something struck Astilbe as so familiar about Elliane that she peered across her drink too hard. Elliane's eye caught her, coy and adept.

Elliane said, "So pleased to make your aquaint, Shelly."

Astilbe extended her arm and offered a cold and cordial invitation to shake. "Uh-Still-Bee." She stressed the *bee*. "And yours, madam." She stressed the *damn*.

Elliane accepted Astilbe's hand, seized it loosely and moved her face forward as though to kiss. Astilbe jumped from her seat and fumbled for her footing.

"Um, I—I haven't eaten anything today. That shot hit me a little hard." She fanned herself, hoping she hadn't blown the deal. "Whew."

Andy strained. His teeth were bared in a smile and a warning light flashed from his earring, a diamond dice-roll of snake eyes.

"Excuse me for a second," Astilbe said. "I think I need the powder room."

Before Astilbe escaped, Elliane said, "And I too, as well."

Trapped, Astilbe fake smiled *brilliantly* as Andy would say if he understood one small crumb of her unease. Astilbe's job was harder than Andy's. No matter who or what he chose to work with, she had to be a good hostess. She had to set herself

214

aside and make the client feel at home. Astilbe led Elliane hand in hand through the pulsing mass of bodies on the dance floor. Her manicure curled through Elliane's long fingers. Moments ago it had been poised to pluck out all of the strange woman's eyes.

Stilettos echoed on the marble steps that led down to the basement restrooms of the restored mansion. The building concealed an exclusive modern club behind a façade of urban decay. "Art deco," Elliane said. "Nothing is old. Your Detroit burns each hundred years."

Astilbe followed an imperative: no matter what, remain engaged and polite. No more sass tonight. She said, "How very interesting. Where did you learn that?"

"I know this. Here we were built on the fur trade. Detroit hatted Europe when all the Russian beaver died. Hunted dead for fashion. We burn and grow, phoenix from such a narrow river. I have this as my home."

"Did you live in Europe before coming here?"

"No, no. Aictaeronon, of old. Now Detroit."

Astilbe had no clue where that was. "We're delighted to have you. But why not Chicago, New York?"

"Look to the maps. These streets make a spider web, a trap, a mad French prophecy of culture coagulating in this dead strait. Such terrible hope. I love this Detroit, who once lived and flowed like an artery of industry, a vein of fresh hope. We grow again now, unextinct. You as well, my charm."

Descending the marble steps with Elliane, Astilbe felt the thrill underneath the decay, the lost world beneath the stone. It was the excitement she'd felt earlier in the car. She couldn't help herself: she squeezed Elliane's hand. The older woman's fingers radiated in return, acknowledging the secret, shared history of an underground city, alive and vibrant, hidden beneath the salt mines until its wings were ready to unfurl.

In the anteroom they waited for a vacancy with fingers entwined like lurid lace. Astilbe dropped her guard and confided, awash in Elliane's allure: "You need to know me if you stay. I don't care who you are or how much you pay: you best keep your hands off my man."

All of Elliane's eyes went wide. Then she began to shake.

It took Astilbe a few moments to recognize the older woman's odd convulsions as laughter. The pulse of muffled music from the club above melded with Elliane's effusive gulps. The beautiful side of her face was more beautiful, the horrid side more horrid.

"Dear, dear," Elliane said, attempting to clear her throat. "Child, no. From Aictaeronon we all kiss hello."

Astilbe didn't unwind her fingers. She looked down to dampen her tears and held tighter. "That was more than hello."

Elliane ceased laughing. All the sides of her face went serious. She placed her free hand on Astilbe's inflamed cheek. "I understand," Elliane said. "All men are vampires."

Years passed, or maybe a fraction of a second.

"They cry, they feed, they sleep. But we harbor alike, you and I. Come now, you must kiss. You are charm, you are lucky with me, yes?"

The voice convinced with expert ease. Music pumped above.

Elliane swept Astilbe into the next vacant stall. Through a veil of shock, Astilbe mouthed a mouth that was soft on one side, all teeth and harsh cubist ligaments on the other. Maneuvering around the multiplicity of the nose made Astilbe giggle and squirm. Close up, all of Elliane's eyes merged in an optical illusion and appeared as one engorged orb.

Astilbe threw off the veil. Elliane erupted.

The edifice under the marble facade stirred. The lost city beneath the salt resurrected. Born from the incomprehensible planes of Elliane's face, the House of Elias rose to ascendancy from the ashes of long-dead Aictaeronon.

Money poured in like lava after fashion week. Andy grabbed Astilbe's ass too hard and said, "We're stinking rich, bitch!"

Astilbe was half awake. She'd passed out rolling coins again. They never ceased mounting up. Her cheek had pressed onto the pile as she slept and some coins stuck to her face until Andy shook them to the floor. He stopped grabbing and shaking and fitted his fingertips into the indentions left by the coins.

"It's a nice look for you, you know," he said.

Astilbe sagged. "Not that again."

Andy's hand dropped.

"Given our position, it's something to consider," Andy said. "You can't go about looking like *this* all the time."

This carried the full weight of Andy's disdain.

Astilbe said, "*This* used to be good enough for you."

"Yes, but it's not just you and me anymore. We have to think of Elliane."

"Don't play me like that and don't play like you know what Elliane wants. You're nothing but her errand boy."

"Am I? Kissing in the little girl's room isn't quite a player's move, darling," Andy said. "Yes, I heard all about your fun and games. When you two have a go again, remember to invite me to watch. If you ask nicely, I might even be persuaded to join in."

Astilbe wanted to hit him. She said, "It got you what you wanted, didn't it? I'd call that a sharp move."

Andy said, "You look a bit tired, love. Have another bump."

He unfolded his pocket square, opened a vial and doled out some pink powder on the broad thumb-side muscle of his hand. The vials were strewn all over the house, broken among landslides of slippery coins. Andy held his hand near Astilbe's nostrils and rubbed her neck. She bowed and sniffed and felt better. She didn't know if it was the pink powder or Andy's rare attention.

"I'm jealous," Andy said. "Can you really blame me?"

He was such a beautiful man. Astilbe wanted to cry.

She said, "What are we doing?"

Andy hoisted her up in a rough bear hug and squeezed her tight and spun her around and said: "Winning!"

Astilbe let him spin her and didn't say stop. Andy had ignored her for days, maybe months. She didn't know how long. She only knew it started when Elliane began bringing the models home.

The house altered and stretched to accommodate them. It grew hallways, attics and additions to fit the new residents. It was a nightmare to clean with all the unknown nooks and changing pathways, with all the accessories and clutter the models left behind. Astilbe was tired, oh so tired of playing Cinderella to their exquisitely ugly demands.

Ugly was in. Deformity was hot. Before fashion week, the House of Elias faced a challenge finding models to fit Elliane's uncanny designs, but Andy was up to the task. He had a few contacts, knew a few people here and there with a few covert kinks.

Okay, Astilbe admitted. He knew a lot.

The Paris premier featured amputees and accident victims, self-mutilators and garage body-mod hackers, and a host of those naturally wracked by progressive and congenital body changes disdained by conventional culture. Several models were gifted with soon-to-be fashionable disfigurements at birth. The climax featured conjoined twins who had survived childhood burn trauma clad in a gossamer moth-wing onesie that seemed to float above the floor. After shocked silence, the audience exploded in adulation.

Jaded by years of insipid, unrealistic beauty codes, the fashion world went wild for Elliane's shocking aesthetic of the forbidden. An impossible body became the most important acquisition of the season, and the catwalk bloomed with grotesque and unreasonable variety. Long legs were fine, but merely having two attached below the pelvis became unthinkable.

Detroit became the medical tourism center of the world. Surgical deformity centers popped up overnight. Andy was willing to pay for anything Astilbe wanted, perhaps one of the stylish amputation-trades sported by the chic set in New York or Hollywood. Or the Mermaid look: Astilbe had the curves for it. Her legs could be fused into one svelte, undulating tube that terminated in an elongated vagina. It was supposed to be wonderful for sex. Men loved it, but Astilbe thought the servants needed after the upgrade way too much of a hassle.

One recent Oscar nominee took the Mermaid look so far she had shark fins implanted on her back. Interviewed on the red carpet in a tiny clamshell bra, lounging on a velvet stretcher borne by four boys in golden thongs, the actress confessed the fins were her new erogenous zones. She encouraged young women to express themselves by claiming the body that felt true for them and to defy society's pressure to remain mundane.

Quoting Elliane, the interview with the actress went viral. She said, "No woman needs to be limited anymore by her physique, only by her imagination. Elliane has set us all free to express our true selves. She's given us wings. Elliane said it best: *I don't design for the body you have. I design for the body you want.*"

Andy set Astilbe down and said, "We're winning. That's the kind of people we are, right? Winners. Feel better?"

Astilbe's head spun. She was afraid she might vomit. She said, "Why does winning feel like losing?"

"But darling," said Andy. "We have everything. Look around."

Astilbe looked around. The house spun in the opposite direction of her head. She was definitely going to vomit. She said, "What about us?"

Andy held Astilbe quiet against his chest for a few moments. Her head and stomach stilled and she basked in his affection. It wasn't like him, not lately. And then, even less typical, he spoke softly in her ear, lower than a whisper, rushing like a river:

"Hang on to me, love. I love you. That's all that matters. Not the hype. Right now it's important to do it all up. It's necessary while she's here. You'll see. We'll come through this together in the end. If you think you've lost me, remember to say this: *resurgemus flumine sanguinis.*"

"Huh?"

"Say it for me. Try."

Astilbe struggled with the unfamiliar words and Andy spoke along, coaxing her to get the phrase right, maintaining his embrace and speaking in a hush. "That's a good girl," Andy said, his breath in her hair, his warmth reminding her of all the good times. "You've got it. When I'm gone, you're the only one who can bring me back. Don't give up on me, my love."

Astilbe wasn't ready to make any promises. She also wasn't ready to let go. She looked up to kiss him. Abruptly, roughly, Andy held her off at arm's length and said, "There's my girl."

His voice was loud. He addressed Elliane over Astilbe's head. Astilbe turned to see Elliane dragging what looked like a canvas duffel bag crammed full of fabric, but on closer view it was one of the models bandaged like a pupa. No face or flesh was visible inside the post-surgical dressings. Elliane hoisted the cocoon toward the ceiling where she spit on her hands and made it stick. A growing collection of models hung there in various stages of convalescence. Astilbe didn't see any mechanism by which they were suspended and wondered if the ceiling in the old house could bear the weight.

"Did you find a stud?" Astilbe said.

Elliane gazed without comprehension. Her coiffure had begun to uncoil.

Andy laughed, but didn't smile. The room behind him warped to accommodate the new occupant.

"I starve," Elliane said, and slumped against Andy. "I perish."

Andy put an arm around Elliane, placed the vial of pink powder in Astilbe's palm and closed her fingers around it. "Clear your head, love. Why don't you make us a nice soup and we'll talk about your upgrades in the morning."

"It is morning. And I don't want any," Astilbe said.

"I die for soup," said Elliane. "I rot, I decay, I crush."

Andy said to Astilbe, "No, love. It's dark out. Of course you do."

"How do you know?" said Astilbe. "The windows are gone."

Andy's eyes swept over the dark, mirrored walls. Models protruded and lurked as the house shifted like a sluggish poison river to welcome their uncommon forms. Astilbe couldn't count how many there were. As far as she could tell, the original models were gone, the proud women who had flaunted body-positivity in opposition to morpho-normative slurs, defiant models who had fought to re-frame beauty as a measure of difference rather than sameness. The newcomers suspended from the ceiling were lit from underneath by the glow of phones and looked indistinguishable from one another in their larval state. Those that recovered un-bandaged rolled and intersected on the furniture, testing the sexual function of their enhancements, exploring their upgrades and gorging their detractions on any available prosthetic, living or inert. Andy's eyes strayed.

He straightened his silk pocket square. Elliane draped languid on his arm.

"Take me out," Astilbe said, drab-bombing his vanity. In the mirror, Elliane's good angle looked like Andy's twin if not for the disparity in age. Astilbe crowded Elliane's image out of the frame. "I want to go dancing."

Andy didn't try to suppress his incredulous snort. He looked her up and down. "Even if I wanted, no club's letting you in like that."

"Parkline will," Astilbe said.

Elliane moaned.

"Oh, we want to go slumming, now do we?" Andy said, getting shrill, keening under Elliane's weight. "The media will have a field day."

"So what? Does that make us their slaves?"

The multiple mirrors that replaced the windows created a funhouse of misperception. Astilbe thought about an old black and white movie that ended with a chase in an abandoned carnival ride called the Crazy House. The lovers shot each other in a maze of mirrors, deceived by distortion. She knew one of them was going to die. Both was the twist.

Astilbe softened her tone, took Andy's free arm and said, "Hey, never mind. Who needs to go out? Come on and dance with me right here."

Andy leaned into Astilbe and Elliane flailed him with limp fists. "Dance, dance, dance. Upon me you shit and you dance."

Astilbe said, "Get over your damn self. We are trying to talk."

"I die!" Elliane exclaimed. "All I do for you! And but this!"

"Ladies," Andy said.

"All you do? Excuse me?" said Astilbe.

Andy's body was a barricade. Elliane clung to him and Astilbe all but spat in his face challenging her.

"What exactly have you done for us? Tell me," Astilbe said.

"We're rich," Andy said. "Isn't that enough?"

"All mistake I embrace. All choice, yet they lay stupid and make no wings. Look, there!" Elliane gestured wildly at the living room. "Butchers, fiends, fools!"

Astilbe said to Elliane, "You put the knife in their hands."

"But I cannot. Butchers do not know beauty. Can I throw useless lumps of flesh upon my runway like your bowling of pins? No. Beauty must rise. Not this. Never this." Elliane drooped. "Please, if it occasion. A soup, for I die."

Andy tried to worm his way out of the fray. "Speaking of useless lumps of flesh, maybe you ladies can, um—"

"Save the sales pitch for the cameras," Astilbe said. "I don't buy that tortured artist act."

Elliane's many eyes grew luminous and she unburdened Andy's arm. "Ah, here is fire. We make the phoenix even yet. You are lucky with me, yes? Come, I dress you for dinner. I see you fly."

"I don't want to be like you," Astilbe said.

"This is true," said Elliane. "All beauty is extinct."

Astilbe swirled around and stomped into the kitchen. Andy dogged her heels. His voice was fast and jittery. "Listen, pet, I'll make you a deal. Fix us a nice soup. Make enough so the girls get something in them besides pills today. Then go tart yourself up with Elliane and I'll take you both out dancing. She works wonders."

"I can dress myself," Astilbe said. "With my normal, boring, functional limbs."

"Yes, yes of course. But—"

"Are you ashamed to be seen with me?"

"That's not how I'd put it. Elliane wants to help. She likes you. Stop fighting her on this."

"Did you mean anything you said before? About us?"

Andy's face stuttered and he didn't speak. He eyed Elliane in panic. Astilbe let him squirm. He was less than human. He was a parasite. The older woman ignored him, her forearm hurled over her head in dramatic fatigue. Astilbe took her cue from Andy's silence.

She left him snagged in his own game, speechless, eyes bugged. It felt like winning and losing all at once.

The cupboards were stocked with energy drinks and vodka. Space shrank in the kitchen as other rooms grew. The ceiling descended so low that Boo could barely raise her backside to stretch on top of the refrigerator. The cat had claimed the spot, made it her territory as more and more models moved in. Astilbe reached up to give her a pat. Boo backed out of reach.

Astilbe scooped a bowl of cat food from the bag blocking the dishwasher. She pushed the bowl onto the top of the refrigerator and said, "There you go, hon. Have some noms." Boo gave Astilbe blinky eyes and sniffed. She waited for Astilbe's hand to withdraw before she approached the bowl.

The stock pot was wedged in the sink. It didn't fit anywhere else. Astilbe maneuvered it out and onto a burner. It sloshed with old water. Astilbe turned up the heat, spotted a box of French onion dip, and dumped the dry shards into the pot. Some overripe tomatoes shriveled on the rim of the sink. She crushed them in her fist over the water. Skins and seeds separated on the slimy surface and floated like shreds of afterbirth. Astilbe considered adding a handful of cat food to the pot and decided not to waste it on the ungrateful entourage.

While the water rose to a boil, Astilbe took Andy's vial out of her bra where she'd stashed it with her lucky penny. She had a big bump, saw no reason not to have another, and ended up finishing off the dregs of pink powder before the water began bubbling.

Elliane had to go. If Andy was too weak to choose, Astilbe must take action.

Astilbe clenched her lucky penny in her tomato-stained fist

and marched through the house. "Breakfast is ready," she said. "And when you're done, you can all pack up your shit and leave!"

She didn't see Elliane. She didn't see Andy. She didn't see anything that looked like people at all. The walls pulsed in accommodation as Astilbe doubled across the room trying to identify residents on the furniture and floor. It was dim except for the glow of screens, silent except for the slot-machine chatter of ringtones. Astilbe looked for evidence of Andy entangled in the warped limbs and gelatinous orifices splayed on the sectional. She circled spiky horns, absent limbs, and tails and fins that slapped and probed. Something moaned, and Astilbe glimpsed golden hair and a diamond snake eyes earring that vanished under a triple jointed haunch. What appeared to be the rough fur of a goat turned out to be an illusion: when Astilbe reached for it, her hand passed through smoke. Something warm spattered her arm and she recoiled. The amalgamation folded over itself like an infinity symbol seared into liquid flesh. Thunder groaned from the friction it caused, sparking in the air. Astilbe shrank from its rumbling heat. Blazing shadows licked at her feet. Astilbe backed into the kitchen, crouching under cocoons and slipping on loose coins until the chorus of the storm was drowned by the glop glop glop of boiling water.

The lucky penny pressed into her hand. Its rough edge drew blood.

Astilbe read the inscription above, now legible: *Dominion of New Aictaeronon, 1701-1985*, and below, *resurgemus flumine sanguinis*. While she sounded out the words, the butterfly-skull-bear face gawked, mouth wide open in hilarity. Astilbe felt strange knowing that the face had pressed into her skin every day, wings and eyes and mouth muffled by the warmth of her breast. She wondered, had she felt a tingle when it laughed?

The light altered. Both dark and bright, an orange glare

scorched the wall. Astilbe's palm was bleeding. Nineteen eighty-five glowed crimson on the coin: the year of Andy's birth.

The hot breath of the storm hunted for Astilbe around a corner of the compressed kitchen. Had Elliane mothered all this? Would Andy reach for Astilbe from the crackling smoke with long fingers of lightning and char her supple skin? The deviant coin cackled at her questions. Astilbe flipped the lucky penny high and aimed for the stock pot. When the coin splashed in the soup, Boo dropped from her perch and weaved her head and tail through Astilbe's legs.

Astilbe didn't have to coax the cat to flee.

The side door and front door were gone. Nothing in the house was right. Familiar furnishings were replaced by bolts of fabric, dressmaker's dummies and obscure medical supplies. Boo hissed at draped discards that gestured and swayed, awoken by Astilbe's sudden motion. Astilbe stumbled over piles of prosthetic flesh, or so she thought until they mumbled and moved. She couldn't tell the models from the mounds of mildewed garments and rusted surgical supports. Psychedelic flowers of water damage bloomed on the ceiling. Boo scampered ahead and meowed.

Deep inside the house, the corridors grew dark. Astilbe found her way by touch and by tracking Boo's meow. The walls swelled like sponges. Things moved under Astilbe's startled hands, and a stormy heat crawled inside of her and clouded her lungs. Her clothes were drenched. Her feet were mired in muck. Astilbe needed the body of a snake to move. She slid down, down, down, blinded by the tight fit of the fleshy walls, breathing their salty sweat like amniotic fluid. There was nowhere to go but further down. Astilbe took a deliberate dive and propelled her body through the dripping coagulation, far under the crumbling house, deep beneath the poison river, straight into the swimming sensation of Elliane's exotic mouth.

"I design for my own pleasure. I make the world in my image."

The celebrity designer's mouth filled the eighty-two inch TV screen. Red lips surrounded white teeth, and inside was a beckoning black: the color palette of propaganda. "I work to please myself. Fashion cannot be for all. Only those willing to make the sacrifice."

The camera panned back into a wide shot. Behind Elliane, the room of cocoons dazzled as individual pupa glowed and became semi-transparent. Liquid forms writhed within, creating hypnotic wing patterns under the sheaths that mimicked the faces of large predators. The illusion corrupted as one by one the models emerged, mangled. The many sides of Elliane's face dissented. One angle stuttered while another hung slack. "Unngh gack gack," she said and choked. The camera dropped and smashed.

An anchorwoman took charge of the screen. "Maven of the moribund, diva of disfigurement, controversial designer Elliane Elias passed away earlier this week on location with Cinema Splice. Foul play has been ruled out. Her tragic death, now deemed accidental, was caused by the ingestion of a small foreign object that ultimately lodged in her trachea. No able-bodied heir has been named to continue her work, and sources say that the famed House of Elias may remain forever entombed at the bottom of the Detroit River."

Astilbe fast-forwarded past the mourners and wailers to the black and white footage caught by a city security camera. The house split open from some internal storm, its structure shot through with a wild light that fissured its frame and forced its walls asunder as it collapsed into the river. A zig-zag of lightening burst forth, and with a tumultuous shout the rushing waters of the ancient strait laid claim to the fragments of the House of Elias.

Scrolling backwards through the video, Astilbe noticed the strange doubling effect when Andy and Elliane were in a frame together. Elliane was both beauty and beast. Andy appeared as her shadow, duplicated in the background as though he were cast from multiple sources of misleading light, a soft version of a shattered funhouse. With repeated viewings, his edges blurred and dimmed.

Before her last interview, Elliane burst ravenous into the frame. Her efforts dressing Astilbe had consumed her. She veered into the kitchen with a dramatic toss of her unraveled up-do and downed the whole pot of soup all at once. It was comic shot: the elegant older woman hoisted the stock pot off the burner with both hands and drank the boiling liquid in one giant gulp. Cocooned off-camera, Astilbe hadn't tried to intervene.

Now set up in her grandma's guest room, Astilbe patted the spot next to her on the bed. Boo crossed the ceiling with sticky paws and lowered on a retractable tail. She purred. Boo hadn't wasted her chance to upgrade before she slashed through the cocoon with her claws.

Astilbe had no regrets. She'd maintained her integrity. Camouflaged, the new organs nestled in her brain heightened her cognitive perceptions, much like a butterfly's compound eyes allow it to see a vast spectrum beyond ordinary light. Grandma was teaching her to sew, she'd learned branding from her experience with Elliane, and when paperwork was done and the rights were cleared, Astilbe wanted Andy back. She admitted he was a sham. She didn't know how much of him remained after Elliane's demise, but she felt certain his vanity would rise intact. Astilbe visualized the heart at the center of the reflections, the small creature exaggerated by the hall of mirrors misnamed reality. Exposed, he bared the seeds of beauty like the hint of a diamond chip.

228

Whether Andy returned to her as man or proxy or churning conflagration didn't matter to Astilbe. She wanted him back. The dimension of history that Andy and Elliane belonged to didn't have what Andy craved. He'd chosen Astilbe and made promises, even if his tactics were inept. Money soaked up more blood than it bought. Astilbe offered substance. She knew there were no rats in the salt mines.

She waited until after dark, when the reporters and rescue teams vacated the waterfront and the curious tourists retired to their casino hotels. Astilbe whispered. The water lay still.

"Resurgemus flumine sanguinis."

The river moved, and the thunder of a thousand hooves began to build in the distance. Undaunted, Astilbe braced herself. The wind whipped up. The clouds glowered and swirled. The din of a herd pounded against the waves, eager to trample the shore. For a moment, Astilbe's confidence failed. She didn't expect the sonic mass that approached, the lover that reached for her with a thousand hands. Its electric embrace broke above the horizon, and as soon as she saw him, her heart leapt. Passion and rage rose within Astilbe like winged twins. Andy had so much to learn. A whole herd of Andys wasn't too much for Astilbe's love to tame. Come to think of it, a herd might be just the thing. Astilbe had big plans for Andy when she premiered her new line from House of Elias: *Payback, The Collection for Men.*

MIRRORS

Billy Chizmar

MASTERS OF MIDNIGHT

It'S NINE-THIRTY on a Saturday morning.

You're walking through your grandson's middle school.

It's Graduation Day.

You pass by a mirror and see a reflection from decades ago.

It's a boy, his hair wild and blonde.

Eyes unobscured by thick lenses stare back at you with a brightness that has become less and less familiar to you, eyes surrounded by clear skin, no scars, no burns. A black AC/DC t-shirt protects a tan and unpunished body. Navy shorts cover where one day there will be a tube, and jutting out of these same shorts are two full, healthy legs, and that's perhaps what you miss the most in this moment.

You walk closer to the mirror, not by your own determination, but out of obedience to the unforgettable, a desire to see what has already been seen.

The mirror transforms into a time machine and you walk through it because you've only just realized that you never thought you would be here and not *there*.

You wonder how much you've forgotten. You wonder who you've forgotten, who has forgotten you.

So you remember what you remember.

Your first football game, freshman year of high school, when you played wide receiver because all anyone knew of you was some skinny kid who could run. The first true friends you made back then (where are they now?), that day the lot of you got into a fight with those older boys from Joppatowne, a fight that, of course, you all won after Stevie Cavanaugh (or was it Casey Tipton?) landed a right hook right to the jaw of their biggest guy and dropped him cold.

233

The first girl you slept with, also the first girl you *thought* you loved, also the first person that really hurt you, but none of those would be the last.

The late nights spent with teammates drinking Bud Light on the darkened school football field talking about what it will be like to get old and forget about each other, then promising each other that such a thing will never happen and truly believing in that promise because back then none of you knew any better.

Back then, when months felt like years.

Suddenly, there's a scruff-covered chin beneath the wild hair, a college man, but those eyes still shine with love—love for everything, the world and all its innocence, because that's how you saw it all back then.

That's how you saw it when you met the first (and last) girl you ever did love, real love, true love.

That's how you saw it when you met your second group of true friends (where are they now?), and even how you saw it when you took a left hook to the nose because your best friend started a fight with the university's lacrosse team because, hey, he was your best friend.

That's how you saw it even when you played your last football game, now a linebacker, because you and the world realized that you could tackle a guy like no one else (when did that go away?).

And yes, you saw the world with such love when you and your teammates drank Natural Light in the darkened football stadium talking about what it will be like to get old and forget about each other, then promising each other that such a thing will never happen, and truly believing in that promise because back then none of you knew any better.

You held onto that youthfulness for some time and you want to say it was forever because you can't remember the moment where it ended (but where is it now?), and so you tell yourself that it's still there.

It was there when you and your wife-to-be moved to New York City, a job in economics (where was it when you got offered the job in journalism?) and you wonder where it was when you let an elderly Jewish man tame your wild blonde hair with a razor just so you could spend a life (sentence?) in a tie behind a desk buried underneath numbers.

You try to think of your wedding, your child's birth, grandchild's birth, but you can't because you've realized all of the lies you've told to all the people you promised to remember. Fragmented names fly in and out, the only ones you can piece together are the dead ones (when will that be you—

Your daughter taps you on the shoulder. Your grandson is standing with your wife, several paces ahead. You blink your eyes and turn away.

REFUGE

William Meikle

I'VE BEEN CALLED MANY THINGS this past month, refugee, illegal, fucking Arab bastard and freeloader being just four. What I haven't been called is what I am, or rather, what I was, doctor, husband, father, brother. But that was another place, another time, before the shell that marks the line between then and now, that place and this.

They told me when I stepped off the plane at Gatwick that I was one of the lucky ones. If lucky is losing all of your family and your home while you're at work, then losing your workplace in the next wave of attacks and getting out while the airport is being shelled, then I suppose I am lucky. But it did not feel that way in my first weeks in this cold, dark, country.

I had hopes of being able to take up my profession here but it appears it is not that simple. Nothing is simple now. My money was not going to last, especially as I took to drink. While there are many of my countrymen in this new land, they are of a more religious bent than I and tend to congregate around their mosques. I have never been a man of strong faith, even less so now. So I looked for work, got called many more names, and finally found employment, of a sort, in a bar in London's East End, and a bed, of a sort, in a cramped room out back.

Lucky to be alive, they said.

And as I have said every day since my arrival, I am not sure of that.

At first I worked and tried to forget. There was hard liquor aplenty for the times when I could not. And sometimes, for minutes, even hours, I was able to keep the horror at bay, at least for long enough to function. But it seems that even here, in the supposed civilized world, there is more than enough hate to go round and remind me of my fate.

He took a dislike to me the first time he saw me. Wilkins is a big, red faced bald man, with eyes too close together in his head, a voice like a foghorn and fewer manners than a feral dog. All he knows is hate for anyone not like him. The first thing I noticed wasn't any of these though. He had a large black swastika tattooed on his neck.

"I'm not having my drink poured by no fuckin' Arab," was his introductory remark, and John, my boss, moved me away to the other end of the bar before I even replied. But all of that first night I felt Wilkins' eyes, unclean eyes, staring at me, the hate coming off him in waves.

He made no other outburst that night, but there were plenty more in nights to come, despite John's best efforts to keep me away from any part of the bar in which Wilkins might be. I learned more names, all of them abusive, and I struggled to keep a civil tongue in my head. My job was insecure, even at the best of times.

But every man has his breaking point, and mine came in a wash of rage, regret and grief that came out of me all at once.

"Why aren't you back in your own country making more towel heads?" Wilkins asked. "Why don't you just fuck off back where you came from?"

I kept my voice low so that only he would hear.

"Because ignorant fascists just like you blew my family out of their shoes. This bar is my home. Why don't you fuck off back to yours."

I don't know what disturbed me more: that I had lost my temper or that casual profanity had come so easily to me. In

240

either case, it caused Wilkins to go so violently red that I feared he might explode. Luckily John got between us as Wilkins moved to climb over the bar.

"Are you going to let that sand-nigger talk to an Englishman like that?" the bald man asked. John ignored him, and looked me in the eye.

"Take the night off," he said. "I'll deal with this arsehole."

He spoke loud enough for Wilkins to hear, but the bald man knew that he'd get thrown out the bar if he tried anything, and he was still sober enough to prefer more beer to violence. As for me, I could have headed for my room, but I needed clean air, a clear head, and an escape from the walls that closed tighter around me every day.

As I left I felt Wilkins' gaze, a weight at my back pushing me out the door.

I walked. I can't remember for how long, I let my feet take me where they would. Light glistened off the road and pavements, fractured twice as it refracted through my tears. I only stopped when I reached the river, the gray thick worm that burrows through the middle of London. I watched it sluggishly flop against the embankment walls, then the rage swelled up, like a wave. I couldn't hit Wilkins, but I needed to hit something, anything. I punched the wall, twice when the first didn't help.

"You can see them again, you know?" a woman said at my back. At first I didn't realize she was speaking to me.

I turned. She was old, bent by it, making her small, barely up to my chest, and dressed all in black like a hole in the night. But she'd definitely been addressing me. There was no one else in sight.

"You can see them again. You can see your family."

"My family is dead, madam," I replied. "And long past talking to me."

She smiled sadly.

"Sahid said you would say that. He asked me to remind you about the fort. About Saladin and the Infidels, to remind you of who won."

I was at a loss for words all of a sudden, taken by a memory of a hot day playing with plastic soldiers around a dusty well. Playing with my son, Sahid.

"Will you come?" the old lady said. "It's just round the corner. We'll have a chat and a wee drink, I'll make you something to eat, and we'll get that hand fixed."

I looked down, surprised to see drops of blood spatter from my knuckles to the wet pavement as she went on.

"And I'll tell you why you came here to find me. And what you need to know."

She was as good as her word. I had expected to be led to a house but was instead shown into a modern warehouse conversion, six flats in a tall slim red brick building on a newly refurbished quayside.

"I'm the concierge," she said, rather grandly, as if it was a title rather than a job description. She was in number one, just inside the hallway door, and although the conversion was new, the sofa was floral, ancient, and the bulk of a small car. The TV set was also older, a boxy wooden cube some three feet on a side, currently showing only dancing static.

She showed me to the couch and I sat gingerly near the front edge, afraid to relax into it lest it swallow me whole while she rummaged through a cupboard, coming up with scissors and a wrap of bandages. I motioned she should pass them to me. I had to cradle my injured hand in the other to avoid dripping on her carpet.

"I'm a doctor," I replied.

"And so am I, of a kind," she said softly. "Let me do this for you. You're a guest, for now."

For an old lady she had quick fingers, and soft, efficient hands. I only felt pain once, when she tightened the bandage before tying it off. As I winced, I heard another voice, young, and happy.

"Do not worry, father. Pain is fleeting."

I looked around. The voice was unmistakable. It was Sahid, my dead son. For a moment I feared that my rage had unhinged me completely. Then the voice came again.

"Remember the fort, father. Remember who won."

The sound seemed to have come from the television set, but it only showed more of the dancing white static.

The old lady saw me looking, and smiled.

"Getting voices from the great beyond are we? I told you that you had come to the right place."

The firmness of her knot as she tied off the bandage did a lot to ground me back in reality, and the half-filled glass of rum she brought me helped some more, so by the time she sat and started to talk I was almost ready to listen.

Almost.

"You'll have questions?" she said.

"I will have questions," I agreed. "Many of them. Here is an easy one to start with. What is going on here?"

She smiled, and for the first time I saw the deep sadness in her. Something in her eyes that told me she had suffered.

"It is an outlandish story, I'm afraid," she replied.

I let her talk. Sense could wait. What I needed now was something to take my mind off the dancing static, and the voice of my dead boy.

243

"There are houses like this all over the world," she started. "Most people only know of them from whispered stories over campfires, tall tales told to scare the unwary," she went on. It was beginning to sound more and more like a pre-prepared speech. "But some of us, those who suffer . . . some of us know better. We are drawn to the places, the loci if you like, where what ails us can be eased. Yes, dead is dead, as it was and always will be. But there are other worlds than these, other possibilities. And if we have the will, the fortitude, we can peer into another life, where the dead are not gone, where we can see that they thrive and go on. And as we watch, we can, sometimes, gain enough peace for ourselves that we too can thrive, and go on.

"You will want to know more than why. You will want to know how. I cannot tell you that. None of us has ever known, only that place is important, and the sigil and token are needed.

"If you wish to stay, you will need a sigil, a tattoo if you like, one that means something to you and yours. And you already have a totem, a lock of your wife's hair in your wallet, or so Sahid tells me. You will also want to know about the boy, and the others, and the why and how of that too. And again, I cannot tell you. You were drawn here. What you see is what you see, and what you take from it is what you take from it. Only the Dreaming God knows."

I scarcely heard a word of it. All I heard was Sahid's happy voice, all I felt was longing. Grief tugged at my heart and a great tiredness washed over me. Unwanted tears ran down both cheeks.

"Please, madam, just tell me what is going on?"

"I'm trying to," she said softly, "as well as I am able. But sometimes it is best if you see for yourself. You'll have number three, for tonight at least, and then we'll see how it goes. Sometimes one night is all it takes."

"All it takes for what?"

But she didn't answer, and when she took my hand again I rose meekly, and let her lead me upstairs, where there was a soft bed waiting.

Darkness called to me and I fell into it gladly.

I woke in the early hours of the morning, not really knowing where I was until I saw the bare brick walls and the exposed plumbing of the warehouse conversion. Snatches of the old woman's conversation came back to me, fragments that didn't make much sense. There had been some nonsense about sigils and tokens and something about being drawn to this place, this house. What with that, and the memory of Sahid's voice, it all took on the blur and fever of a bad dream. It wasn't as if I had not had plenty of them in recent weeks.

I found my jacket at my feet on the floor when I stood. I bent to lift it, intending to sneak out without having to face the embarrassment of apologizing for falling asleep in a strange house. As I lifted the jacket something tinkled—metal on wood— the small locket in which I kept Asha's hair falling out of my wallet onto the floor.

I picked it up.

Light flickered in the corner as a TV set woke up, white dancing static, and a hissing that became a drone, distant, but definitely getting closer.

Sahid's voice spoke from inside the TV set, clear as day.

"Hello father. It is good to see you again."

The next thing I knew I was standing out in the hallway, looking back into the empty room, with dampness at knuckles

245

where the wounds had seeped and a hot burn in my palm where the locket sat. My breath came so heavily I felt light-headed, almost dizzy, and my legs refused to move.

I almost leapt in the air when a hand touched my shoulder.

It was the old lady. She wore a dressing-gown three sizes too big for her wrapped tight around her small frame.

"Come downstairs," she said. "We'll have a coffee and see what's what."

I wasn't listening.

"I heard him. It was Sahid, clear as day," I said.

"And you'll probably see him too, soon enough, if that's what you want? All you need now is the sigil."

I pulled away, heading for the stairs.

"You don't understand," I said. "This isn't right."

"Right and wrong don't come into it, not here," she replied. "There are only the dreams of the Sleeping God, and what we can understand of them."

I pushed past her and made for the stairs, the hallway, and once again out into the damp London air. I heard Sahid's voice in my head all the way back to my room at the back of the bar.

"Hello father. It is good to see you again."

The next morning, I decided to get a tattoo.

John gave me directions to a parlor he said was reputable off Whitechapel Road, and I got a life-sized representation of Asha's locket done on the inside of my forearm, in a deep yellow that glowed like a heart-shaped pool of gold on my skin.

When I got back to the bar, John wanted me to work the lunchtime shift, as there'd be less chance of Wilkins coming in.

"Give him a chance to calm down," he said. "He's a hothead, but he's got the attention span of a goldfish. In a couple of days he'll have forgotten all about you and be on to thinking about football again."

I kept an eye on the door all through my shift, but Wilkins didn't come in. The place was almost empty so I had plenty of time to think about the night before.

I still could not process the events into a sequence of facts that made sense, but one thing was always at the front of my mind. Sahid was there. He'd spoken to me. And if he wanted to speak again, I certainly wanted to listen.

I could scarcely wait for the shift to end. As soon as the last patron was out and the glasses were washed and put away, I was out the door, determined to head straight for the building on the quayside.

Unfortunately I was not the only man on a mission that afternoon. Wilkins, and two other men almost indistinguishable from him in build, tattoos and lack of hair, stood on the first corner. All three looked at me as soon as I left the bar, like hunting dogs spotting their prey. I could have gone straight back into the bar and safety. But that would have felt like betrayal, both to myself, and to Sahid, who might be waiting for me. Instead I turned and walked away.

Evidently I was their sport for today. They came after me, staying twenty yards behind as I headed down streets I hoped would be busy with either traffic or pedestrians, for I knew that as soon as all was quiet, the walking would quickly turn into running.

We played cat and mouse for the next twenty minutes as I made my way, the long way, south towards the river. Any thought they might become bored and give up the pursuit was shattered at a set of traffic lights were Wilkins, emboldened at a quiet junction, slid a long, evil looking knife out of his belt and waved it at me.

"My old granddad got this off a Gerry in France," he shouted across the top of a car sitting at the red light. "They knew how to deal with bastard mongrels like you. I'll be showing you soon."

I walked faster. I did not have a plan, beyond reaching the converted warehouse and hoping that a locked door would be enough to fend off an attack. I turned the last corner. The old lady stood in her doorway, a smile on her face, waving me forward.

The three men behind me broke into a run when they saw where I was headed.

"Get inside," I shouted. "He's got a knife."

I reached the door only a yard ahead of Wilkins and threw myself inside, expecting her to close the door at my back. But when I turned, she was still there in the open doorway. Wilkins and the other two stood on the doorstep, as if unsure of their next move. The big man had the long dagger in his hand.

"He said you would come," the old lady said. She wasn't talking to me.

"Come on, George," one of the other two men said. "We can get him later."

Wilkins didn't reply, didn't even notice when his two partners sidled off out of view. He still had the dagger in his hand, but it hung at his side. His attention wasn't on me, but on the old lady.

"What the fuck is this? You're from my dream."

"You were called," she said. She reached out and stroked his neck where the tattoo seemed to pulse with a life of its own. "You have a sigil, and you have a totem," she pointed to the dagger. "You can come in. You can see him again."

A door creaked open to my left, room two, directly across the hall from the old lady's room.

"Georgie? Is that you, lad?" a London accented voice called out. Wilkins looked from the old lady, to the door of the room.

"What the fuck is this?" he said again, louder this time, as if it would make the answer come faster.

"Georgie!" the voice admonished. "I've told you not to swear."

"Granddad?"

Wilkins stepped over the threshold into the house. The door swung shut behind him with a loud click, but I could tell that the bald man only had attention for the open door of room two. I stepped out of his path but he had forgotten me completely, and I was reminded of John's analogy of the goldfish.

"Come on in, lad, don't be shy," the voice said from inside the room. There was a television on or at least it sounded like it, as bullets whistled and bombs exploded amid faint, far away screams. A war movie was my thought.

"What the fuck is this?" Wilkins said, his mind stuck in the same, querying loop, but now overlaid with something else. At first I thought it to be fear, before I saw the tears in his eyes. "You died when I was a boy."

"Dead and alive don't come into it, not here," the old lady replied, and shepherded the man toward the room. "There are only the dreams of the Sleeping God, and what we can understand of them."

That went over Wilkins' head. By this time his eyes had glazed with tears, and he walked, stiff legged toward the open door of room two.

"Granddad?"

"In here, lad. Everything's going to be fine."

He reached the door. The dagger still hung, loose in his hand by his side.

"Ah, I wondered where that had got to," the voice said from inside. "Come on in, lad. Don't be shy."

Wilkins walked into the room. Just before the door shut the bursts of weapons fire got so loud that it sounded like it came from the room itself. More bullets flew. There was a soft, moist noise, and a grunt.

"What the fuck is this?" Wilkins said, then the door shut and the hallway fell silent and still.

I moved forward to put a hand on the door but the old lady held me back.

"He was drawn here. What he sees is what he sees, and what he takes from it is what he takes from it. Only the Dreaming God knows."

I might have remonstrated with her even then, for Wilkins' question was also my question. But all of that was forgotten seconds later when another door opened, upstairs. I knew in my heart it was room three, knew it even before I heard my wife singing, knew it as I climbed to stairs to go and play Crusaders and Saracens with my boy.

I remembered who had won.

PULSATE

Espi Kvlt

MASTERS OF MIDNIGHT

I GRIND MY TEETH together as my burning flesh cries out for mercy. There is nothing I can do. The artist keeps the buzzing gun pressed solidly against my skin and seems to have no intention of stopping.

Until he does. And, looking very pleased with himself, he soaks paper towels in green soap and wipes them across my leg. Again, I grit my teeth, and again, my skin cries out for help.

"So, you should wash your new tattoo three to five times a—"

"I know," I say, cutting him off as I try to hand him the money I owe him. "Ain't my first rodeo."

"Okay, but you should really—"

"Sorry, but I don't have time to hear the spiel again. Places to be." I start towards the door, then turn back around to notice his stunned expression. "Thanks, by the way."

The frigid Reno air sends bullets into my bare legs, and even though I knew my new tattoo would sting, I'm not prepared for it to send a shockwave through my leg that causes me to end up on the cement before I even register that I am falling.

Several moments pass before I even attempt to get up. My leg continues to pulsate.

I feel a heart growing in the place where I have been tattooed.

My mother is tapping the dining table with her fork. "Peter? Peter?"

I look down at my hand which I have subconsciously been

running back and forth along my throbbing leg. I then look up to meet my mother's wide eyes, as she bites her glossy lips. "Sorry. What?"

"You're rubbing your leg. What's wrong?"

"Oh. Nothing. I got a tattoo today, and it hurts. That's all."

"Another one? What now?"

"Yes, another one. I'd show you, but it's hidden under my pants, and I don't think a restaurant is the place to pull them down."

"Oh, Peter," she says with a laugh, as she brings a fork full of spaghetti up to her shiny lips. I try not to let her see my disgust as her wet chops wrap around the prongs. "By the by, I asked you about Julie. You haven't mentioned her in a while."

"Yeah, that's probably due to the fact that I haven't seen her in a while."

"Define 'a while.'"

I rub my hand along my leg again, this time consciously. "Um, about one date."

"One date? I finally find you the perfect girl, and you never even give her a chance. Why do you always do this?"

Because I have no desire for physical intimacy with another human being and am repulsed by the natural functions of my fellow man. "I don't know, I guess I just have difficulty connecting with people."

My mother giggles, and I make the mistake of attempting eye contact. I bring my napkin to my mouth as I try to remove the image of her half-chewed meatballs from my mind. "No you don't, sweetheart."

"How can you claim that? You aren't living my daily life."

"Because I see you constantly sabotaging yourself. Like when you quit your job and lived five years in poverty."

"I wasn't in poverty just because I wasn't as rich as you are."

"Well, you moved into an apartment and were eating frozen meals every day."

"So? That's what I wanted to do. And why are you trying to tell me how I feel?"

"I'm not. But you can't say you have trouble connecting with people when you spend so much time with me. That doesn't make any sense."

"We have a natural connection. It's unavoidable."

"So you'd avoid it if you could?"

"That's not what I meant. Can we just drop it, please?"

"Is this about your father?"

"What?" I didn't mean for it to come out as a shout. "What are you talking about?"

"Well, maybe if he hadn't left when you were little, maybe if he hadn't done all the things he did, you wouldn't have these issues."

"They're not issues. I'm fine. I just don't want to date anyone, okay? Can you please just accept that?"

"But are you happy?"

"Yes, Mother. I'm happy."

Truth be told, I have never understood the meaning of the word. I've never understood sadness, either.

I am perched inches away from my body at all times, as I attempt to navigate through the fog that surrounds me.

The apartment is hardly any warmer than outside. As I walk through the door, I am hit by the smell of piss. I flip on the light switch and turn to my left, where Angel has once again peed on the blanket that is spread along the green couch. She is trotting away towards the bedroom already, and I see her tail just as it disappears into the hallway. I should have been mad, but I couldn't bring myself to care.

I pick the blanket up off the couch and bring it to my bedroom to throw it in the laundry hamper. Angel is sprawled out along the bed, her tortoiseshell stomach begging to be petted. Even though I know she doesn't deserve it, I walk over to the edge of the bed, get down to my knees, and rub her belly. The vibrations from her purrs ricochet through my body. One of the few things in the world that gives me the true feeling of peace.

"Just try to stop being a brat, okay?" I ask her, as I pet her behind her ears.

Angel tilts her head back to lick my fingers. I take it as a yes before heading to the kitchen for a beer.

The pulsating coming from my new tattoo begins to feel less like a heartbeat and more like the tearing of my flesh. I cry out and fall to the floor, leaning my back against the wall as I rub my hand against my leg. Despite the feeling of my flesh tearing itself from my body, my skin doesn't feel any different than normal against my hand.

I put my other hand up against the wall in order to push myself forward. My knees find their way into the carpet, and I begin to unbuckle my belt and drop my pants. I then fall back against the wall and pull my pants off the rest of the way.

The tattoo I am looking at is not the same one I got this morning. Despite it still being in the general shape of an hourglass, it has twisted and warped and looks far larger, spreading across a wider section of my leg. A heart is at the bottom of the tattoo, jutting out from a section of broken glass that I am sure I had not asked for. As I look closer, and gaze at the sand in the bottom of the hour glass, I notice a face—a shadowy face, with two black eyes, a dark nose, and a wide grin. The heart below it begins to pulsate.

I pull my cell phone from my pants and dial the number of the tattoo artist. At the very least, I can find out if he took some liberties on the design. I saw the stencil, but I was in such a hurry to get out of the shop, I hadn't taken a good look at it. Maybe he changed it as he tattooed. Maybe it was supposed to be like this.

"Viking Ink. This is Michael. How can I help you?"

"Hi, Michael," I say, still running my hand up and down my leg. "It's Peter. I just got home and took a look at the tattoo. I was wondering if you changed anything after the initial stencil."

"Uh, changed anything? Like how do you mean?"

"You know. Added anything, warped the design somehow, anything like that."

"No, man. The stencil was how I tattooed it. Why? Is something wrong?"

I consider telling him everything. Then I consider only telling him about the face. It's the least shocking and could have unintentionally been put in the design. Like how some people see Jesus in their toast. But eventually, I say, "No" and let him go.

Angel is rubbing her head against my leg. I quickly pick her up and carry her back to the room. She mews at me as I place her back on the bed and pet her head until she lies back down.

"I'm sorry, Angel," I say, as I run my fingers through her soft fur. "I don't want you to get hurt."

I consider lying down myself. It's only 6 P.M., but I am one rough day away from needing a full 24 hours of sleep. But will I even fall asleep if I try?

I decide I won't, and go to the spare bedroom where my paintings are. After I told my mother I'd quit my job at the tax agency, I lied and told her a few months later that I picked up a job as an accountant for a big company. I never specified a company in particular, except to say "they deal in electronics." Her response was, "How painfully boring," and she never asked too many questions about it after that.

The truth is, I finally began to pursue my dream of becoming a painter. I sell my pieces online while I work a part-time job as a waiter. It's rough reliving my twenties, and at first, I was worried the lack of real job security would wind me up back in the hell that was the suit-and-tie. As it turns out, I'm fine living in an apartment and serving people who give me 5% tips as long as I get to do what I really love.

I begin to paint a baby's skull detached from its body, trapped inside of an hour glass. The rest of the child's skeleton is in an unmarked grave. The skeleton's heart lies on top of it, weeping. Its tears flow down into the ground to be reunited with its body, while the skull smiles.

My mother had blood dripping down her legs. She held my confused, four-year-old body in her arms. All I could think about was my soaked t-shirt, and how it felt the way her legs looked. She whispered in my ear that my sister was gone, but I didn't know what she meant by that.

My grandmother picked me up that night and told me my mother needed to be rushed to the hospital. I asked her where my father was, and she said she hoped he was in Hell.

After my mother returned from the hospital, my grandmother stayed with us for a while. I heard them talking when they thought I was asleep. That is how I found out he raped my mother and caused her to miscarriage. That is how I found out they thought he was a murderer.

I waited by the window at 5:30 P.M. every day. I always thought he would come back if I just prayed for it hard enough.

I am woken up by my burning leg. The skin stretches and pulls. The muscle beneath feels like a mass of bruises. It's still dark in my room, and when I force my head to the side to look at my alarm clock, it reads 4:35 A.M.

258

I sit up and turn on my bedside lamp before pulling away the blanket. The hourglass no longer looks like an hourglass, but has warped and stretched so far across my leg that it now looks like nothing more than uneven circles with more uneven circles inside of it. Still, the face inside looks exactly the same, but has grown larger and now covers nearly my entire calf. The heart protruding from the hourglass is no longer contained within my calf, but has now grown so large that it reaches all the way down to my foot. The pulse is now rapid.

I climb out of bed, and when my foot meets the carpet, the heart's pulse speeds up even more. I go to the bathroom and get in the shower, but as the water begins to hit my tattooed leg, it feels like my lungs are filling up with hot water. I push open the shower door and fall to my knees in front of the toilet. As I dry heave for what feels like ten solid minutes, the tattoo's heartbeat slows down to a crawl.

Despite still feeling water in my lungs, I can't cough anymore, and I fall down to the floor. The longer I stare at the ceiling, the more vividly I see the face from my tattoo. As it comes clearer into focus, it begins to laugh. Then the laughing turns to screaming. Then the screaming turns to crying. I'm about to crawl back to my bedroom to get away from it when its mocking is interrupted by Angel crawling on top of me and peering down at me.

"Thank you," I say with a groan, as the world around us warps and blurs. I force my eyes shut and keep my hand firmly on her back, as I attempt to keep myself grounded in reality.

What if she isn't real, either? What if the only intruder in this world is me?

Michael looks at the tattoo and back at me multiple times. I am close to yelling at him to tell me what he's doing when he finally says, "So, what am I supposed to be seeing here?"

"Is that a joke?"

"Uh, no, man. I have no idea what's wrong with it."

"How can you not see what's wrong when everything is wrong?" I walk over to the full-length mirror hanging on the wall. The tattoo is even more warped than when woke up this morning. The top of the hourglass has shrunk to the point that it is impossible to tell what it used to be. The bottom of the hourglass has ballooned out so much that it appears to be nothing but a black oval. It's impossible to read any part of the tattoo—besides the face and the heart. "Are you really going to stand there and tell me you don't see how much of a mess this is?"

He walks up next to me and looks in the mirror. "I really have no idea what's wrong. What are you seeing that I'm not?"

I look him dead in the eyes. He is not smiling or holding back a laugh. He doesn't see it. I pull out my wallet and hand him a twenty. He starts to ask me what it's for, but I am already halfway to the door and have no intention of stopping. The world is blurring around me. I am watching myself walk to my car. I am screaming with my head against the steering wheel, but I can't hear anything. I start driving, but I don't know where I'm going.

It isn't until I've walked halfway across the cemetery parking lot that the pulse in my leg forces me back into my body. The force is so great that it pushes me into the cement. My hands are against it, and I am able to push myself back up and keep walking.

The pulsing in my leg is going faster than it ever has as I stand in front of the unmarked grave. I sit down in the grass, which is still wet from the morning rain, and lift up my pant leg. Below the heart, new tattoos have formed—tears which cover my foot.

My pants feel more and more wet. Images of my mother's bloody legs flash through my mind. But all I can really think about is my father.

I know I should be crying for my sister who never had a chance to live. I know this grave has the remains of her fetus beneath it, not his. But I might as well have asked them to carve "David" into the stone, because that's who I cry for each time I fall upon this spot. I beg God to forgive him when no one else will.

I hand the painting to my mom, and she stares at it for a long time. The overwhelming amount of lit candles in her living room is making me gradually more nauseous, but I need to hear her say it. She hasn't said it since the day it happened.

"When did you have time to paint this?"

My nails are digging into my arm before I realize it. That's all she can say? "After work. But what do you think of it?"

"You always tell me how busy you are. I'm amazed you managed to find the time to paint something so grand."

"Mother," I say, as I scoot next to her on the couch and place my hand over hers, "do you like it?"

When she finally looks at me, she's crying. "Is it . . . ?" She trails off, but she sets the painting down on her lap and places her hand over her stomach.

"Yes, it is. I've been thinking about it so much lately. I'm not sure why." I eye the unmarked grave in the painting, then look back at her. "What were you going to name her?"

My mother looks back at the painting, and slides her fingers along the headstone. "I wanted to name her Delilah, but your father hated it. He wanted to name her Mary. That's why your name is Peter, you know."

"What do you mean?"

"Well, I wanted to name you Mars. Maybe it's a little out there, but—"

"No, Mother. I love it." I take the painting from her hands and place it on the coffee table. I sit down next to her and pull her into my arms. "And I love you. I'm sorry I have such a hard time showing it, but I do."

"I know you do, Peter. I love you, too."

As I hold her in my arms, my legs begin to burn more than they ever have before. It feels like I am dropping my leg into a fire as someone pulls the skin away from my body.

But as I cry, it's not from the pain of my leg. The pain my father has caused my mother has finally hit me, and for the first time it is Delilah I miss, not him.

I call in sick to the restaurant, as I can't even get out of my bed. Every time Angel tries to rub up against my burning leg, I grab her and make her sit on my chest. Each time, she attempts to crawl back down towards my leg, and each time, I pull her back up.

By the time noon rolls around, no amount of television is able to distract me from the pain. I shut it off and set the remote down on the pillow next to me, which Angel immediately tackles. With her purring body away from me and no television noise canceling out the buzzing in my ears, I turn my attention to my leg.

I can't keep living like this.

I have to do something.

I have to get away.

Why am I forced to live in the Hell my father deserved? If I hadn't sat there waiting for him every day, if I hadn't cried for him so often, if I hadn't tried to ignore all the pain he caused the people around me, would things be different now? Would I be serving coffee with a new tattoo, instead of lying in bed and trying to distract myself from the pain?

Why can't I let him go? Why can't I stop avoiding my pain? Why can't I face everything he's done head on and allow myself to heal like a normal person? Like a person who doesn't fly out of their body every opportunity they get, like a person who isn't afraid to let people into their lives?

I attempt to sit up, but it's useless. The pain from my leg has now spread and every time I try to lift myself up, I feel like I am being stabbed in every square inch of my body. So instead, I fall. Fall right onto the floor, face first. It feels like my nose is bleeding, and my head begins to pound, but I start to crawl to the kitchen.

It takes me half an hour and I have to take several breaks, but I reach the cabinet under the sink. I open the door and looking back at me are my cleaning supplies and tools. I reach for the hand saw, set it down beside me, and then grab my pocket knife.

I pull my cell phone from my pocket and dial my mother's number. When she picks up, she tries to start asking me why I'm not at work.

"Mother, please. Can you please do something for me?"

"You don't sound good, Peter. Are you sick?"

"Yes, I am, which is why I need your help, and why I'm not at work."

"Well, what do you need help with?"

"Can you come by tonight and feed Angel? I haven't gotten out of bed all day, and I need to sleep some more. Can you please do this for me?"

"All right, dear. I'll see you later then?"

"Yes, I'll see you later. I love you, Mom."

"I love you, too, Peter."

I set the phone down and then force myself to sit up. I set my back against the flat part of the counter wall. I undo my belt and place it into my mouth.

I then pick up the pocket knife.

Delilah has long black hair. She rides her bike down the street behind me. She falls off and scrapes her knee. I carry her back to the house and place a Band-Aid over it. I kiss it and tell her how strong she is.

Delilah has short hair. The night after her first day of high school, she comes to my apartment and tells me about the bullies that follow her home. They throw rocks at her and call her names. I wait half-way between the high school and my mother's house and beat them up as they follow her home the next day.

Delilah dyes her hair blonde. She dates a boy named Kyle and changes her major to be able to spend more time with him. He gets her pregnant and runs away. I hold her hand in the car outside of the abortion clinic and promise her I won't tell Mom.

Delilah has long black hair. She marries a man named Rainn. They have two boys and a girl.

David is a shadow. Delilah never even asks what his name is. She doesn't have room in her life to care about the man who never loved our mother. She only has room for love.

I remove the skin from my leg and am now looking at my bone. I have the saw in my hand as I picture Delilah's death. Delilah has gray hair. She dies of a stroke. She is sixty, and she is loved.

She is loved.

I hack through the bone and am overwhelmed by pain. I focus on the grinding as my teeth clamp down on the belt. I am here. I am real.

I make my way through my bone and though I would love to embrace my body's desire to black out, I have to finish. I have to let it go.

The saw finds its way to the other side of my leg. I think of

Julie. I think of how much I would love to hold her only once, just to see if I can.

I look at my detached leg. The tattoo is an hourglass—now impossibly small—with black sand inside of it. I laugh, and fall down to the floor. I hear Angel meowing. I hear myself laughing.

I feel Angel's fur against my face. I hear her purrs.

"I'm sorry," I say. "I love you, Angel."

As I close my eyes, I see the face from my tattoo. It fades into focus and becomes Delilah, whose long black hair cascades around me as she leans down to kiss my forehead.

"I'm sorry," I whisper.

One Thousand Words on a Tombstone

Josh Malerman

DOLORES RAY
1774–1784

Here lies Delores Ray
who saw, one day, the Blue Hag through a spyglass
while watching for birds in the back meadow of the Ray home.

Beloved daughter who asked, always,
to borrow her father's glass, and who handled
the device with meticulous care, adoration, it seemed,
as if the glass were not only an assistance for her own eyes
but a way by which to be with the birds,
to actually be with them, in the sky, to fly.

Beloved daughter who asked each day upon waking
if it was Saturday, the day on which she'd step
into her rain boots, cradle her notebook and pen
under one arm, ask Father for the use of his glass,
and tramp out the home's back door,
crossing the deck and down the decks stairs,
to the marsh before the meadow,
the swamp through which she had to pass before reaching
the meadow better known as Ray Field.

Beloved sister
who asked her younger sister Priscilla Ray
to join her the day she, Delores, saw the Blue Hag
through Father's fine glass.

Delores and Priscilla in matching
boots, the muck nearly to their knees, as Priscilla stopped
to catch a frog and Delores said, that very day,
Never mind with toads today, sister!
There are extraordinary things in the sky!

Delores Ray, beloved granddaughter,
Grandma Ruth's favorite
as Ruth introduced the girl to the wonders of nature,
life in the marsh, life in the meadow,
and gave Delores her first book on birds.

Beloved aunt to baby Ralph who cried suddenly
within the Ray home, cried and would not be consoled,
not by his mother January nor his father Nathaniel
to whom Delores was indeed also a beloved sister.

Beloved neighbor, spotted by the Banner Clan,
jaunting into the meadow with her sister Priscilla,
the glass in Delores's hand, always in Delores's hand.
The neighbor June Banner closing the drapes
after witnessing the girls arrival in the meadow.

June Banner who later said she felt a storm coming
but wrote in her journal she was afraid of the sky
that day, the very day, claimed she saw a fissure above,
said the sky was held together by ribbon in a steel boned corset.
Said she feared it coming undone.

Beloved neighbor to Douglas Banner, too,
who watched from his bedroom window the sisters
even as his mother June turned from the sight
of the two young girls playing in the tall grass,
one of them with a spyglass to her eye, trained on the sky.

Beloved sister of she, Priscilla, who looked up just in time
to see a shiver ripple down Delores's body, she, Priscilla,
who looked up to the sky to see a single bluebird or,
as she described to Doctor Mayfair,
A flying thing coated in blue fur.

Delores Ray, beloved neighbor
of that same Douglass Banner whose hair went white
from the sight of the same bird in the sky.

Beloved daughter of Harrison Ray
who saw first Priscilla running too quick through the marsh,
screaming, Delores! Delores!

Delores saw something rotten in the sky!
It wasn't until the younger of the two sisters fell
in that same muck that Harrison saw Delores,
on that day, walking steady behind, far behind,
her hair hanging over her face, obscuring whatever it was
she tried to remove from her face. Walking like blind.

Beloved daughter of Nell Ray
who ran past Harrison and assisted Priscilla
to standing before rushing to her eldest daughter
(no rain boots for Nell, muck to her naked knees)
and there saw what her husband could not from the back porch
of the Ray home, saw that Delores's dark hair obscured
new eyes, navy eyes, orbs of furred blue, witch's eyes,
punishment for having seen a witch in the sky.

Here lies Delores Ray who, on that day,
saw the Blue Hag split the ribbon of the boned corset,
saw more of her than anybody is allowed to see.

Beloved master to Barley, hunting dog,
who loved dear Delores most of all
but who would not watch birds with her,
refused to ever cross the muck to the meadow.

Beloved neighbor of Sammy Banner who,
having seen her brother turn white,
rushed to the Ray home to seek help,
arriving rather to discover damnation in the kitchen
as Delores Ray swiped at her own eyes,
attempting to pluck the blue fur from her sockets,
succeeding enough to send
tiny blue feathers to the kitchen floor.

Beloved sister of Nathaniel Ray
who couldn't quiet baby Ralph
and so left said duty to January
before taking a musket from the pantry
and setting off to kill the Blue Hag in the sky.

Here lies Delores Ray
who spoke in the kitchen, as all other but Nathaniel
listened, as she said these words: She looks back.
Beloved daughter of Harrison and Nell,
parents who carried Delores to Doctor Mayfair,
showed him the furred eyes, demanded he help.

Beloved member of the congregation of Father Lawrence Cantor
who saw Delores when Mayfair said no more,
there would be eyes no more, only blue.
Father Lawrence who took the girl, here lying,
to the foot of Christ and asked the savior for a miracle,
but fled said church as Christ looked down
upon him with furred eyes of his own.

Beloved daughter, sister, granddaughter,
neighbor, master, friend to all, evidenced by the funeral line
who attended the ceremony,
who were asked not to look her in the eye,
for Aaron Buck could not close them,
all who respected these wishes, this command,
by blindfolding themselves, one by one,
touching the side of the casket,
weeping into black fabric upon their faces.

Here lies Delores Ray,

who saw the Blue Hag in the sky that day.

And so it is known that one ought not to look into the sky,

not when the color blue is nearby, for a witch, too, has eyes.

Blue eyes. The color of color's ending.

Chiseled by Aaron Buck, 2 August, 1784

ABOUT THE AUTHORS

Michael Bray is a bestselling author and screenwriter. Influenced from an early age by the suspense horror of authors such as Stephen King, Richard Laymon, Shaun Hutson, James Herbert & Brian Lumley, along with TV shows like *Tales from the Crypt* and *The Twilight Zone,* his work touches on the psychological side of horror, teasing the reader's nerves and willing them to keep turning the pages.

Billy Chizmar's short stories have been published in various anthologies including *Fearful Fathoms* and *Dead Harvest.* His essay, "The Role of God in Stephen King's *Desperation*" was published in the non-fiction collection, *Reading Stephen King.* In 2017, he directed/co-wrote/starred in a short horror film, *Gone,* which has been screened at numerous film festivals around the country.

Israel Finn is the author of *Dreaming At the Top of My Lungs,* and a winner of the 80th Annual Writer's Digest Short Story Competition. He writes dark stories about everyday people in extraordinary circumstances. He lives in southern California.

Author **Joanna Koch** writes literary horror and surrealist trash. Her short stories have been published in journals and anthologies including *Doorbells at Dusk.* Joanna is a Contemplative Psychotherapy graduate of Naropa University who lives and works near Detroit.

Espi Kvlt is a nonbinary writer who specializes in speculative fiction. They are also an editor in the investigation industry by day and a sex worker by night. They obtained their B.A. in English-Writing from the University of Nevada, Reno in 2016. They have previously been published in *Gender Terror*, as well as the now tragically ended *The Fem*. They live with their significant other, three cats, and a snake in California. When not writing, they enjoy playing video games, watching horror movies, and covering themselves in blood for photo shoots. They are also a Mercy main.

Patrick Lacey was born and raised in a haunted house. He currently spends his nights and weekends writing about things that make the general public uncomfortable. He lives in Massachusetts with his Pomeranian, his over-sized cat, his fiancée, and his muse, who is likely trying to kill him.

Andrew Lennon is the author of *Every Twisted Thought* and other books in the horror and thriller genres. He has been featured in various bestselling anthologies, and is becoming a recognized name in the horror and thriller writing community. Andrew is a happily married man living in the North West of England with his wife Hazel & their children.

Lisa Lepovetsky has published fiction and poetry widely in the small press, professional publications and anthologies. Her work has appeared in *Ellery Queen's Mystery Magazine, Cemetery Dance* and many other magazines, and such anthologies as *Dark Destiny, Blood Muse,* and *HORRORS!,* among others. She earned her MFA from Penn State, and her most recent book is *Voices from Empty Rooms,* a collection of dark poetry.

Evans Light is a writer of horror and suspense, and is the author of *Screamscapes: Tales of Terror, Arboreatum, Don't Need No Water* and more. He is the editor of the well-received anthology *Doorbells at Dusk*, and is a co-creator of the *Bad Apples* Halloween anthology series and *Dead Roses: Five Dark Tales of Twisted Love*. He lives in Charlotte, North Carolina, surrounded by thousands of vintage horror paperbacks, and is the proud father of fine sons and the lucky husband of a beautiful wife.

John McNee is the writer of numerous strange and disturbing horror stories, published in a variety of strange and disturbing anthologies as well as the novel *Prince of Nightmares*. He is also the creator of Grudgehaven and the author of *Grudge Punk*, a collection of short stories detailing the lives and deaths of its gruesome inhabitants, plus the sequel, *Petroleum Precinct*. He lives on the west coast of Scotland, where he is employed as a journalist. He can easily be sought out on Facebook, Goodreads, Twitter and YouTube, where he hosts the horror-themed cooking show *A Recipe for Nightmares*.

Josh Malerman is an American author and also one of two singer/songwriters for the rock band The High Strung, whose song "The Luck You Got" can be heard as the theme song to the Showtime show *Shameless*. His book *Bird Box* is also currently being filmed as a feature film starring Sandra Bullock, John Malkovich, and Sarah Paulson. *Bird Box* was also nominated for the Stoker Award, the Shirley Jackson Award, and the James Herbert Award. His books *Black Mad Wheel* and *Goblin* have also been nominated for Stoker Awards.

Mark Matthews is a graduate of the University of Michigan and a licensed professional counselor who has worked in behavioral health for over twenty years. He is the author of *On the Lips of Children, All Smoke Rises*, and *Milk-Blood*, as well as the editor of *Garden of Fiends: Tales of Addiction Horror*. He lives near Detroit with his wife and two daughters. His story in this book was inspired by the Pearl Jam song, "Black".

William Meikle is a Scottish writer, now living in Canada, with over thirty novels published in the genre press and more than three hundred short story credits in thirteen countries. He has books available from a variety of publishers including Dark Regions Press and Severed Press and his work has appeared in a large number of professional anthologies and magazines. He lives in Newfoundland with whales, bald eagles and icebergs for company. When he's not writing he drinks beer, plays guitar, and dreams of fortune and glory.

Paul Michaels is the pseudonym for horror writer Paul M. Feeney. Under his real name (Feeney) he has published numerous short stories in a variety of anthologies, and has had two novellas released, *The Last Bus* (limited edition paperback now out of print) and *Kids*. His intention with the Paul Michaels name is to write and publish work on the quiet, literary end of horror, less genre-infused than his other writing. As of this bio, "Angel Wings" (included in this collection) will be the first published story using the Paul Michaels name. Paul currently lives in the north east of England, where he is busy working away on stories under both names. He also contributes an occasional review to This is Horror, one of the internet's premier horror resource sites.

In his head, **Jason Parent** lives in many places, but in the real world, he calls New England his home. The region offers an abundance of settings for his writing and many wonderful places in which to write them. He currently resides in Rhode Island.

In a prior life, Jason spent most of his time in front of a judge . . . as a civil litigator. When he wanted a change, he traded in his cheap suits for flip flops and designer stubble. The flops got repossessed the next day, and he's back in the legal field . . . sorta. But that's another story. When he's not working, Jason likes to kayak, catch a movie, and travel any place that will let him enter. And read and write, of course—he does that too sometimes.

Ryan C. Thomas is an award-winning journalist and editor living in San Diego, California. He is the author of thirteen novels (including the cult classic, *The Summer I Died*), numerous novellas and short stories, and can often be found in the bars around Southern California playing rockabilly guitar. When he is not writing or rocking out, he is at home with his wife, son, daughter, two dogs and cat watching really bad B-movies.

Monique Youzwa grew up in a small town in Manitoba, Canada. Though she has worked at various jobs, from restaurants to bars to pharmacies, writing has always been a part of her life. A couple years ago she made it her full-time career and has since written hundreds of articles and blogs for a variety of websites. Fiction has always been her passion, though, and recently she has begun submitting her short stories for publication. She is also at work on a novel, which she hopes to complete in the near future.

Don't miss the next thrilling volume...

IN DARKNESS, *DELIGHT*

CREATURES OF THE NIGHT

EDITED BY
ANDREW LENNON & EVANS LIGHT

Available 2019 from CORPUS PRESS

CARVE YOUR PUMPKINS AND TURN ON THE PORCH LIGHT.

MORE FROM THE EDITORS

 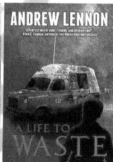  

ANDREW LENNON

EVANS LIGHT

WANT MORE?

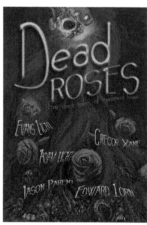  

HORROR AND WEIRD FICTION AT
CORPUSPRESS.COM

Printed in Poland
by Amazon Fulfillment
Poland Sp. z o.o., Wrocław